RUTHLESS DADDY

BOSTON MAFIA DONS

BIANCA COLE

TWISTED ROMANCE PUBLICATIONS

CONTENTS

1. Fabio — 1
2. Gia — 17
3. Fabio — 29
4. Gia — 41
5. Fabio — 51
6. Gia — 59
7. Fabio — 69
8. Gia — 79
9. Fabio — 89
10. Gia — 99
11. Fabio — 109
12. Gia — 117
13. Fabio — 127
14. Gia — 141
15. Fabio — 151
16. Gia — 165
17. Fabio — 175
18. Gia — 185
19. Fabio — 197
20. Gia — 205
21. Fabio — 213
22. Gia — 221
23. Fabio — 231
24. Gia — 245
25. Fabio — 257
26. Gia — 265
27. Fabio — 273
28. Gia — 281

29. Fabio	289
30. Gia	299
31. Fabio	307
Epilogue	321
Glossary	333
Also by Bianca Cole	335
About the Author	337

Ruthless Daddy Copyright © 2021 Bianca Cole

All Rights Reserved.
No part of this publication may be reproduced, stored, or transmitted in any form or by any means, electronic, mechanical, photocopying, recording, scanning, or otherwise without written permission from the publisher. It is illegal to copy this book, post it to a website, or distribute it by any other means without permission.

This novel is entirely a work of fiction. The names, characters and incidents portrayed in it are the work of the author's imagination. Any resemblance to actual persons, living or dead, events or localities is entirely coincidental.

Warning: the unauthorized reproduction or distribution of this copyrighted work is illegal. Criminal copyright infringement, including infringement without monetary gain, is investigated by the FBI and is punishable by up to 5 years in prison and a fine of $250,000.

Book cover design by Deliciously Dark Designs

Photography by Wander Aguiar

Editing: Rainlyt Editing

❦ Created with Vellum

1

FABIO

I open the door to Salvatore's apartment and drop to my knees. The scene in front of me knocks all the air from my lungs as if someone punched me hard in the gut.

What I'm looking at is horrific. I expected the worst when I saw a blood-stained knife and my best friend's watch on my doorstep with the message *stiamo venendo per te* written on a scrap of blood-stained paper. The message was written in Italian and meant we're coming for you.

Salvatore is no longer in one piece. They've severed his head and positioned it on the coffee table, looking straight at me. Bile rises in my throat at the vacant look in his still open but lifeless eyes.

Blood covers the luxurious beige carpets and white walls. It's a bloodbath so graphic that most people would throw up. But the terrible truth of this life is that the more blood and gore you encounter, the more difficult it is to be shocked or feel anything when you come across it.

Sorrowful pain and all-consuming rage slam into me all at once. First, they took my wife and now, ten years later, they've taken my capo and best friend. I won't rest until I have every member of the Moretti family's head on a fucking spike for this.

The echo of fast-approaching footsteps fills the air as my lieutenant approaches. "Boss, what is—" Lorenzo retches and doubles over, almost throwing up. "Fuck, we better call the cops."

I remain on my knees, my eyes fixed to the vacant stare of my best friend. The man I'd always hoped I'd call a son one day once he married Aida. Aida may not have liked the prospect, since she didn't know Salvatore as I keep her at arm's length from the family business to protect her. However, I always expected her to marry him one day.

The Moretti family is here in Sicily, which means no one I care about is safe. The only person I care about on this godforsaken earth now is my daughter.

Sicily and the Alteri family could fall.

"Call the cops and tell them. I need to make plans to protect my daughter." I stand and stare for one last, long moment at the only man I considered worthy of the position. "You will step in as interim capo while we sort things out."

Lorenzo's eyes widen slightly, but he bows his head. "Of course, sir. I won't let you down."

I don't respond to him, as none of my men are worthy of the position. Lorenzo is the best of the men I have, but no one will ever compare to the man I just lost. "Make sure the police know we need to have a funeral for him soon. I will alert his family."

I grit my teeth. I know Salvatore's ex-wife was on speaking terms with him. They have a child together, but she lives in Rome. It will be a tough conversation to have, but I owe it to my friend and his child to ensure they get his inheritance.

Life has become a lot darker now that the Moretti family just snatched away my daughter's future. Aida has no one to protect her anymore once I'm gone, and I'm not getting any younger. I march out of the apartment block and get into the town car that's waiting for me.

"Home," I order my driver, Paolo.

He nods and fixes his attention on the road, driving me through the streets of Palermo. A place I once loved, but as my enemies rip away the people I care about, my love for my home country diminishes.

Aida isn't safe here. I have no option but to find her a suitable husband. I need to find someone who can provide her protection from the Moretti family and give me the power to force them to back down.

It won't be easy, but it's my only option.

Two months later...

I stand on the edge of the clifftop, wondering if it would be easier to jump off and allow the cresting waves to take me away from this desolate and cruel life.

Today I have to do something that will hurt my daughter, but if I allow her to see any reluctance, I'm not sure I'll be able to go through with it.

The Moretti family has already issued threats against her. In the two months since Salvatore's death, they have become more aggressive with their tactics. They want to take control of Sicily. If that were to happen and Aida was here, I know all too well the gruesome fate she'd fall prey to. I won't risk her life, even if the only way to protect her isn't exactly great either.

Milo Mazzeo was the only man to bite at the chance of partnering with me, and I had to push for him to marry Aida as part of the deal. The crunch of the ground underfoot catches my attention, making me aware that my daughter has arrived.

I turn to face her, feeling an ache in my chest at how beautiful she is—as beautiful as her mother was. "Aida, please join me," I say, holding out a hand to her.

Aida takes my hand. We stand in silence for a moment, gazing over the view of the azure Sicilian sea. "How are you, father?"

I swallow hard, wishing I didn't have to do this. "As well as I can be. As always, work is stressful." I don't talk to Aida about my work, shielding her as best as possible from the terrible things I'm involved in.

I glance at Aida and squeeze her hand gently, wishing things were different. "I asked you to meet me here as I have some news, amore."

Aida smiles at me, which only makes my chest ache more. "What is it?" she asks.

I pause for a moment, grappling with the words about to come out of my mouth. "I've found you a husband."

Aida's eyes widen in shock. "What?"

I smile, but it's forced and unnatural. "I've kept you safe, Aida, but now it's time another man takes the role of your protector." I clench my jaw, knowing the type of man I'm sending her to. It's ridiculous that he is the better option. "Milo Mazzeo wants to marry you in his hometown, Boston."

Aida drops my hand, stepping away from me. There's silence as she processes the news before she shakes her head. "No, I won't marry that man. He's as evil as they get, father. I don't need a protector. I want to marry a man I love, not by an arrangement."

I drop the false smile and narrow my eyes at her, knowing that the only way is to take the hard line and pretend I don't care. "You'll do as you are told, Aida."

"Why would you give me to a man like him?" she asks, her voice cracking with emotion.

"It was always my intention to marry you to a man who can increase the power of our family's business,

Aida." I grab her shoulders, knowing that I'm breaking her heart. "I don't want any disobedience. You will marry Milo Mazzeo, end of discussion."

"I thought you cared about me," she murmurs, and those words stab me like a knife to the gut.

I do care about her. She's the only thing that matters to me in this world. My gaze remains pinned to the blue of the azure sea, as I know if I look at her, I'll crack. "Your mother's death changed me, Aida. I hate how much you remind me of her. If you're in Boston, that will solve the problem." It kills me inside to say these words to her since they're not true, but I know it's the only way to get her to leave and not come back. I block out my emotions and glare at my daughter. "I don't want you here."

Aida's eyes quickly fill with tears. "What would mother think if she could see what you are doing to her only child?"

The mention of Lianna snaps something inside of me. It's a reminder of what I've lost and what I'm still going to lose. "Don't fucking talk about her." I grab her wrist. "She can't see because she is dead and gone, Aida." I shake my head. "There's no such thing as happy endings in our world, so you will have to accept your fate with dignity." It's a truth that has become too real for me of late.

She fights away from me and rushes back the way she came, putting space between us. I watch, hating that I'm hurting her. These will be my last moments with her before she's on the plane. Milo expected me to attend the wedding, but this is bad enough. I can't trust myself to attend, or I'll end up breaking it off.

Aida walks dangerously close to the cliff edge, making my heart accelerate. "Aida, come away from there," I call.

My dutiful daughter obeys, walking toward me again. She wipes the tears from her face. "When will I be leaving?"

I glance over her shoulder at Aldo and nod. "Right away."

Aldo grabs her shoulder. "The car is waiting to take you to the airport. We've packed all of your things, and they are already on the plane."

Aida stares at me in shock. "Won't you at least let me say goodbye to my friends?"

I shake my head, knowing it's too risky. "I won't risk you running. Aldo is to take you straight to the airport."

Aida breaks away from Aldo, looking up at me for a moment, before rushing toward the descent off the clifftop. I nod at Aldo for him to follow, knowing she won't get far. Aldo grabs her before she starts her descent down the cliff. He drags her back toward me.

"Stop this at once, Aida." I grab her wrists to stop her from fighting. There's a moment of hesitation before I give Aldo the signal. Guilt coils through me like a disease as Aldo stabs the needle into Aida's neck, administering a dose of sedatives.

"What the hell?" Aida exclaims, clutching her neck.

I have to remain strong, knowing that any sign of weakness could crumble my resolve within an instant. "It is best if you can't fight. By the time you wake up, you will be in America."

Aida shakes her head. "You drugged me?"

"It's for your own good," I say, knowing that's the only thing I've said on this clifftop that is not a lie. Aida can't stay in Sicily, not when we're on the brink of war.

My little girl has always been so strong. She stands there, fighting not to cry, glaring at me.

"You will be in Boston and married before you know it. Your life here will be a memory. Embrace it," I say, keeping my gaze cold. "Goodbye." I turn away from my daughter, feeling tears welling in my eyes. With every step I take away from her, the pain in my chest grows.

"Aldo, please don't do this," I hear her plead with her bodyguard.

"I'm sorry. I don't have a choice," Aldo replies.

The tears fall down my face. It's been ten years since I cried. Even at Salvatore's funeral, I couldn't cry. Losing Lianna was the hardest thing I've ever had to deal with, but losing Salvatore and now Aida in such quick succession takes first prize.

Once I'm certain Aldo has taken Aida out of sight, I drop to my knees. The weight of the empire I hold on my shoulders is crushing, and the guilt over not protecting the people I love is heavy.

Tears stream down my face as I stare up at the sky,

knowing that my world has become darker still. The Moretti family has forced me to send away the only love and light in my life.

Ten months later...

The image of blood painting the walls of my best friend's apartment is impossible to get out of my mind, especially when Benito Moretti sits at the other side of the boardroom table, smirking at me. Benito is the reason Salvatore's dead. I should get up from this chair and strangle the life out of him, even if it will cause my death.

These board meetings are fucking pointless and dangerous. I could never comprehend why the firm would ever want to bring enemies into the same room for a meeting. The shares I own in the financial firm in Rome are a front for laundering cash from our operations, as is the same for the Moretti family. They own Naples, and just over ten months ago they started to make a move on Sicily.

The Moretti family has been a thorn in my side for too long. Thankfully, they have little power over me since my alliance with Milo. Benito is the cocky twenty-eight-year-old son of my enemy, Rafa Moretti. He's a coward who has no business sitting among the men at this table, and yet here he is, smirking at me.

The other people at the table are inconsequential to

me. Alfeio Sabbatelli runs the north of Italy, and he keeps to himself. We've never had a run-in with each other, but we're not exactly on friendly terms either. Ricci Alo runs west Italy. Tonio Busa runs east Italy, including Rome. Finally, of course, the Moretti family runs the south of Italy, including Naples.

All the shareholders of this company are mafia. Five of us in total. Our ancestors set up the company to keep the peace between the different regions and launder money for all five families. It made sense when it was established as there were no wars for territory, but in time the situation in Italy has become less stable.

"Are there any objections to the proposed moves for the company?" Tieri Fernando, the CEO, asks.

I am here to satisfy the shareholders. If I didn't make an appearance, I know Benito wouldn't hesitate to undermine me. The entire meeting, I've hardly listened as it's all bullshit.

"I'm glad to see no one objects." Tieri claps his hands. "In that case, I will end this meeting."

Everyone stands, but I remain seated. It irritates me when Benito also remains seated, giving me that stupid smirk. If it weren't for the risk of war, I'd kill him right here and wipe that smirk from his face permanently. After a few moments, everyone else has left, leaving both of us sitting opposite each other.

"Aren't you going to leave, Moretti?" I ask.

He tilts his head. "I could ask you the same question."

I shake my head and stand, not intending to play games with this man. He's childish and pathetic. "If you didn't have protection," I glance at his bodyguard, who steps forward, "I'd kill you right here and now," I say, glaring at him.

He pales slightly. His father has shielded him from true brutality. He's a puppy dog, and I'm a wolf ready to devour him. It's because of these assholes that I had to break my daughter's heart—an act that has haunted me ever since.

It was the only way to ensure Aida was safe, even though I knew I was taking a risk giving her to a man like Milo. Thankfully, Milo assures me she's safe and happy, which is as much as I can ask for. He has frequently asked me to visit Boston, but I won't leave Italy until I'm confident that my new capo can handle operations alone.

I want to rip Benito's fucking heart out and ship it to his father as revenge, but I know that doing so would throw the whole of Italy into chaos. It's tempting, though, as I could take down his bodyguard and him.

"Watch your back," I say before walking out of the boardroom. I've been at this far too long, and there is no end in sight. Salvatore was like a son to me, and I always expected him to take over the business.

I'd hoped that Aida might have married him instead of Milo, but the one thing I've learned is nothing in life turns out how you expect. When Salvatore learned about their plans to take Sicily, he got the message to me before the Moretti family killed him in cold blood.

They had intended to invade my country and take it over, forcing my daughter to marry Benito. There was no way that I was going to let that happen. So I knew I needed backup and a powerful ally, even if that ally is in Boston.

Once the Moretti family found out that I'd partnered with Milo Mazzeo, they backed off instantly. It was a necessary move to protect everything, including Aida. The only proper way to bind our organizations was to offer Aida to him as a wife, hoping they'd provide an heir.

I had to break her heart to force her to leave. It was easier if she hated me, yet the look she gave me will haunt me until my dying day. All I can hope is that she finds happiness with Milo.

I walk out of the boardroom and bump into Tieri, the CEO of the company.

"Fabio, it's great that you could come for the meeting." His brow furrows. "How are relations between you and the Morettis?"

I shake my head. "As bad as they ever were, but we're at a stalemate."

He smiles. "So a cold war, essentially?"

I nod. "You could call it that, yes."

Tieri runs a hand through his long dark hair. "That's got to be better than an active war." He looks wistful. "I'm so sorry about Salvatore. I know you two were close."

I clench my jaw. "I expect casualties in a war," I say, not letting Tieri know how much Salvatore's death hurt me. Tieri might not be a threat, but I let no one know my true feelings. If you do, enemies can exploit the part of you that cares.

His expression turns stern. "Indeed. Are you staying in Rome?" he asks.

I shake my head. "No, and that's why I must leave now. I intend to be back in Palermo by the evening."

Tieri looks surprised but nods. "Of course." He steps out of my way. "I will be in touch about when the next board meeting is."

I grunt in reply and walk away from him. These board meetings are a hassle that I don't need. Salvatore always attended them before he died. Lorenzo, the man I'm training to be my capo, doesn't have my trust yet.

I step out of the building and onto the streets. The Rome streets are busy, and the air is polluted. It's one reason I hate coming here. Sicily is my favorite place on this earth, and I don't particularly appreciate leaving it.

The car is waiting outside of my building, and Aldo gets out when he sees me. He used to be Aida's bodyguard, but after I shipped her away, he became mine.

"Good meeting, sir?" he asks as he opens the door for me.

I shake my head. "A meeting can't be good when a

Moretti is in attendance." I clench my fists as I get into the car.

"Of course. Sorry I asked, sir." He shuts the door and gets into the driver's seat. "The jet is ready for take-off as soon as we arrive," Aldo says.

I nod. "Good, I want to be back in Sicily before nightfall," I say, desperate to get out of the city. Unfortunately, the traffic in Rome is always bad, so the likelihood is we'll be back in Sicily later than I hoped.

"I'll try to get us to the airport as fast as possible," he says before raising the privacy screen between us in the car.

The car moves for a few blocks only to come to a halt in traffic. I sigh heavily, sitting back in the chair and trying to relax. The empire I hold upon my shoulders has become a heavy burden, one which I have no choice but to shoulder.

Lianna and I didn't have a boy. After Aida was born, we were told we were lucky to conceive her, as Lianna wasn't very fertile. I never worried about succession because I loved Salvatore like a brother and knew he would look after the empire and Aida. I always hoped he and Aida would continue the legacy my ancestors built

Instead, the Moretti family stole that from me too. It wasn't enough that they killed my wife. They had to steal away everything else that mattered to me. I am not a stupid, hot-headed man. My plan to exact revenge against them has been in play for a long time, but every time I think I'm getting close to executing it, they thwart my plans.

I loosen the tie around my neck. The longer I remain in control of the Sicilian mafia, the more it weighs me down. My father died when I was twenty years old, and I took over. It's been twenty-nine years of blood, war, and deceit. Twenty-nine years of losing the only people I care about in this world. All I'm left with is a darkness that grows with every year that passes.

Aida was the only light I had left in my life. When the Moretti family forced me to send her away, they left me with nothing but a pit of eternal darkness. A darkness that threatens to consume me every single day.

2

GIA

"Happy twenty-first birthday," Siena says, clinking her glass against mine.

It may be my birthday, but I can't help feeling down because my other best friend isn't here. Aida left Sicily about ten months ago now, and I rarely hear from her at all.

Siena waves a hand in front of my face. "Why does this seem more like a funeral than a birthday celebration?"

I sigh heavily. "Sorry. I just can't believe Aida isn't here."

Siena smiles sadly. "I know. Nothing is the same without her." Her brow furrows. "Has Aida not gotten in touch?"

I shake my head. "No, it's the first time I haven't seen her on my birthday." I sigh heavily. "I reckon she's too caught up in her new life to remember us."

"That's not true. Aida has a lot going on with the war her husband is fighting." Siena digs her phone out of her pocket. "Why don't we try to call her?"

"We can. It will be late morning in Boston." I shrug. "She probably won't pick up."

Siena finds Aida's number and attempts to video call her. It rings for a while before cutting out.

I sigh heavily. "It's as if Aida's forgotten about us entirely since she moved." My brow furrows. "I hope she's okay with that terrible man."

Siena grabs my hand and squeezes it. "She's fine. The last time we spoke to her, she said she was happy with him. They're newlyweds, so it's not surprising that she doesn't have time for us at the moment."

I nod and take a drink of my Chardonnay, trying to forget about the hole that Aida has left. Her father is an asshole for sending her away the way he did. "I think we ought to go to Aida's house and give her bastard of a father a good telling off."

Siena shakes her head. "Don't be a fool. You know who her father is."

I'm well aware of who he is. Fabio Alteri practically runs Sicily. He has more power than the government does on this island. "Are you suggesting he might kill us if we go over there?" I ask, downing my third glass of wine.

"I'm suggesting that going over to a mafia don's house drunk and telling him off for shipping his daughter away is a terrible idea." Siena grabs the glass out of my hand. "Why don't you slow down, Gia." She places a hand on my shoulder.

I shoot her an irritated glare. "Because it's my birthday," I say, snatching the glass back.

I love Siena, but we've certainly clashed more since Aida left. Aida was the glue that held us together and the buffer whenever Siena and I disagreed. We're hopeless without her. At least we've resisted killing each other for ten months. The worst part of it is that she hasn't yet bothered to wish me a happy birthday.

Siena places her glass down. "Why don't we dance?"

I glance at the dance floor, feeling my stomach churn. Since Aida left, everything has been less exciting. Ever since we were kids, it's always been the three of us. "I'm not sure."

Siena shakes her head and stands, hooking her arm with mine. "You need to get out of this slump. Come on. We're going to dance whether you like it or not." She forces me out of my chair and drags me onto the crowded dancefloor.

It's as if she planned it as one of my favorite songs of all time plays—Get Lucky by Daft Punk. It's impossible not to move to the song as we both sing along, laughing. The moment I'm on that dance floor, the sadness I'd felt that Aida forgot about my birthday fades away.

We dance together, allowing the music to take over the night. The buzz of the wine makes it even more enjoyable until we finally stop and sit back down, laughing. "I needed that." I smile at my friend. "Thank you for always trying even when I'm an impossible grump."

"Always." Siena takes my hand and smiles. "More wine is in order too," she says, getting the server's attention.

The server comes over. "What can I get for you?"

"Two more glasses of Chardonnay, please," Siena says, handing her the empty glasses.

I glance at my watch and notice that it's almost eleven o'clock. I have to be up early to open the shop in the morning. "Maybe we should cancel the wine and call it a night?"

Siena shakes her head. "No way. You only turn twenty-one once."

I sigh. "I've got work in the morning."

"One more hour. I wanted to check out a new bar. We will finish our drinks and then head straight there, okay?"

I hold back my remark that one hour always turns to two. It's not worth trying to argue with Siena. If the shop opens a little later, it won't be a big deal. Thursday is always our slowest day. "Fine."

The waitress brings us our drinks, and Siena talks about a party a girl from our high school is throwing tomorrow night.

"Do you think either of us will be up to drinking more alcohol tomorrow?" I ask.

Siena laughs. "You know me; I'm always up to drinking more alcohol."

I shake my head. "I don't think I will want to drink, but I'll come along for the party, anyway."

"That's the spirit," Siena says as she knocks back the rest of her wine in record time. "Now drink up. We need to check out this new bar everyone is talking about."

I knock back the rest of my drink, feeling queasy the moment I do. When I stand up, I can't walk straight so I grab hold of Siena's arm. "I hope you can walk straighter than I can right now."

Siena chuckles. "Not sure, to be honest."

I shake my head as she leads me out into the streets. We're about to step into the road when a limousine blares its horn at us. It slows right down, and the guy shouts something out of the window.

My heart skips a beat when I see Fabio Alteri sitting in the back. It instantly brings my attention back to my anger over Aida being taken from us.

"That son of a bitch almost ran us over too."

Siena's brow furrowed. "Who are you talking about?"

I point after the car. "Mr. Alteri was in the back of that car."

"Seriously? We should have stopped it and given him a good telling off."

I shake my head. "I thought you said it was a bad idea to tell him off about anything."

"I did when I was more sober and before he almost ran us over with his fancy-pants limousine."

I laugh. "You make no sense. Come on, let's get to this bar you've been going on about. What is it called?"

Siena nods up the street. "Topaz."

My stomach sinks as I remember reading about it in the local newspaper. "Great. A place run by the man who almost knocked us down and stole our friend away."

Siena stares at me with wide eyes. "He owns Topaz?" she asks.

I nod. "Let's be honest. Mr. Alteri owns Sicily."

Siena sighs. "Unfortunately, you are right." She hooks her arm with mine again and leads me toward Fabio's new fancy bar.

I can see why the place got featured in the newspaper. It's a beautiful bar with the best view of the beach. "Wow, this is a nice place."

Siena nods. "Yeah, I'm sure the prices are nice, too. One drink, and then we go home, agreed?"

"Agreed," I reply, walking toward the bar in the center of the courtyard.

A man grabs hold of my hips before I make it there. "Hey, sweet cheeks. Do you want to dance?" he asks.

I yank his hands off me and spin around. "No, I don't. Keep your hands to yourself, creep," I say.

He holds his hands up, swaying slightly. "Calm down, bitch."

I roll my eyes, knowing that nothing good can come

from arguing with a sexist piece of shit like him. Siena hadn't noticed that I got caught up as she searches the crowd for me.

I join her at the bar. "Men can be real idiots," I say.

Siena raises a brow. "What happened?"

"Some dick back there grabbed my hips and called me sweet cheeks." I roll my eyes. "A pig, basically."

Siena wrinkles her nose. "They're all pigs on this fucking island." The bartender passes her two glasses of wine. "We need to find nice men in Rome or something."

"No chance. My life will always be in Sicily." I take a glass of wine and knock half of it back. There's one thing I'd never do, and that's move because of a man.

Siena makes a dismissive noise. "Fuck that. If some rich and handsome man who lived in Rome wanted this," she gestures to her body, "I'd move there in a heartbeat." She drinks some of her wine, glancing around the bar. "Unfortunately, we know every man worth knowing on this island, and they are all disappointing."

I sip the rest of my wine, feeling down about my future. Siena has a way of making prospects on this island seem hopeless, but then she's never loved it the way Aida and I do. I think it's because she moved here when she was eight years old.

"I'm empty," I say, holding up my glass.

Siena downs the rest of hers. "Fair enough. Are you ready to go home?" she asks.

I sway a little, shaking my head. "You go ahead. I'm going to walk along the beach alone for a bit."

Siena's eyes narrow. "It's a bad idea to be on your own. I'll walk with you."

"Don't be silly. I want some time alone." I hug Siena, hoping she'll understand.

She looks at me uncertainly before nodding. "Okay. Be careful, and I'll see you in the morning."

I nod, turning away from her. "See you tomorrow."

Siena says nothing else, allowing me to head down the alleyway toward the beach. I know I've drunk a few too many glasses of Chardonnay when I almost trip over the cobblestones.

My head is pounding. I pull out my cell phone and sigh when I see my screensaver, a photo of the three of us on the beach last year. I decide to try Aida's cell phone since Siena couldn't get through.

The dial tone sounds a few times before cutting to her messaging service. I sigh and stow my phone back in my purse. It's as though she has forgotten about me entirely. I take off my high heel shoes and step onto the sand, enjoying the softness beneath my bare feet.

The sound of the water gently lapping at the shore is calming. I feel angry and hurt that Aida forgot my birthday, but I know she's got a lot going on in Boston. She has a new life now that doesn't include Siena or me.

As I walk along the beach, I realize that I'm heading straight toward Aida's home. A place I remember from many days spent there as a young child. After Aida's mother died, she no longer wanted to have us over, always insisting on getting out of the house.

The man who stole her away lives in that same villa. Deep down, a part of me wanted to walk along this beach to get answers. As I get closer, the temptation to walk in there and demand an explanation for why he sold his daughter to some cruel, vindictive bastard on the other side of the Atlantic gets stronger.

Aida trusted him, and he broke that trust. I don't understand why he sold her to a man known for his cruelty.

The fancy villa sits back from the beach and is dimly lit. Fabio has many guards, but Aida always boasted about the secret entrance only she knew about. The cellar is easily accessible from the beach and leads into the main heart of the villa.

Aida kept it a secret from her father, as it was her only way to escape without Aldo. She didn't take the chance too often, though, since getting caught would have been disastrous.

I make it to the small hatch on the beach that leads into the home and lift it. It's impossible not to be a little nervous as I stare into the dark, cavernous hole. The sensible part of me knows this is a bad idea. The drunk, angry part of me wants answers from the man who never struck me as cruel when we were little.

He may be dangerous, but he doted on Aida. It made no sense when he sent her away, telling Aida he can't bear to be around her because she reminds him of her mother. Fabio Alteri always struck me as a ruthless man, but one that cared about his family above all.

I haven't spoken to him since I was eleven years old, when his enemy murdered his wife. Perhaps her murder changed him in ways I can't understand. I've seen him around Palermo many times, and I always attend the annual ball he holds.

There was no way I'd ever approach him, though, not since Aida stopped asking us over to their home.

I shuffle onto my knees and drop through the hole into a small, compact tunnel. My shoes remain on the beach by the opening since I can't carry them and go through. It's the first time I've gone into Aida's home like this. We always met her on the other side. The passage is cramped. Luckily, I'm not claustrophobic.

The tunnel is long, but it finally opens up to a vent, which I push open. Carefully, I drop out of the vent hole and into the basement of the Alteri residence. My eyes widen when I see the hundreds of bottles of wine carefully stored in stunning wooden racks made to fit every side of the basement.

Fabio must like his red wine to have this many bottles.

I sneak out of the basement and into the main corridor of the home. It's hard to get my bearings since I was eleven when I last stepped in here.

Fabio's study was the one place we could never go, so it's the first place I intend to start my search for the don. My heart is pounding so hard I can hear it. There's no doubt that what I'm doing is certifiably insane. If I was sober, there's no way I'd sneak into a mobster's home.

The study is down a small corridor and to the left. We used to sneak in here when Fabio was out because we were told not to. I reach for the door, trying to still my fast heartbeat. When I open the door, I find the study empty.

I exhale a breath I didn't realize I was holding, stepping into the study. Although Mr. Alteri banned us from coming in here, it was always my favorite room because of the floor-to-ceiling bookshelves on one side. Mr. Alteri has so many books I often wondered how he got the time to read them.

I walk toward the bookshelf and run my hand along the spines of the number of expensive first edition books.

The click of a gun being cocked behind me turns my legs to jello. "What are you doing here?" a deep voice rumbles behind me, sending goosebumps prickling over every inch of my skin.

I don't need to turn around to know that Fabio Alteri is standing behind me, aiming a gun at me. That deep, booming voice has haunted my fantasies for as long as I can remember.

Slowly, I turn to face him with my hands up. I swallow hard as I haven't seen him up close like this for quite a while, let alone spoken to him. He's wearing a pair of black pants and a white t-shirt that shows off his bulging muscles and tattooed arms.

His hair is a stunning gray that only a man as gorgeous as Fabio can pull off. My heartrate accelerates as our eyes meet. His dark, almost onyx black eyes flash with recognition. My stomach flutters, and I quickly turn into a little girl with a crush again.

"Gia?" he asks, his voice softening as he lowers the gun.

I'm surprised that he recognizes me. I nod in reply. "Hello, Mr. Alteri."

There's a tense silence that falls between us as Fabio's eyes wander slowly down my body. I feel the heat rising to my cheeks at the way he takes in every curve. His eyes pause on my exposed cleavage, making me hotter than fire. He moves his attention back to my eyes, and the look in them knocks the air from my lungs.

Fabio stares at me with a desire that sets my soul on fire. He looks like a hungry wolf, ready to devour his prey.

The problem is, I'm the prey.

3

FABIO

I stare at my daughter's friend, wondering how on earth she got in here. A muscle in my jaw ticks, as it's almost impossible not to notice her perfect, curvy figure. Gia is all grown up now.

The last time I saw Gia she was only eleven years old. Aida stopped bringing her friends here after her mother died. I know deep down that Aida always blamed me for her death, since my enemy killed her in the crossfire of a war I'd been fighting.

"What are you doing here?" I ask again.

Gia swallows hard. "I'm here for answers," she says, setting her hands on her hips to look confident.

The movement draws my attention to her curvy body again. It's impossible not to notice her tempting, full cleavage in the tight black dress she is wearing. Her hips are round and perfect for grabbing.

I swallow hard, realizing how wrong it is to think

about her like that. She's twenty-one years old, and it's clear from the glassy look in her chestnut eyes that she's drunk. I'm knocking on fifty years old in just over three months.

Nothing could ever happen between us. Not to mention, Aida already hates me enough for sending her to Milo. "Answers to what?" I ask, indulging her for a moment. The girl has some guts to break into my home and demand answers to anything.

She sighs heavily. "Why the fuck you sold your daughter to some cruel mafia don all the way in Boston."

Her question snaps me out of the lust-filled daze she had drawn me into. "It's none of your business." I stalk toward her, forcing her to take steps backward until she's pressed against the wall. "What right do you have to break into my home and demand answers from me?"

There are only a few feet between us now, and I can smell her sweet strawberry scent. It fuels the desire blazing inside of me—desire that I haven't felt in a very long time. Ten years it's been since my wife was taken so cruelly from me. Lianna was the love of my life, and her death changed me. Since then, I've not wanted a woman the way I want my daughter's friend.

"Answer me," I order.

She jumps at the tone of my voice. "I—I miss her so much..." She shakes her head. "I want to know why you would send away your only daughter like that." Gia looks up into my eyes and there's a sadness in them—a sadness I want to soothe but know I can't.

"Gia, I had no choice and we will have to leave it at that." I can hardly believe the softness of my voice.

The column of her throat bobs as she stares into my eyes. I'm surprised when I see what looks like desire in the depths of hers. "Okay, I guess I'd better be going…" she says awkwardly, still not breaking our lingering eye contact.

A brief silence lingers between us, filled with tension. "Would you like a drink?" I ask.

Gia's cheeks flush, and she finally breaks the gaze. "Oh, I don't know…" She looks down at the floor. "Siena reckons I have already had too much to drink."

I can't help but smile at her endearing bashfulness. "Were you out celebrating a special occasion?"

Her eyes meet mine again, and she nods. "My birthday."

I clench my fist, resisting the urge to confirm her age. It doesn't really make my questionable desires any better if she's twenty-one or twenty-two. She's too fucking young. "I insist. You must have a drink with me to celebrate."

Gia smiles at me and it's such a beautiful smile. "Okay. Thanks, Mr. Alteri."

I almost wince at her calling me that. "Call me Fabio. You're an adult now."

She nods, cheeks reddening more. "Sorry, Fabio," she says, her voice quiet. I can't understand why hearing her say my name drives me crazy. I shouldn't have asked her to have a drink with me.

"Follow me," I say, leading her out of my study and toward the open-plan kitchen and living room.

Gia follows quietly, and when I turn around, she is standing awkwardly in the center of the room.

"Take a seat." I gesture toward the sofa.

I can't help but watch as her hips sway temptingly with each step she takes. It's as if everything about her was made to draw me in to take a bite. I grind my teeth, focusing my attention on getting her a drink. "What is your poison?"

Gia licks her bottom lip out of nerves, but it adds fuel to the fire that is blazing inside of me. My cock is harder than a rock in my tight boxer briefs, making it almost impossible to think of anything but pushing her against the wall and making her mine.

"Do you have any Chardonnay?" she asks.

I nod. "I'm sure I can find you some." I walk into the kitchen area and open the wine fridge, selecting the most expensive chardonnay I have. "Will this do?" I ask, holding it up for her to see.

Her eyes widen. "That's expensive. Don't you have a cheaper—"

I wave my hand dismissively. "It's nothing." I open the bottle and grab two glasses. "I'll share it with you."

She smiles again, and I feel that desire building. It's been too long since I've felt like this. I have had many brief flings with women since my late wife's death, but they were nothing more than a way to take out my frustrations. The desire I feel now was always lacking.

I pour us each a glass of wine and pass hers to her. Our fingers touch as I pass the glass and it feels like a shock of electricity snaps through my body. I know she feels it too as her eyes widen and her lips purse together.

My cock is still hard as she discreetly clenches her thighs. I know Gia wouldn't be able to handle the shit I'm into and that's not even mentioning how wrong it would be for us to cross that line.

"Thank you," Gia says, trying to diffuse the sexual tension in the air.

I sit next to her, watching as she takes a long sip from her glass. Gia is mesmerizing. "How is it?" I ask.

Her eyes move to meet mine and her cheeks turn red again. "It's great." She glances at my glass. "Why don't you try it?"

I'm too busy staring at her, but I don't tell her that. "That would be a good idea, but I wanted to get your opinion." I grab my glass and take a sip. "It's good, but I prefer whiskey."

Gia's nose crinkles. "I'm not a fan of whiskey."

I laugh. "Few women are."

She looks irritated by my comment. "That's a sexist remark."

I don't respond, as I did not intend it to be sexist. It's the truth. Most of the women I've met don't like whiskey. "How did you get into my home and past the guards?" I ask, intrigued that she could outsmart them.

She shakes her head. "I didn't need to get past the guards." There's a hesitation before she carries on. "I guess it doesn't matter now that Aida isn't here. She has a secret escape from the basement to the beach."

My eyes widen. "A breach in the security of my home?" I ask, feeling frustrated that Aida would have kept it from me considering the danger that surrounds our family.

Gia shrugs. "Yes. Aida used it to sneak out now and then when she wanted to go to a party without Aldo trailing behind."

Aida always was resourceful, and it's a credit to her she didn't get caught. The mention of my daughter only irritates me. Ever since I broke her heart and forced her into Milo's arms, I try not to think about her.

"I can show you where I got in if you want, so you can block it up?" Gia suggests.

I wave my hand. "No, don't worry. I'll get my men to find it in the morning." Our eyes meet again and it feels like my entire body is on fire.

There's no way I'm imagining it. Gia wants me as much as I want her. I can see it in her stunning chestnut eyes. "What do you do for a living?" I ask, trying to break the tension between us.

She knocks back the rest of her first glass of wine. "I opened a little flower shop in the center of Palermo."

Gia smiles. "I've always loved flowers and working with them every day is a dream."

I admire Gia for following her dreams and opening her own business. It takes guts to do something like that, not knowing if it will work out. "Are you doing well with it?"

She nods. "Yes, I'm booked solid and have had to employ two flower arrangers to help me."

I grab the bottle of wine and go to fill up her glass, but she stops me. "I'd best be going," Gia glances at her watch. "It's two o'clock in the morning." She sets the glass down on the table and stands.

"Are you sure you can't stay to finish this bottle off?" I ask, knowing I don't really want to drink it.

Gia shakes her head. "No, but thank you for the drink."

I set the bottle down on the table and stand. The unbelievable desire to act on my perverse fantasy with this girl is difficult to ignore. I grab hold of Gia's hand. "You don't have to rush off, tesorina," I murmur, using the term "little treasure" in Italian. It's what a man would normally call his girlfriend, but it just feels right calling her that.

She pulls her hand away. "I need to get back or Siena will wonder why I've been so long."

My brow furrows. "You live with Siena?" I ask, remembering the other little girl that my daughter used to have over to the house.

Gia nods. "Yes, ever since my mother died four years ago from cancer."

I didn't know her mother had died, but I've been out of the loop of general Sicilian society for a long while. Her mother was a well-known seamstress and owned a shop in Palermo, too. "I'm very sorry to hear that." Her worthless father abandoned Gia and her mother when she was only three years old. To have lost her mother so early in life must have been hard.

A tension falls between us as we are silent.

"Let me walk you out," I say, placing a hand on the small of her back.

She tenses at my touch, turning even redder in the face. Once we get to the front door, she moves away and spins to face me. "Sorry that I stormed in here asking for questions," she blurts out.

"Don't be." I step closer to her and set my hands on her hips possessively. "I enjoyed meeting you all grown up, tesorina."

Our eyes lock, and the desire that mounts between us is palpable. It's as if it draws all the oxygen from the air, as Gia starts to breathe heavily. Her chest rises and falls in quick movements. All I can think about is having her naked and writhing beneath me. I clench my jaw and let go of her hips, knowing how wrong it is to want her.

She takes a step away from me. "It was nice to speak with you, Mr. Alteri." She puts her hand out to me.

I shake my head. "I told you to call me Fabio, Gia,"

I say, grabbing hold of her hand and pulling her closer to me again. "Did you forget?"

She licks her bottom lip, which draws all my attention to her lips. "No. Sorry, Fabio." She stares up at me with lustful eyes, and it breaks all my control.

"Fuck it," I growl, wrapping my arms around her waist and lifting her against the front door. "I've wanted to do this ever since you broke into my home, naughty girl," I say, before pressing my lips to hers.

Gia instinctively wraps her arms around my neck and her thighs around my waist. Her mouth parts eagerly as my tongue delves inside, searching it with frantic need. I feel my cock leak into my boxer briefs as she moans into my mouth. The clawing need to be inside of her only increases.

I set her back down on the ground and spin her around. My body remains tight against her as I let her feel the hard press of my cock against her ass. "I want you, tesorina," I murmur into her ear, teasing it with my teeth. "Can you feel how much I want you?"

Gia visibly shivers, arching her back. "Yes, I can feel it," she whispers.

I run my hands down her hips, making her tense. "Do you want it, naughty girl?" I ask, gently moving my hand under the skirt of her dress and teasing my fingers over her inner thighs.

She shudders. "I-I don't... We shouldn't—"

I spin her back to face me and kiss her lips again. "I

always get what I want." I hold her against the wall and move my finger between her thighs.

Gia looks torn between giving in to temptation and doing what is right. The right thing would be to stop this before it goes too far. I'm not one who often does the right thing, though.

I feel the lace of her panties and slide a finger through them. The fabric is wet, meaning she's wet for me. I groan and slide my finger through her soaking wet lips. "So wet for me, Gia."

She moans softly as I slide a finger into her perfect pussy. "This is wrong," she says, but she doesn't tell me to stop.

I kiss her neck. "Why does it feel so right then?"

She moans as I move my finger in and out of her, groaning at the thought of her perfect, tight pussy wrapped around my cock. Her eyes fall shut as she leans her head against the door. I wrap my fingers around her throat and squeeze. "Be a good girl and let me look into your eyes," I order.

Her eyes open and it feels like she sets me on fire with her lust-filled gaze. I capture her lips, continuing to thrust my finger in and out of her perfect pussy. I pull back and hold her gaze as I move my finger to her clit.

She moans softly as I tease her. "That feels so good."

I bite her shoulder softly, continuing to push her toward her climax. "Ci spogliamo," I murmur into her ear, saying let's get naked in Italian.

It seems my suggestion snaps her to her senses. "No." She places a hand on my chest and pushes me away forcefully. "We shouldn't have done this. I've got to go." She reaches for the door handle before I can stop her.

I watch as she flees my home, leaving me sexually frustrated. I slide my finger into my mouth and taste her juice. "Amo il tuo sapore." I murmur the words as I watch her rush away—words that I would have said to her.

I love how you taste.

My cock is harder than a rock in my pants. I shut the door of my home and lean my back against it, unzipping my pants and pulling my cock out. I groan as I pump my fist up and down, thinking about the beauty that just escaped me. The last time I was so wound up that I had to take matters into my own hands I was a young man and had recently met my first wife.

I think about all the filthy things I wanted to do to the young beauty that just left. My cock throbs as I bring myself closer and closer to climax.

The image of her panting and writhing beneath me, tied to my bed as I fuck her roughly, is enough to bring me to the cliff edge faster than ever.

I roar as I come undone, shooting cum onto the travertine floor of my villa. The mess doesn't bother me. I'm lost to my urges like a primal beast.

Gia drives me as crazy as my late wife once did. I

never thought I'd find that desire again. In fact, I thought those urges had died along with her.

It's a dangerous game. Gia is my daughter's best friend—my daughter who hates me enough already after what I did to her. We may have crossed a line tonight, but no one ever needs to know. It's best we keep far away from each other and try to forget about it.

I can't understand why a niggling voice in my mind tells me it's impossible to stay away. The voice tells me that Gia is mine already.

4

GIA

I run from the wolf's den, sprinting down the beach toward Palermo, carrying my shoes that I grabbed on the way past. I'm not sure why I'm running, as I know he won't chase after me. Part of me knows that if I don't run, I'll fall into his trap and take things too far with him. My heart is racing faster than my feet can carry me.

There's no doubt in my mind that I'm the worst friend in the world. I crossed a line that should never have been crossed. Despite how much alcohol I've had, I feel sober. Our encounter sobered me up, so I can't even blame it on being drunk.

Once I'm a suitable distance from Fabio's home, I slow down and walk more leisurely back to the apartment. My mind won't stop replaying the hot, passionate kiss that I shared with my best friend's father. Let's be honest, it wasn't just a kiss. If I hadn't broken away from him, I'd be in his bed right now.

I groan, placing my hand on my forehead. Ever since I was old enough to notice men, I've had a secret—or not so secret—crush on Fabio Alteri.

He's the epitome of a silver fox in every sense of the word. Beautiful gray hair, stunning dark brown eyes, and muscles that would put a lot of twenty-year-old men to shame. I want him more than I've ever wanted anyone.

My phone buzzes, and I pull it out of my purse. It's a text from Aida.

I'm so sorry I didn't take your call. I didn't want to ring, as I know you will be asleep now. Happy birthday. I'll call you tomorrow.

I let out a deep exhale of breath and set the phone back in my purse. I unlock the door to the shop and head inside, going up the back steps to the apartment. Carefully, I sneak through to my bedroom without making a sound. Siena is probably fast asleep, but I'm not sure how I'd explain a walk on the beach taking close to two hours.

Aida would kill me if she knew what happened between me and her father tonight. I hate that our moment of passion was the highlight of my birthday.

There's been a deep ache between my thighs ever since he kissed me. I undress and get into bed, glancing at the alarm clock on the nightstand. It's two thirty in the morning and I'm not even tired.

I am sexually frustrated and reeling from the passionate moment with Fabio. I reach between my thighs, rubbing my clit. My body is overly sensitive after what just happened. I bite my lip to not make a sound and slip my fingers into my pussy.

I shut my eyes and remember how good it felt when his thick finger slid inside of me. The entire situation was intoxicating and beyond exciting. My nipples harden as I finger fuck my pussy harder, biting my lip to stop myself from moaning. Siena is in the room next door, and I don't want to wake her.

The overwhelming desire I felt when Fabio touched me was unlike anything I've ever felt. It was as if his touch burned me. Maybe it's the forbidden aspect that made it hot, or maybe it's because I've admired his stunning good looks since I was about fifteen years old.

It doesn't really matter why I felt so drawn to him. All I know is it's fucking wrong, and once I've climaxed, I need to forget about the entire night. It will just be a hot dream that I had one night and nothing more.

I rub my clit, feeling myself getting closer to the edge. My body is on fire as I think about his rough beard grazing my skin and his muscular arm lifting me against the wall. The way he thrust his fingers inside of me, as though he had the right to do whatever he wanted, was hotter than I'd expected.

He was rough and frantic, as if he had no control over his urges. When I felt his hard cock against my ass, all I wanted was to feel him inside of me.

"Fabio," I murmur his name as I feel myself getting close. The thought of him fucking me is all that it takes and I come undone. The force of my orgasm is stronger than anything I've felt before. Fabio is the reason for the intensity—my best friend's father.

I quickly feel the guilt and shame coil through me as the pleasure wears off. There's something very wrong with me for a wanting a man like him—a man who stole her away from me.

Tonight was a dark and forbidden fantasy come true, but one that is dangerous to reflect on anymore. I need to forget what happened between us.

I ARRANGE a mix of stunning powder pink peonies with white roses, making sure the bouquet looks perfect. I'm working on an arrangement for a wedding tomorrow. It's been a year since I opened Natural Beauty Florist and ever since I've been booked solid.

It's been two weeks since I broke into Fabio's home and we crossed a line that we shouldn't have crossed.

I'm pretty sure I'm going insane. All I can think about is the man I shouldn't want. His powerful muscles, his masculine scent of whiskey and musk, his stunning silver hair. Everything about him drives my hormones into overdrive. That's not even mentioning the way it felt when he grabbed my hips so possessively, pushing me against the wall as if he couldn't control himself.

A snap in front of my face pulls me out of the lust-filled daydream I'd fallen into. "Are you alright?" Siena asks, standing there and staring at me.

I nod. "Yes, why?"

"I literally came in and asked how you are and you just stared into space like you were deaf or something," Siena says, looking at me questioningly.

I shrug. "Sorry. You know how I get when I'm focused on work. I was in my own world." My world where Fabio and I were crossing the line. I could never tell Siena what happened that night. She would be as mad at me as Aida would be.

She shakes her head. "Yes, I know. Did Aida ever ring you?"

I sigh heavily. "No. The last time I heard from her, she sent a text in the early hours of the morning after my birthday." I shrug. "She said she would call the next day but never did."

Siena sets her hands on her hips. "She may have moved half-way across the world, but the least she can do is wish you a happy birthday over the goddamn phone." She shakes her head. "It's not acceptable."

"It is what it is," I say, finding it hard to be angry at Aida after what I did with her father.

Siena's brow knits together. "You've changed your tune since your birthday."

"Yeah, well, as you said, she's a newlywed and has a lot going on in Boston." My chest aches as I say it. "I think it's about time we accept that she's gone and she isn't coming back."

Siena sighs this time. "You're right." She shakes her head. "I just always thought that maybe she'd escape and come back, you know?"

I nod in reply. I'd hoped for that too. The last time I spoke to her, she had changed her opinion about her husband, though. She said that although he had been cruel at first, she'd fallen for him. I couldn't quite understand it after the things she told me he did, but then we can't choose who we fall in love with.

I honestly believe fate brings people together.

If that's the case, why did I wind up in my best friend's father's arms?

"I know we both had hope, but I think there's only so much you can have." I shake my head. "It's time we both move on and when Aida can, she will visit. I'm sure of it."

Siena doesn't look so convinced. "What are you working on?"

I look down at the centerpiece I'm putting together. "Centerpiece for a wedding this weekend." I glance around the shop. "I've got a lot more arrangements to do for the wedding, including the bridal bouquet."

"Where are the two girls you employ?"

I shake my head. "Both booked this week off for

holiday. That's the trouble when you employ a couple. They always want their holiday at the same time."

Siena laughs. "Well, you shouldn't employ a couple in the future. Do you want me to give you a hand?"

"No, don't worry. I'll get it all done easily. I've got tomorrow to finish." I brush her offer to help off as last time her arrangement was a little too messy. Siena doesn't have the patience for flower arrangement. My brow furrows. "Why aren't you at work today?"

She shrugs. "No real estate viewings so I've got the afternoon off." She sighs. "It's been a little rough lately."

I tilt my head to the side. "Why is that?"

Siena rests her elbows on the counter, her face in her hands. "I don't know. It seems foreign investment has dried up." She glances down at the flower on the table and picks it up, twirling it between her fingers. "Hopefully it picks up soon or they might lay me off."

I set my hand on her arm. "Whatever happens, at least we won't lose the apartment."

Siena smiles. "I know." Her parents moved back to Rome two years ago, leaving us to get an apartment for ourselves. I had been living with them since my mother died. My mother had left me an apartment in her will, and I sold it to buy this shop and our apartment above it.

"I'll finish up soon. I need to go to the shop. Do you need anything?" I ask.

Siena looks at me thoughtfully. "I'm making pasta,

but I think we're out of parmigiano. Can you get some?"

I nod in response. "Of course."

She walks toward the back of the shop to go up to our apartment.

I finish the centerpiece floral arrangement and set it down carefully on the table before grabbing my purse and heading into the streets.

I had only intended to go to the shop, but the moment I step out into the center, I find myself heading somewhere else first. I cross the road and head down the same cobbled alleyway I took the night of my birthday two weeks ago.

The fact is, I have no intention of breaking into his home again, but I can't sit by and do nothing while I go insane.

Once I get to Fabio's house, I place my business card through the door. There aren't many guards at the front and none of them ask me what I'm doing. As I walk away, I immediately regret posting the card through his door.

Now the ball is in his court, and if I don't hear from him, I'll probably go insane. The thought of waiting makes my stomach twist as I head back toward the shop to get Siena's cheese.

There is definitely something wrong with me for trying to continue the forbidden path I started on with Fabio. He is off limits. Not to mention, Fabio is broken in ways I can't comprehend.

It's a shame that I've always had a tendency to attempt to fix things that are broken. Fabio is the ultimate challenge—a challenge I should keep my distance from.

So why the hell did I just post my business card through his door?

5

FABIO

"Sir, Milo Mazzeo has requested you attend a party in Boston next month," Lorenzo says, leaning against the doorframe into my home office. "How should I respond?"

I run a hand through my hair, shaking my head. "How long does he expect me to be in Boston for?" There are only so many times I can refuse his invites. After all, I was absent from my daughter's wedding. Aida couldn't understand the danger she was in here in Sicily. She believed my capo's death was just a deal gone wrong, not a feud reigniting—the same feud that killed her mother.

Lorenzo clears his throat. "He didn't say. The party is on the third Saturday in May."

I look at my capo, trying to gauge whether he can hold down the fort for a weekend. "Are you ready to step into my shoes if I go to Boston for the weekend?"

Lorenzo nods. "Of course, sir. I can handle everything while you are in Boston."

I know Lorenzo's careful and competent, but I've never had to trust anyone but Salvatore. "Very well. Tell him I will be there." I run a hand through my hair, knowing that Milo needs my support in the war he's facing in Boston. The Irish have been coming at him hard lately and he's losing men.

"I'll let him know." Lorenzo lingers in the doorway.

"Is there something else?" I ask.

His brow furrows, and he slides a hand into his pocket. "Someone left this card through the door. Does it mean anything to you?" he asks, stepping toward my office desk. He places a card down on my table and I pick it up.

The front of the card has flowers on it and the name Natural Beauty Florist. I turn the card over and instantly know who left it.

On the back it reads "Call Gia Dicampo" and her cell number. I feel my cock harden as memories of that night two weeks ago come flooding back to the forefront of my mind. A day hasn't gone by when I don't think about the moment our lips touched. If it hadn't been for Gia pulling away, then I would have had her in my bed that night. "Yes, it's for me. Thank you, Lorenzo."

Lorenzo looks a little surprised, but doesn't ask me about the card. Instead, he nods. "If that is all, sir?"

"Yes, please leave me."

He walks away stiffly and shuts the door. I stare at

the card for a while, contemplating my next move.

Could Gia have been thinking about our moment of passion as much as I have?

I pull my cell phone out of my jacket pocket and add Gia as a contact before typing a text to her.

I got your card. Have you been thinking about me, naughty girl?

I hit send and place the phone down on my desk, staring at it impatiently. What we did was wrong and taking it any further is a bad idea. However, I can't seem to resist her.

I turn my attention back to my work. There's a planning application for a new hotel to be built close to mine on my desk. All planning applications in Sicily have to go through me before they get put to the council. I have no intention of approving this one, especially when the guy applying is some Russian I know nothing about.

The government's willingness to accept our power in Sicily makes my situation unique. I rule the island and everyone on it, even if it's thinly veiled. The Alteri mafia family has had strong roots here for centuries and that will never change.

I press a denied stamp on the bottom of the page and toss it into the denied pile. My cell phone buzzes and I check it, seeing Gia's name on the front. I feel my cock harden, wondering what she's going to say.

Yes. I can't stop thinking about what we did.

I groan, rubbing my hand across my cock, which is

already painfully hard. The past two weeks it has felt like I'm a teenager again, jerking off constantly and thinking about Gia.

Have you played with your perfect pussy while thinking about me?

I send the text, knowing that I shouldn't be pushing this. Aida hates me enough as it is, the last thing I need is to add in an affair with her best friend. I grind my teeth together, feeling my common sense and my cock fighting each other.

The phone buzzes, and I groan at the sight. There's a photo of Gia in a pair of lace panties and bra with her hand in her panties. The message accompanying it drives me wild.

Every time I touch myself, I think of you.

I glance at the door to my office, which Lorenzo left open. Instead of getting up to close it, I free my cock from my boxer briefs and fist it in my hands. There's no stopping me when I'm like this. I feel like a horny teenage kid, but I can't help it.

The picture is fucking perfect. I take a photo of my cock and send it to her, along with another message.

Such a dirty little girl. I'm thinking about being inside your perfect, tight pussy right now, tesorina.

I focus all my attention on her photo as I take myself in hand. The fantasy of her thick lips wrapping around my shaft as she takes me into the back of her throat flashes into my mind. I grit my teeth, fisting my cock even harder. The image quickly turns to me grabbing a fist full of her hair and fucking her throat so hard she can hardly breathe.

"Cazzo," I growl fuck in Italian as my balls ache for release.

The phone buzzes again and I look at the screen, feeling my cock twitch when I see the image. Gia has sent a photo of her tight little pussy, dripping and wet.

My pussy is soaking wet and ready for your cock, sir.

I clench my jaw, knowing that this innocent young girl can't handle me. She's playing with fire.

The image is alluring and I think about her tied to my bed, blindfolded and gagged. My cock throbs, and I know I'm near my release.

The thought of taking her rough and hard is all it takes to send me over the edge. I lift my shirt up and cum on my abs, roaring as the release hits me. Once I've drained every drop of thick, pearly cum, I grab my phone and take a photo.

My cum should be deep in that perfect pussy of yours.

My breathing evens and I grab a tissue from my desk, cleaning myself up before pushing myself back into my pants. There's something deeply wrong with me for crossing that line with her, even if it is via text message.

The phone buzzes and there's another photo of Gia with her dripping wet pussy and a damp patch on her bed.

Mine should have been all over your enormous cock.

I groan as I stow my phone back into my jacket

pocket, knowing how dangerous we're being. If we start this, then there is no going back. The last time I desired a woman the way I desire Gia, I married her.

I've always been a rough lover. Dominating a woman is the most exhilarating experience, and my late wife loved to submit. It's why we fitted together so well.

The women I fuck accept my rough and ruthless ways during sex, since I'm rich and they want to experience the high life. Gia isn't like that. She's not like the women who like to fuck me for a ride on a yacht or in my jet to London or Paris.

I get up from my desk, feeling restless despite relieving myself. Gia is going to be the death of me at this rate. The only thing that calms me when I'm like this is a long swim along the coastline or a jog. Since it's April and still a little cold in the sea, I opt for a jog.

I get changed into my workout clothes and head out of my living room door and down onto the beach. The sea air clears my head as I try to stop thinking about the tempting twenty-one-year-old girl that has captured my attention like no other woman has in years.

I start along the beach toward the center of Palermo, although I normally run the other way. The pull of stumbling into the woman who is driving me crazy is the only reason, even though it's unlikely.

I force one foot in front of the other, jogging as fast as I can. The sea breeze against my face is calming as I head along the stretch of white sand. A jog helps me relieve tension whenever I'm frustrated.

As I run, I can hardly keep Gia out of my mind. Working out is an easy way to clear my head, but today I can't seem to clear it. She's infected me like a disease and I can't stop thinking about her.

By the time I get to Palermo, I'm more frustrated than I was when I started running. I sit down on the sand and rest my head in my hands.

Ever since Salvatore's death, I've been reeling. On the edge of losing control and barely holding on. He was like a son to me. To top it off, I lost my daughter too. I clench my jaw, feeling regret weigh me down.

My way of life has lost me everyone I care about and I'm left an empty shell of a man with nothing but darkness and hatred.

I sense someone watching me and tense. It's rare that I'm in Palermo, alone without a bodyguard, despite not having many enemies on the island itself.

When I glance over my shoulder, I instantly relax. The beauty I can't get out of my mind is staring at me, frozen like a statue. There's indecision in her eyes, as if she was wondering whether to approach me.

I should turn away and ignore her, but I can't. The first night was a slipup, but the texts were a confession that she wants me as much as I want her. There's no way I'm going to keep away from her, not now that we've crossed the line twice.

Gia is the ultimate prize, and I don't back down from a challenge. She will be mine, consequences be damned.

6

GIA

"Why are you constantly checking your phone?" Siena asks, handing me a tray with some pasta she made for dinner.

I shake my head. "No reason." I stow my phone back in my pants pocket. The reason I keep checking it is that Fabio hasn't replied to my last message, and it's been forty minutes. Our texting quickly descended into sexting in record time.

It's clear from his messages that he wants me as badly as I want him. I tuck into my pasta, which is delicious, but I hardly have an appetite. There's silence between us as we eat, other than the blaring radio that Siena will never turn off.

I pick at the food, keeping my attention on my cell phone, which is on the coffee table in our living room.

I need to stop thinking about the man who is off

limits and totally forbidden. Siena finished eating long before me, running the faucet to wash up the dishes.

I can't stomach any more of my pasta. So, I take the dish to the sink and throw my left overs in the bin.

Siena grabs the bowl. "Didn't like the pasta?" she asks.

"I loved it. I'm just not very hungry."

Siena raises a brow. "When are you ever not hungry?"

"Tonight," I say, laughing.

I walk back to the living room and sit on the sofa, grabbing my cell phone and checking it.

There's still no message from Fabio. I notice it's about ten minutes until the sunset.

"I'm going to go out for a walk," I say.

Siena looks over my way, nodding. "Okay. Do you want some company?"

I shake my head. "No, I want some time alone if that's alright?"

Siena looks disappointed, but waves her hand. "Sure. See you later."

We are two opposites, Siena and me. She has to be with people and talk all the time, whereas I like the quiet and time alone. Aida was more like me.

I grab my purse, slipping my phone into it. "How about some gelato for dessert on me?" I ask.

"I thought you weren't hungry?"

I laugh. "You know there's always room for ice cream."

Siena nods. "I can't argue with that. You know my favorite."

"I do." Siena's favorite is salted caramel, while I love chocolate. I head down into my florist shop and then out of the back exit onto the cobbled alleyway behind and head straight down to Main Street.

I take the first street that leads to the beach. Sicily is a beautiful place to live, and it was an amazing place to grow up, even if my father didn't think so. He abandoned my mother when I was only three years old. Other than a few photos I've seen of him, I can't remember him at all.

My mother rarely dated again and when she got cancer five years ago, it was the hardest time of my life. She battled for a year before finally losing her fight. If it weren't for Siena and her parents, I don't know how I would have made it through. Aida was a support too, but Siena's family took me under their wing and supported me in ways I can never repay.

When they left for Rome because Antonio, her father, had transferred to the main headquarters, it was a bit of a shock. Thankfully, Siena had no intention of returning to Rome because of her job.

I always count myself lucky that I have such natural beauty on my doorstep. The white sandy beach comes into view, and I walk faster toward it. A cool sea breeze encases me as I wrap my arms around myself.

It's quiet on the beach this evening, most likely

because of the cool wind. The moment I get closer to the water's edge, I wish I'd grabbed a coat before I left.

The sun is slowly descending toward the horizon, painting the sky in a deep crimson and orange hue. I glance to my right, feeling my heart skip a beat.

Fabio is sitting with his feet in the surf, staring out at the sunset too. He's wearing sports clothes, and sweat glistens on his forehead, suggesting he's been running.

I swallow hard as I try to decide whether or not to turn around and walk away before he sees me. Especially after the texts I sent him barely an hour ago. Common sense screams at me to turn around and walk away, however, another part of me is egging me on to approach.

Fabio decides for me when he glances over his shoulder. Our eyes meet instantly, and I'm frozen to the spot by his intense gaze.

Fabio's silver hair catches the dimming light, and his face is almost golden. He smiles at me in a way that makes him look heartbreakingly handsome.

I feel heat filter through every inch of my flesh as I remember the photos he sent me and I sent him. There's something very different when you are actually in front of the person, rather than behind a cell phone screen.

Fabio pats the spot of sand next to him. "Gia, come and sit with me."

I swallow hard, glancing around the beach.

What would people think if they saw me watching the sunset with Fabio Alteri?

Palermo is a small town. Hell, Sicily isn't exactly a big island. Everyone knows everyone and gossip can spread like wildfire, whether or not it's true.

Thankfully, the beach is almost deserted, and all I'm doing is sitting. It's not like I'm going to jump his bones in public.

I sit next to him with a few feet of space between us. "What are you doing this far down the beach?" I ask, keeping my attention on the setting sun. Fabio's home is two miles up the beach.

Fabio clears his throat. "I needed a jog and came this way. When I saw the sun setting, I paused a moment to watch it."

I can feel his intense gaze on me, and it's a little intimidating.

"Why are you on the beach?" he asks.

I finally glance at him. "I needed some fresh air and time alone."

He laughs. "Oh, I'm sorry to have interrupted your alone time."

I shake my head. "Not from you. Living with Siena can be a bit much." I tear my eyes from his. "I enjoy the quiet and she's always got to be loud."

Fabio sets a hand over mine, making my heart skip a beat. "I enjoy the peace too. Have you found it comforting since losing your mother?"

I swallow hard, feeling a lump form in my throat. I have found that whenever I'm down, the peace and solitude is a comfort. Life is too hectic and taking a moment to pause and reflect helps. Before my mother's death, I was a bit more like Siena, but her loss changed me. "Yes," I say simply.

Fabio says nothing, merely holding my hand as we enjoy watching the sunset in silence. I hate the way my stomach flutters with butterflies at his touch. It's wrong to even flirt with this man, let alone consider taking this further than it has already gone.

"The sunset is beautiful, isn't it?" Fabio asks, breaking the tense silence between us as the sun finally disappears beyond the horizon.

"It is exquisite," I say, meeting his hot and heavy gaze.

There's so much tension between us it draws all the oxygen from the air. The darkness in the air cloaks us from prying eyes, making the temptation to cross the line again even stronger.

I shake my head. "I wouldn't have come here if I'd known—"

Fabio places his hand on my thigh, stopping me mid-sentence. "I jogged in this direction in the hope of seeing you, Gia."

My heart skips a beat at the sentiment, and I shuffle uncomfortably in the sand. This man is off limits and even thinking about crossing the line again is wrong. It's also dangerous. If anything happens between us, I'll lose Aida.

"This is a bad idea," I say, standing and glancing around to see if anyone saw us sitting together.

The beach is deserted and getting darker by the minute.

Fabio stands and grabs hold of my wrist, tugging me close. I instinctively place a hand on his chest, trying to keep the distance between us.

"What are you doing?" I ask, staring into his dark, almost black eyes.

He yanks me closer, wrapping his arms around me tightly. "Whatever the hell I want, tesorina."

He knocks the air from my lungs as he lowers his lips to mine. I tense, painfully aware that we're in a very public place.

Fabio's tongue probes at my lips, demanding entrance. His masculine scent floods my senses as I give in, allowing his tongue to plunder my mouth.

I moan, unable to get a handle on my urges. No matter how much I tell myself to stop, my body has a life of its own. I've wanted this man too long to resist his advances.

Fabio tightens his grasp on me, groaning into my mouth. "I want you, Gia," he murmurs against my lips.

I'm about to say it's a bad idea when he grazes his teeth up my neck before nibbling on my earlobe. He makes me forget everything. It's hard to believe this is wrong when it feels so natural.

When he finally stops, I'm panting for breath and too turned on.

"Come to my home for dinner tomorrow evening," Fabio says, eyes full of passionate desire.

I swallow hard, searching his dark brown eyes. It's an invitation I should decline without hesitation.

"What time?" I ask.

Fabio smiles handsomely. "I'll text you to confirm." He kisses me again, stealing the breath from my lungs for the second time. "See you tomorrow, tesorina." He turns away and jogs in the opposite direction without another word.

I watch after him, wondering if I've truly lost the plot. Tomorrow night I'm going to Fabio's home and there's no way we're going to resist temptation.

The sensible thing to do would be to text him and tell him I can't come. I head back toward Main Street and stop by the gelato shop. Siena wouldn't forgive me if I forgot her ice cream.

When I get back, she's got the music blaring louder. I turn it down when I walk in. "Ice cream," I say, sitting down next to her on the sofa and passing her the caramel ice cream.

"Thanks," she says, taking it. She begins talking about some friend at work, but I can hardly hear her.

My mind is consumed by the man I agreed to have dinner with tomorrow night and how wrong it is. I play with my cell phone in my hand, considering sending

Fabio a text to cancel tomorrow evening right away. It's a bad idea, and yet I can't find it in me to cancel.

It's clear that I'm walking a dangerous path. Fabio is not only my best friend's father, but the most dangerous man in Sicily. Death and destruction follow him, but it seems I do too.

7

FABIO

*L*orenzo knocks on my door, looking uncertain about entering.

"What is it?" I ask.

He is clutching a file in his hand. "I've finished the report on the Moretti family's movements for the past month."

I nod and gesture for him to enter. "Any important findings?"

My capo looks torn, setting the report down in front of me. "One." He runs a hand across the back of his neck. "Every Thursday the entire family gets together at a restaurant in the center of Naples without fail."

I smile at my capo, knowing this is exactly the information I was looking for when I set him this task. "Perfect. You know what to do."

Lorenzo stares at me for a few beats. "Are you sure about this?"

I glare back at him. "Am I sure about annihilating the people that murdered my wife and best friend?" I shake my head. "Are you sure you want to ask me that question, Lorenzo?"

Lorenzo clenches his jaw. "Revenge never brings the people you love back. It only deepens the dark wounds that fester inside of you."

I narrow my eyes at him. "Careful. I don't appreciate being questioned."

Lorenzo doesn't back down. "If I am to be your capo, then I must question you. It's my job as your second in command. Who else will if I don't?"

For the first time since I appointed him, I feel a small sense of admiration for the man standing in front of me. He's right. Salvatore always brought my decisions into question, challenging me. However, there is no one on this earth that can dissuade me from seeking revenge on the Moretti family. No matter the fallout. I have nothing left to lose.

I nod. "You are right. As my capo, you have a responsibility to question my decisions." I run a hand through my hair. "However, there is nothing you can say to stop me from pursuing revenge against the Moretti family."

Lorenzo nods. "Very well. I'll make the arrangements." He lingers a moment. "Is there anything else you need?"

I shake my head. "No, I have plans tonight." I check

my watch, noticing that it's half-past six. Thirty minutes until Gia is due to arrive. "I'll see you tomorrow."

"Yeah, I'll keep you posted on Naples." He turns his back on me and walks out of the office.

I shut down my computer and head out of my study, planning to freshen up fast. I head to my bedroom and strip quickly, turning on the faucet of my shower.

I get under the spray and wash myself. As soon as I'm in the shower, the memories of Gia come flooding back. My cock hardens as I wash myself, finding it impossible not to slide my hand around my shaft and jerk it a few times.

I groan at the thought of being inside of Gia. It's sick that I want her so badly, considering how young she is. I let go of my cock, knowing that there's no use relieving myself now. By the time Gia walks through the door, I'll be hard again.

I clench my jaw as I wash, trying not to think about the tempting, forbidden beauty coming to dinner. My daughter would hate me more than she already does if she knew. I'm a selfish man. It's not new for me to put my needs before others. The only people's needs I ever gave a damn about were my wife's and my daughter's.

I step out of the shower and towel myself off before walking into the closet. I put on a cream shirt and button it half-way up, before selecting a pair of black pants to go with it. Once I'm satisfied that I look good, I head out of my room and into the kitchen, where Alejandro is already preparing our dinner.

"How is it coming along?" I ask.

He looks up and smiles at me. "All on time, sir."

The doorbell rings and I feel my heartrate speed up. There's no going back from this. I turn away from the kitchen and walk slowly toward the front door. My head is at war with itself, as I know I shouldn't be doing this. I reach for the door handle and open it.

The moment that I set eyes on Gia, I feel that war settle a little. A certainty spreads through me that this is right, no matter how unconventional it may be. Her blonde hair is curled into gentle waves, and she's wearing an exquisite turquoise dress that frames her beautiful curves perfectly.

I reach for her hand and lift it to my lips. "You look beautiful, Gia," I say.

Her cheeks turn pink, and she pulls her hand away. "Thanks." She drags her eyes down the front of my suit. "You look good too."

I step to one side to allow her inside. As she walks past me, her sweet, berry scent overwhelms my senses.

Once I've shut the door, some of the tension in her shoulders eases. "You have such an amazing view here," she says, staring out of the floor-to-ceiling windows of the open-plan kitchen and living room. "Last time I was here I couldn't admire it." She laughs. "When I was a kid, I cared more about what toys Aida had to play with. It really is stunning."

I set a gentle hand on the small of her back. "It is beautiful, isn't it?" I sigh as I stare out over the azure sea. "One of the best places to watch the sunset is from my terrace."

Alejandro has already set out canapes on the terrace and the wine on ice. I lead Gia out of the bifold doors onto the terrace. "I thought we'd dine out since it's warm today."

Gia smiles, and I feel the desire inside of me increase. "Sounds perfect."

I pull out a chair for her at the intimate dining table and she sits, reddening a little. "Thank you for inviting me to dinner," she says, her voice so sweet it makes me groan.

The thought of having such a delicious woman submit to me is enough to drive me insane. "You're welcome, tesorina." I grab her napkin out of the wineglass, placing it on her lap and allowing my hand to linger. "The chef is making us his famous ravioli." I grab the bottle of Chardonnay out of the cooler and pour her a glass.

I return to my side of the table and sit down opposite her. A tense silence falls between us as we stare at each other from either side of the table. Gia reaches for an olive and pops it into her mouth, a move that isn't intended to be sensual, but somehow is.

I watch her intensely, feeling mesmerized by every one of her quirks.

Gia shuffles uncomfortably and meets my gaze. "About those texts we sent—"

"Don't worry, baby. They will remain our little secret."

Her face reddens more, and she shakes her head. "Are they the reason you asked me to dinner?"

I feel my cock hardening at her question. There's no way I'm letting her escape me tonight. She's walked into the wolf's den and she's not getting out until I say so. "Yes. I thought that would be obvious, Gia."

She bites her bottom lip in a way that makes my cock even harder, shaking her head. "They should remain a fantasy."

"I beg to differ."

Alejandro steps onto the terrace with two dishes. "I hope you are both ready to eat, sir."

I beckon him over. "Yes. Thank you."

He places a plate in front of Gia first and then me. A flash of recognition passes through his features when he sees Gia, but if he knows her, he doesn't acknowledge it. Gia glances after him as he swiftly heads back to the kitchen without another word.

"What is your chef's name?" She asks.

I raise a brow. "Alejandro. Do you know him?"

She swallows hard. "Aida and I went to high school with him." Gia sets a hand on her forehead. "He's going to tell everyone about this."

I laugh. "He isn't stupid enough to spread any

gossip from my home. Alejandro signed a nondisclosure agreement before he stepped foot over the threshold."

Gia visibly relaxes. "Oh. Of course." She shakes her head. "Sometimes I forget who you are."

I run a hand across the back of my neck. "That's a dangerous thing to forget, tesorina." I pick up my fork and taste the ravioli, which, as always, is divine.

Gia picks up her form. "It smells delicious," she says.

I tilt my head to the side, observing the woman in front of me. It's odd how she makes every single thing she does alluring without even trying.

"Back to the subject we were discussing before the chef interrupted. You're not leaving here until I've made you mine," I say simply, forking more ravioli into my mouth.

Her red face deepens in shade as she keeps her attention fixed on me. She shakes her head. "What about Aida?"

The mention of my daughter brings the biggest issue to the forefront of my mind. Aida would hate me more than she already does if I fuck her best friend. The likelihood that Aida will never find out is the only reason I'm flirting with the idea. "Aida is thousands of miles away."

Gia looks torn. "She is, but if she ever found out…" She shakes her head. "I'd lose my best friend."

She's right. We both should resist the twisted temptation and think of my daughter. There's a chance that in time she will understand my actions on the clifftop and give me a chance to explain everything to her, but if I cross this line with Gia, all will be lost.

"What if we make sure she never finds out?" I ask.

Gia looks torn as she stares into my eyes from across the table. It's as if we both know that if this starts, we won't be able to stop. "I think it's a bad idea."

I rap my fingers on the table, looking at the family crest on my ring. It is a bad idea, as Aida should come first, but I'm a selfish man. Gia didn't come here thinking that nothing would happen. She wants this as much as I do, even if she's getting cold feet now.

"It may be a bad idea, but I always get what I want, Gia." I meet her gaze across the table. "And I want you."

Gia's cheeks flush, and she clears her throat. "That's cocky."

I smirk. She knows who she's dealing with. "I own Sicily, tesorina. Don't you think I have a reason to be cocky?"

Gia doesn't answer me and instead turns her attention to her food, shaking her head as she tastes the ravioli for the first time.

"How is it?" I ask.

She barely looks at me, shaken by my previous statement. "Delicious, thank you."

I can't understand why she's trying to back out now, when she's come this far. The last thing anyone should do is tease me, as I'm not one to back off if I want something.

"I'm glad you like it. How did you get into flower arranging?" I ask, curious to learn more about the intriguing young woman she's become.

Gia takes a sip of the Chardonnay I'd selected for us. "I've always loved creating." She shrugs. "Unlike my mother, I wasn't that interested in fashion but flowers always fascinated me."

"Your mother's boutique was famous in Sicily. I bought a few dresses from her for my late wife and after her death, for Aida." I knock back the rest of my whiskey, hoping it will take away the sting of losing both of them.

Gia probably thinks I'm a cold-hearted son of a bitch who doesn't care about his only child. It doesn't matter what she thinks. I know the truth.

"My mom had a lot of clients." She gazes into her wine glass wistfully. "I have quite a few of her dresses at home, but I can't ever bring myself to wear them in case I ruin them."

I shake my head. "Your mom would want you to enjoy wearing them. She made them for people to wear and enjoy, not for them to be shut in a closet never to see the light of day."

Gia contemplates me. "I never thought about it like that."

"Many people don't." I run a hand across the back of my neck. "It's not until you lose the people you love that you realize how brief life is. You must live in the moment and seize every opportunity. If you don't, you will only regret it on your deathbed." As the don of a powerful crime organization, I have many regrets about the way I have lived my life.

Love is the only thing in this world worth fighting for, but I couldn't find that truth in time to save the only thing in this world that mattered: my family. As I gaze up from my dish and meet Gia's light chestnut eyes staring at me, I feel a tug in my chest.

"That's so very true." Gia looks sad. "There were so many things my mom still wanted to do when she died."

I draw in a deep breath, trying to stop myself from feeling sorry for the girl sitting opposite me. She's had things hard in life up until now. I love how resilient she is despite it all.

Alejandro returns. "Sorry to interrupt. I wanted to check if you are finished?"

I glance at Gia. "Have you had enough?"

She nods. "Yes, thank you."

Alejandro takes our plates. "Shall I bring dessert straight out?"

I nod. "Yes, please." I'm impatient to get him out of here so the real fun can begin. Gia will be at my mercy and begging me to fuck her before the night is through. She may be shy now, but deep down I know that she's a dirty girl who needs a good punishment for the filthy pictures she texted me.

8

GIA

I finish my last spoon of chocolate dessert, feeling more nervous now than I was before dinner.

Fabio had already clarified that he has no intention of letting me go without fulfilling the fantasies we detailed in our text messages. A part of me wants that more than anything, despite the consequences.

Fantasy only takes you so far. Sitting opposite him has made this too real. The betrayal of my best friend is too much, but it's clear from Fabio's recent actions that he doesn't care much about Aida.

Whenever I stop thinking about the consequences, it feels so natural between us. My few relationships have always been hard work, and yet sitting and talking with Fabio is as easy as breathing. Perhaps it's because he's mature and understands how life can change so drastically when you've lost someone close.

"How was dessert?" he asks, dark brown eyes fixed on me intently.

I smile. "As delicious as the rest of the meal. Thank you."

He nods. "Alejandro is an amazing chef."

I shudder as a cool sea breeze gusts through the air, tugging my shawl tighter around me.

"Are you cold?" he asks, eyes almost glimmering in the candlelight.

"A little," I say, shrugging. "It is only April."

He smiles and the corners of his eyes crinkle attractively. "Why don't we go inside?"

I hug the shawl around my shoulders tighter. If we go inside, it'll only lead to one thing. A part of me wants this night to go that direction and the other part of me doesn't. "If you would like," I say.

Fabio stands and offers me his hand. "It is getting cold."

I hesitate a moment before placing my hand in his. It's clear that all the reservations about what we are doing are one-sided. Fabio doesn't seem fazed about the idea of fucking his daughter's best friend.

Fabio pulls me to my feet and leads me back into his home, which is now empty. I can only guess that Alejandro left after bringing us our dessert. "Have a seat," he says.

I sit on the plush velvet sofa and he takes his place next to me. There's barely a foot between us, and his masculine scent is overwhelming.

Fabio places his hand on my thigh, making me shudder. "You need to relax, baby," he murmurs, his voice like silk.

I swallow hard as his touch and voice racks my entire body with a desire so strong it feels like I'm going to explode if we don't fuck tonight. "I need you, Fabio," I murmur, knowing how dangerous those words are.

A knowing smirk tugs at his lips. "I know, tesorina. All in good time." He squeezes my thigh before letting go and pouring me another glass of wine. "First, a toast."

I begrudgingly take the glass of wine from him. "A toast to what?"

He holds his glass of whiskey up and taps it against mine. "A toast to you becoming mine tonight, Gia."

I raise a brow at him, feeling my stomach twist. "Yours?" I shake my head. "Even if we make those texts a reality, no man will ever own me."

He chuckles, and it's not exactly a friendly laugh. "Oh, Gia, you have got a lot to learn about me." Fabio places down his whiskey glass and grabs my throat softly. "I own everything on this island. You will be mine."

A sinking dread ignites in the pit of my stomach. All this time I've been lusting after the man I've had a crush on and forgotten about who he is and what he stands for. He's dark and dangerous. He means what he says. Perhaps I've walked straight into a trap, deceived by what appeared to be empathy and an electric chemistry between us.

"Tell me you understand," he orders.

I swallow hard, wishing he would let go of my throat. "I understand."

"Good girl," he purrs before releasing his grip. "In the future, I want you to call me sir."

I stare at him in disbelief. "What?"

His eyes narrow. "I said I want you to call me sir."

I shake my head. "No," I reply simply.

He snatches my wine glass out of my hand and sets it down before turning his frantic gaze back to me. "I don't think you understand what is happening here, Gia."

I shift away from him on the sofa, which only seems to enrage him.

He grabs hold of my wrist and drags me closer. "I am in charge. What I say goes." He searches my eyes with a wild look. "I want you to call me sir, and you will."

I feel a surge of defiance at being told to do something. Discipline was never something my mom taught me as a child. I was frequently allowed to do whatever I wanted since my mom was so busy with work. "I'd like to see you make me," I spit.

Fabio smirks. "I love a challenge." He stands and lifts me off the sofa as if I weigh nothing, forcing me onto my knees. He pulls a pair of handcuffs out of his pocket. "You'll learn that I don't like disobedience, tesorina." He clamps the handcuffs around my wrists tightly.

"What the fuck—"

Fabio brings his hand down hard against my ass, making me squeal. The force is unforgiving. He does the same on my other ass cheek before lifting the hem of my dress.

I try to fight out of his grasp, but he's too strong. "Let go of me."

Fabio spanks my ass again. "Not until I have taught you a lesson, tesorina."

It's hard to believe that the same man who I'd just engaged in a deep conversation with over dinner is treating me this way. "That's not how this works," I say.

He places a finger through my panties and tears them from me. "That's exactly how it works, baby. I'm going to make you scream all night long," he says, before plunging two thick fingers inside of me.

My mind recoils at his touch and how fast this all happened, but my body reacts. I feel myself getting wetter as he moves his fingers in and out of me. "So fucking wet, tesorina," he groans.

My nipples harden, and that desperate desire inside of me grows. I arch my back as he finger fucks me, making me forget all reason. Suddenly, he stops and then spanks my ass again, even harder than before.

The sharp pain only serves to amplify the incredible pleasure he's enticing from my body. His fingers plunge deep inside of me again, and he hooks them in a way that hits the perfect spot. My nerve endings ignite, and it feels like I'm on the edge of a cliff, ready to tumble over at any moment.

Never has a man gotten me to the edge that fast. Fabio backs off the moment he realizes how close I am. "Such a naughty girl," he says, spanking my ass again. "You love being punished so much you almost orgasmed, but I control those too, tesorina."

"Is there anything you don't control?" I ask breathlessly, feeling unsatiated after being left on the edge of climax.

"No," he says simply. "Come sei bagnata," he says.

I feel him part my thighs further. "What are you—"

He doesn't allow me to finish the question, burying his face between my thighs. All rhyme and reason float away on a sharp exhale of breath.

It's so wrong that this man who is old enough to be my father is licking my pussy, and yet it feels so right. "Oh, fuck," I cry, arching my back as he licks my clit.

Every lap of his tongue sends my senses into overdrive. I feel the edge of climax approaching faster than before. Then he stops.

I groan. "Ti prego," I beg him in Italian.

Fabio stops and grabs hold of my throat from behind. "What do you want, baby? Tell me."

The force of his hand around my throat is strong, but not enough to hurt. "I need to come."

He chuckles. "Is that right?" He rubs his finger over my clit. "Only good girls get to come, and I don't think you've learned your lesson yet." He stops rubbing me and spanks my ass harder than before.

"Fuck," I cry, feeling the harsh pain radiate through my flesh.

Fabio spanks my other cheek as hard, before burying his face between my thighs again. I have never felt so aroused in all my life.

This man does things to me I never knew were possible. The way he doles out the perfect amount of pain and pleasure to amplify the need inside of me is masterful. "Please make me come," I cry, feeling the frustration build inside of me.

He spanks my ass again before parting my ass cheeks wide.

I gasp as he licks my asshole, making me tense. It's such a filthy thing to do. "Fabio—"

He spanks my ass again. "No talking. I know you love me licking your asshole because you're a dirty little girl, and I don't want to hear anything to the contrary."

I feel my thighs shudder as he continues to lick me. It's the first time a man has ever ventured to that part of my body, and it feels better than I could have imagined.

The pressure inside of me becomes unbearable as he rubs my clit at the same time. I grit my teeth, knowing he's about to send me over the cliff's edge.

I moan when he doesn't stop, finally allowing me to come. "Fuck, yes, sir," I moan as he sends me over the edge.

"That's it, tesorina. Come for me so I can lap up

every fucking drop," he growls, before sliding his fingers into my pussy.

"Fuck," I cry, shocked at how intense my climax is. Every muscle in my body spasms at the force of the climax. I squirt all over his sofa, making a mess. It's beyond thrilling as he spanks my ass, amplifying the pressure.

By the time I come down, I can hardly think straight. My body is racked with exhaustion as I slump onto the sofa, face first. The handcuffs are still tight around my wrists, forcing me to stay in the same position.

Fabio spanks my ass again. "Don't relax. We've barely even started."

He walks in front of me and leans down, forcefully grabbing my chin. "I'm going to fuck you all night long, baby." He kisses me, forcing me to taste myself.

I moan like a whore, as that's what he's turned me into. A dirty whore who can't get enough.

Despite my pleas for him not to cross that line, he did it anyway. I can't understand why him ignoring me is a turn on. It's sick and twisted.

Fabio doesn't care whether or not I want him to fuck me. He wants me and he always gets what he wants.

"I didn't say I want you to fuck me," I point out.

He lets go of my chin and smirks down at me. "Do you think you have a choice?" He shakes his head and grabs his cell phone, pulling up the photos I sent him.

"Are you saying these photos were just to tease me, tesorina?"

I swallow hard as I look at the text messages and pictures I sent him. They were not just to tease him as I want to cross the line with Fabio, but my relationship with Aida comes to the forefront of my mind. "No, but I don't want to hurt my best friend."

He stows away his phone. "You should have thought about that before you posted your card through my door." He crosses his arms over his chest. "Better yet, before you sent me a picture of your perfect little pussy ready for my cock." He moves back to stand behind me and spanks my ass hard. "I don't stand for being teased. Girls that tease need to learn true discipline." He spanks me harder than ever before, making me cry out. "I'm going to make you learn your lesson."

I hate the way my thighs clench and my pussy aches at the thought of being taught a lesson by him. "You're insane. Undo these fucking handcuffs now."

He chuckles. "Oh, Gia. Careful what tone you take with me. I don't like being told what to do." He grabs holds of my throat from behind, choking me so I can't breathe properly. "I take what I want, when I want. You are no different."

A cold dread creeps through my veins as I realize the dangerous mistake I made ever getting involved with this man. The line I crossed was wrong, but the taboo aspect made me forget to question the man Fabio is.

Dark, damaged, and ruthless. A man who doesn't care who he hurts if he gets what he wants. I've made a grave mistake in more ways than one. "You have problems," I spit when he releases my throat.

He ignores me and spanks my left ass cheek hard before spanking my right. He spanks me over and over, wordlessly.

I hate the way the desire inside of me rekindles at his rough, dominant treatment. There's something very disturbing about my desire to be dominated and disciplined by a man who's so broken.

9

FABIO

I'm pretty sure my little treasure underestimated how dark and depraved I am. Many people forget what kind of man I am when they meet me in a public setting. The politics of Sicily dictate that I have a different public persona, and it fools many.

"Have you learned your lesson yet, tesorina?" I ask.

Gia glances over her shoulder at me with a mix of shameless desire and rage in her eyes that could burn any man alive. "Never," she spits.

I love how determined she is not to fall into my trap, even if physically her body is responding to everything I do to her. "That will change, baby." I run a hand over the curve of her ass gently before spanking her again. "Your pussy is so wet that your juices are making a mess on my sofa." I slide my finger inside of her and she gasps, bucking her hips in a way that makes my cock leak. "I think it's about time you take my cock."

Gia tenses and looks over her shoulder at me "You wouldn't dare."

She has underestimated the man that I am. "You told me how badly you want my cock, Gia. I will just fulfil that wish." I unzip my pants and free my hard, throbbing cock from the confines of my tight boxer briefs.

Gia doesn't look back at me, stiffening even more. "You are insane," she says.

I grab hold of her hips and drag her closer to me. Slowly, I drag the head of my cock through her slick, wet juices. "It doesn't matter how much you try to deny it. I know you want me."

Gia doesn't deny it, shuddering as she feels the head of my cock bump against her clit. Instead of pushing forward, I pull away and walk to stand in front of her. "Succhiami il cazzo," I order.

Her eyes are blazing with a fierce mix of anger and lust as she takes in my size. "Succhiatelo da soli," she spits.

I growl softly and grab hold of her chin between my finger and my thumb. "Don't make me get my open mouth gag, Gia." I kiss her lips. "I'm not sure you're ready for me to have unrestricted access to the back of your pretty little throat."

"You're a pig," she says.

I let go of her chin and fist my cock in front of her

face. "Mettilo in bocca," I say. If she resists me again, I will be forced to get the gag.

Gia doesn't resist this time, opening her mouth for me.

I slide the head of my cock into her mouth, groaning as she wraps her thick, plump lips around my shaft. "That's it, baby, suck it like a good girl."

She glares at me as she moves her head up and down, allowing my cock to slip back into her throat each time.

The violent need inside of me to dominate is always there, clawing at my control. All I want to do is grab a fistful of her beautiful blonde hair and fuck her throat so hard she chokes on my cock. The thought of Gia gagging all over my cock, saliva spilling down her chin, makes me lose control.

I grab her hair and force her head forward, pressing my cock deep into her throat.

Her eyes widen as she gags, frantically begging me with her eyes to stop. She has no control since I handcuffed her wrists. I don't stop forcing her to take my cock over and over. "Breathe through your nose, tesorina," I order.

Tears prickle at her eyes as she tries to relax, breathing through her nose as my cock continues to pound her throat. "Cazzo, e'incredible," I groan, loving how good her mouth feels.

When I finally pull my cock from her mouth, she

gasps frantically. "Are you trying to kill me?" Her eyes are wide.

I lean down and grab her chin between my finger and thumb. "Open your mouth," I order, ignoring her question.

She hesitates before opening her mouth.

I spit into it, making her moan despite her reservations. "You're my dirty little whore, Gia." I kiss her, searching her mouth with my tongue. "Mine to do with as I please." I walk around the sofa again so I'm behind her and drag the tip of my cock through her dripping wet pussy. "Ti scoperò col mio cazzo e urlerai di piacere." My dirty talk makes her arch her back.

"This is a bad idea. We shouldn't do this." She glances over her shoulder at me helplessly. "Please don't."

It's cute the way she thinks she has any power here. I tighten my grip on her hips possessively and pull her back, forcing her tight, wet pussy to take every inch of my cock.

Gia moans, arching her back, so I slide as deep as possible into her pretty little pussy. The insatiable yearning for this woman only grows the moment her tight muscles squeeze my cock. It feels like I belong inside of her.

"You feel perfect wrapped around my cock."

Gia moans again, glancing over her shoulder at me as I fuck her. The look in her eyes is no longer one of anger, but of passionate lust. She wants this as much as I do, despite her feeble attempts to stop me.

I fuck her harder, moving in and out with vigorous strokes. The sound of skin slapping against skin fills the open plan living room and her moans punctuate the air too. I can't find it in me to care that the spot lights illuminate my villa and with the floor-to-ceiling glass along one side we're visible from the beach.

All I care about is claiming and possessing the woman in front of me in every single way imaginable. My eyes fix on her tight little asshole. From the way she tensed when I licked her there, no man has ever fucked her ass, and I intend to take her anal virginity.

I move in and out of her tight, wet heat, grunting as she pulls me in deeper. "You are fucking perfect, Gia," I groan, spanking her already red ass.

She moans softly at my treatment of her. A hope has ignited inside of me that she could be the submissive I crave. It seems too convenient that the first woman I've desired in so long could fit my lifestyle so perfectly.

The control I normally have is slipping through my fingers. I'm an animal as I take her rough and hard.

Her moans only push me further into my animalistic tendencies, tendencies I haven't explored in a long time.

Sex for so long has been clean and clinical. All about control and domination, but never about the primal and basic need to fuck. Gia brings that need to the forefront and drives me over the edge. "That's it, baby, take my cock," I growl, tightening my grip so hard on her hips that I know that I'll leave bruises. In fact, I want to leave bruises. Gia makes me so crazy that I want to mark her and brand her as mine.

"I want to feel that tight little pussy come on my cock," I say, spanking her ass. The way her body responds to the mix of pain and pleasure is perfect.

"Fuck, yes, sir," she cries as she tumbles over the edge. Her already tight pussy clamps down on my cock so hard that I feel my release come at the same time. My cock explodes deep inside of her pussy, filling her with my seed. The perfect way to brand her as mine is to mark her with my cum.

Gia is panting as I finish pumping in and out of her, draining every drop. Once I'm finished, I pull my still hard cock out of her and walk toward the kitchen.

"Aren't you going to undo the handcuffs?" Gia asks.

I glance over at her, smirking. "We're not finished yet."

Her eyes widen as they travel down to my hard cock.

I grab a bottle of olive oil off the kitchen counter.

Gia watches me, brow furrowed. "What are you going to do with that?"

I don't answer her question. I know if I tell her I'm going to fuck her ass, she'll freak out.

Instead, I walk behind her again and pour some straight onto her tight little hole. Before she can say another word, I slide my finger through her tight ring of muscles.

She tenses at the sensation, clamping down hard on my finger. "Fabio, stop—"

I spank her ass cheek. "Remember, tesorina. I'm in control." I press my hand against the small of her back. "Relax and enjoy it."

Slowly, I move my finger in and out of her hole, getting her used to the sensation.

Gia moans, signaling that it feels good. Once I'm certain she's used to one finger, I add more oil and slide another finger in too. "Oh, fuck," she cries as I plow two fingers in and out of her tight little hole.

"Has anyone ever done this to you, baby?" I ask.

Gia shakes her head. "No. It feels..." She trails off as I add a third finger. "Fuck me."

I love her dirty little mouth. It's so fucking hot. My cock is leaking all over the sofa as I kneel behind her.

The way her ass grips my fingers makes me long for my cock to replace them. "I want to fuck your tight little ass, Gia." I continue to move three fingers in and out, stretching her. "I want to be the first and only man to fuck you ass," I growl, feeling the possessiveness take hold.

"No way," Gia says, voice full of disbelief. "That would hurt too much."

I add a fourth finger, increasing the oil. "Does this hurt?" I ask, fucking her with four fingers now. Her ass is practically gaping for my cock, ready to feel every inch slide inside.

"No, but—"

I spank her ass with my free hand. "No buts. I need to claim every one of your holes tonight." I pull my fingers from her ass and she whimpers. My cock is harder than a rock as I pump it a few times, coating it in oil. I line the head up with her tight little hole and push forward without warning.

She takes the head of my cock easily.

"Fabio, please don't—" I slide further inside, forcing her to stop mid-sentence. "Fuck, that's too big," she cries. Her puckered hole clings to my cock tightly as she takes every inch.

I only stop moving once she's taken every inch into her ass. "Sei la mia puttana, Gia." I spank her ass. "You've taken every fucking inch, baby."

Gia half-moans, half-cries as I move my cock out slowly.

I'm fascinated by the way her tight ring of muscles clutches around my cock as if desperate to keep me inside. Once I'm half-way out, I slide all the way back in again.

"Fuck, yes," she cries.

I chuckle softly. "It looks like my little whore loves being fucked in the ass," I murmur, reaching forward and grabbing hold of her throat softly. "Do you love having my cock in your ass, Gia?"

Gia tenses at the question, as if it brought her back down to reality. "No," she says, but it's a feeble lie.

"Liar," I growl, grabbing hold of a handful of her hair and fucking her harder in the ass. "You just screamed 'fuck, yes.' I don't like liars, tesorina."

I fuck her harder and rougher, making her moan.

"I'm going to fill your ass up with my cum so that you are dripping from both holes," I growl, feeling that primal side of me take control. "Then I'm going to continue to fuck you all night long."

Gia's thighs visibly quiver at my promise. "Yes, sir. Please fill my ass with cum," she cries, finally accepting the truth. This is right. Me and her fucking had to happen, no matter the consequences.

I groan as she comes again and squirts her juice everywhere, making it impossible to hold out any longer. "Fuck, Gia. Take my cum like a good girl," I growl, letting my climax come. I fill her ass with my seed, grunting as her tight muscles drain every drop from my balls.

We remain silent in the same position, neither of us saying a word. Finally, I pull my cock out of her ass and undo the handcuffs around her wrists, stroking the marks where the metal dug into her.

Gia looks exhausted and a little delirious as I lift her in my arms and carry her toward my bedroom. My little treasure doesn't realize that I've hardly even started with her. I can't satiate the insurmountable urge for her until I've had her a few more times.

10

GIA

The rays of sun streaming into the bedroom disorientate me. I sit up, blinking a few times.

I take a moment to realize that I'm not at home. Fabio is asleep next to me. My heart skips a beat, and I scramble for my cell phone on the nightstand. There are seven missed calls from Siena and a bunch of texts asking me where I am.

I swallow hard and quickly type a reply to her.

Sorry, I met a guy last night and one thing led to another. See you later.

Last night was nothing like my fantasy. Fabio is darker than I ever imagined and his need to dominate is sadistic. It didn't matter what I said. He was having me whether or not I liked it. A part of me liked the way he took control, but I've never felt more conflicted before as I watch him sleeping by my side.

I get out of bed carefully, wincing at the soreness between my thighs. I make sure I don't wake him. My dress is in a corner on the floor, and my panties nearby are in shreds. I grab the dress and move to pull it over myself when I feel two large hands grip my hips.

"Where do you think you are going?" he murmurs into my ear, hot breath hitting the back of my neck.

I swallow hard, hating the way my body responds to him. "I need to open the shop."

"You must think I'm stupid, Gia. It's a Sunday."

Fuck. He's right. It is a Sunday, which means the shop can't work as an excuse to get the hell out of here.

"Right. Siena is worried and needs help at home," I lie.

He forces me around to face him, his dark eyes full of desire that make my thighs quiver. "You're not a very good liar, baby," he says, eyes fixed on my lips. Fabio tightens his grip possessively on my hips and pulls me close, kissing me passionately.

The kiss is hot and heavy. It's even more charged with need than any kiss we've shared before.

I rest my hands on his hard chest, feeling the short hair that covers his skin. His tongue searches my mouth demandingly, forcing me to moan into him. Fabio grabs my ass, making the hunger inside of me insurmountable.

Despite how he treated me the night before, I need him to fuck me. It doesn't matter how wrong this is. I'm hooked on the dangerous don who is totally off limits.

"I need you inside of me," I say as he breaks the kiss. When I look into his eyes, there's a torn look in them. "Ti prego," I beg in Italian.

The look softens, and he smiles handsomely. "Since you asked so nicely, tesorina." He wraps an arm around my waist and lifts me, forcing me to wrap my legs around his hips. "I have a meeting in forty minutes so we will have to fuck and shower at the same time." He kisses my lips, driving me wild with a craving unlike any I've experienced before.

After the way he so roughly took me despite my protests, I should run out of here as fast as possible. Instead, I'm hooked by his dominant side. The way he commands and disciplines me is oddly appealing.

Fabio carries me into the bathroom and sets me down on my feet. He turns on the faucet to the shower.

I'm already totally naked since he stopped me from putting my dress on, but he's wearing a pair of tight boxer briefs. Slowly, he tugs them down and steps out of them. It's impossible to keep my eyes from dipping to the huge, thick length of his cock.

"Guardami," he orders.

When our eyes meet, the inferno of desire glowing in his dark brown eyes is enough to scold me.

He grabs hold of my hips and pulls me close. "Mi fai impazzire."

I shudder as he tells me I make him crazy. The feeling is mutual. "Fuck me, ti prego," I murmur, wanting him inside of me more than anything.

He smiles against my neck before lifting me again. Fabio carries me into the shower, pressing my back against the wall "My pleasure, baby," he purrs, thrusting his hips forward and burying himself deep inside of me.

"Fuck," I cry, digging my nails into his shoulders as he roughly fucks me against the wall.

There's no teasing or playing this time.

"Cazzo, come sei stretta," he growls, fucking me harder.

My hard, peaked nipples graze against his muscular chest. There's a frantic urgency as we fuck under the spray of the shower.

Fabio pulls his cock out of me, leaving me empty. He sets me down on the floor. "Piegati," he orders.

I do as he says, placing my hands on the wall and bending over.

"You are too fucking perfect, tesorina." He thrusts his cock back inside of me, filling that deep, cavernous hole he left.

I moan, loving the way it feels as he grabs hold of my hips dominantly. Fabio is in complete control and it's a breath of fresh air. There's nothing unsure or awkward about this. He is so self-assured about what he's doing to me.

"Fuck me, Fabio," I beg, which earns me a sharp spank.

He stills inside of me. "I told you to call me sir, tesorina."

I feel the passion between us increase at his unforgiving tone. "Sorry, sir." I arch my back, but he remains still inside of me. "Fuck me, sir."

He roars like an animal behind me, digging his fingertips so hard into my hips I'm sure he will leave bruises. "Sei la mia puttana."

I should be pissed that he calls me his little whore but I'm surprised how much of a turn on it is to be called that.

"Yes, sir," I cry as he fucks me hard and fast, forcing me toward the cliff edge with no reservations.

The sound of wet skin clashing against wet skin fills my ears, along with his beast-like grunts. It's as if he has no control of his urges—as if I make him lose control. It's a position that makes me feel empowered.

"I want to feel your pretty little pussy come all over my cock, baby," he orders behind me, grabbing hold of my ass before spanking it. "Then, I'm going to fill you with my cum until it's dripping down your thighs," he growls.

"Give me your cum, please, sir," I cry, feeling that mounting pleasure overwhelm me. I've never been one to talk dirty, but Fabio brings it out in me. He's the most dominant and sexy man I've ever met.

He spanks my ass, fucking me roughly and grunting like an animal. "I'll give it to you once you come and not before," he says, reaching down and rubbing my clit.

That's all it takes, as every nerve ending in my body

is set ablaze. My vision turns white and my muscles spasm as he fucks me through my orgasm.

He growls behind me, biting my shoulder as he comes undone. It's not soft and he will certainly leave a mark on my shoulder, but for some twisted reason I want him to.

I want him to mark me as his, even though this can never happen again. We lived out a fantasy that proved to be so different in reality, but in amazing ways.

My ass is sore from his rough fucking last night, but he opened my eyes up to how good things I've never thought of can feel.

I feel a gush of his hot cum drip down my thighs as he pulls his cock from me.

He wraps his arms around my waist, forcing me around to face him. His lips capture mine with a conflicting tenderness as he kisses me lazily. When we break apart, we're both panting for breath.

"I wish I could stay here with you all day," he murmurs between us.

I hate the way my stomach flutters at the statement. Fabio is rough and unforgiving. A man who knows how to get you hooked but will never let you off it.

He grabs hold of the shampoo bottle and squirts some into his hands. He strokes it through my hair without saying another word.

It's an oddly tender move from him. One that I find unsettling.

Once we're washed, I go to get dressed in my old dress, but Fabio stops me. "Wear something of Aida's."

I meet his gaze and shake my head. "No chance. How would I explain that to Siena?" I pull my dress over my head, knowing that it would be unexplainable. "I better get going."

Fabio grabs my hand and pulls me back to him, kissing my lips. "See you soon, Gia."

I swallow hard, not replying as I walk away from him and out the back door onto the beach. No matter how badly I want to see him again, I know it can't happen.

Last night and this morning were a big mistake, and one I won't make again soon.

"I NEED EVERY JUICY DETAIL," Siena says as I walk through the door, making my entire body hot with embarrassment.

"There's not much to tell." I shrug. "I met a guy and we hooked up. That's all." The guilt spreading through me is sickening. I just spent the night in Aida's father's bed. It was the best night of my life, but that doesn't change the sick reality. I'm the worst friend in the world, particularly for wanting to do it again.

"Well, who was it?" Siena asks. "There are few guys we don't know on the island."

I meet her overly excited gaze. "A guy on holiday

from Rome." I shrug. "He's leaving today so I won't see him again." It makes me feel even more guilty that I'm lying to Siena.

"You seem way too deflated for a woman who just had sex. Was it terrible?" she asks, tilting her head slightly.

My cheeks are burning as the memories flood my mind. It was certainly not terrible. "No, I guess I'm disappointed that it won't happen again." It can't happen again, no matter how badly I want it to.

Siena sighs. "I told you we both need to move to Rome." She shakes her head. "It's where all the good guys are."

I laugh, shaking my head. "That's never going to happen." I flop down onto the sofa next to her. "Maybe the perfect guys from Rome need to move here." I indulge her, despite knowing that the perfect man is already living on this island. Fabio Alteri is the best lover I've ever had, which means forgetting about him will be difficult.

"Yeah right." Siena rolls her eyes. "The woman always has to follow the man."

I sigh. I know Siena is right, even though it's an archaic construct. "Well, it looks like we will remain single forever, then. No man is worth leaving my shop or this island for."

As I say those words, I know they are true. The only man I want is off limits. We may have indulged in a night of dirty fantasies, but that's as far as it can go.

Aida is my best friend. I can't end up in a relationship with her father, no matter how badly I want to continue things with him.

"What do you want for dinner tonight?" I ask, knowing it's my turn to cook.

Siena shrugs. "I've had a craving for Tierry's pizza for ages. Do you want to go out or get take-out?"

My brow furrows. "I'm supposed to cook tonight."

Siena waves her hand dismissively. "Cook tomorrow night. In or out?" she asks.

"We'll get take-out," I say, knowing that I can't handle facing the public right now.

Although no one knows what happened, the sense of deep shame inside of me is difficult to overcome. I can't face the thought of sitting in a restaurant tonight as if nothing happened.

"Yeah, that's probably best. There's supposed to be a storm tonight," Siena says.

I stand and head toward my bedroom. "I need to get changed."

Siena doesn't reply, turning the sound on the radio up as I head into my room. I flop down on the bed with my head in my hands, hardly able to believe what I've done.

11

FABIO

A flood of rage hits me. "What do you mean it went south?" I growl, making my capo pale.

"I sent two contractors as agreed to take the family out, but somehow they knew and boycotted the restaurant." Lorenzo shakes his head. "Ever since that day their entire routine has changed."

I stand and throw my whiskey tumbler against the wall. "Cazzo." I pace the floor, clenching my fists as the violence of my rage inside of me consumes me entirely. "This is your fault, Lorenzo. I asked you to do this one fucking thing for me and you fucked it up." I stop deadly still and stare at him. "How did they know?"

Lorenzo shakes his head. "I don't know. We have a few informants in Naples. I can only assume one of them betrayed us."

"How can I trust you to oversee this place in a couple weeks while I'm in Boston if you can't even get this right?" I shake my head. "Informants don't need to know our plans. Only the fucking contractors hired to take them out."

I take a deep breath, knowing that if I don't calm the rage, it will have a life of its own. If I'd been handling this myself, the Morreti family would be dead, buried in a pile of rubble. If Salvatore had been alive, I know he would have got this right. He knew how much my revenge means to me.

"I'm sorry, sir. I had to ask the informants to find me the contractors." His brow furrows. "If I'd been able to go to Naples in person—"

"Stop. I don't want to hear any more excuses." I hold a hand up. "This was a mistake, and it's on you." I run a hand across the back of my neck. "Get me another angle by the end of the week. You know you can't step foot in Naples unless you want your head blown off." I loosen the tie around my neck. "I need a sit-down with all of my men tomorrow." My brow furrows as I glare at the paperwork Alex brought me yesterday morning. "It seems we have a thief in our ranks."

"A thief?" Lorenzo asks.

"I'll reveal all at the sit-down. Can you arrange it?" I ask, hating being questioned by a man who is so inept that he fucked up my first real chance at revenge.

"Of course, sir." He turns to leave.

I clear my throat. "Lorenzo."

He turns to glance at me. "Yes, sir?"

I glare at him. "Don't fuck it up with the Moretti family this time or there will be severe consequences," I say, making sure he knows how serious his mistake is.

Lorenzo is a good guy, but he's clearly not up to the challenge, despite all the training I've given him. It's been a year and five weeks since that fated day when the Moretti family murdered my capo. He should be better than this by now.

Lorenzo's Adam's apple bobs as he swallows. "I won't."

I wave him away dismissively, feeling the pressure of my rage constricting my lungs. It feels almost impossible to get enough air as the weight of the anger and sorrow I carry around threatens to crush me.

Lorenzo leaves my office, shutting the door behind him gently.

Revenge is the only thing I have left. It's what I cling to—an anchor that grounds me. Lorenzo fucked it up. I should have handled it myself, but contractors rarely like to deal with me directly because of my reputation. They are freelance and they value their lives above all.

Lorenzo is the best of my men, the only man I could trust with this, but even he can't pull it off. A deep sadness tugs at my chest, heightening the rage. I haven't had time to grieve for Salvatore. I'm not entirely sure I ever even grieved properly for my late wife. Their brutal murders are images I struggle to erase from my mind.

Nights are sleepless as the terrible scenes haunt my

dreams. Guilt is a crushing burden on top of it all—guilt that I couldn't protect either of them.

The things I've seen in my life would shock most, but the most scarring image of all is finding someone you love brutally violated. It hasn't only happened once to me, but twice. When I found Lianna raped and brutally dismembered in our own bedroom, something inside of me snapped. The tether that grounded me to a moral code and basic decency was destroyed that day, and I've never been the same since.

I knew from that moment that life would change. Revenge has been my sole aim, even though I knew I had to go about it carefully. For years after they had her killed, the Moretti family moved around a lot. They knew I wanted to come for them.

They found a foothold in Naples, and the Busa family protected them. The Busa family allowed them to take control of Naples, making it virtually impossible for me to touch them.

If one problem isn't enough, Alex, my spy, has brought me some damning evidence. Two of my men have been skimming off the top and stealing from the Alteri mafia. The sit-down tomorrow will be bloody.

My phone buzzes and I eagerly pick it up, hoping Gia might have finally come to her senses and answered me. I feel my stomach sink when I realize that it's Lorenzo, confirming the time and place for the sit-down tomorrow.

It's ridiculous. I'm not the kind of man who sits around waiting for a woman to reply.

It's been three weeks since I crossed the line with Gia. Three weeks since I had her writhing beneath me. That Sunday morning, I never should have let her leave. I should have locked her in my bedroom so I could have my way with her whenever the fuck I wanted. There's not a moment I don't think about her, and it's driving me mad.

I've had a short fuse ever since she ignored my last text two days ago. As the leader of a powerful mafia organization, I'm not used to people ignoring me. Gia obviously thinks it's okay not to reply, which means she needs to be taught a lesson.

It's pathetic that every night I run down the beach, hoping to bump into her. She's never there. I have tried calling her, and she ignores my calls, sending them to voicemail.

No one ignores me. I feel my rage increase.

All the shit going on just overwhelms me. First, Gia ignores me. Second, I find out men who I'm supposed to trust are stealing from me. Third, Lorenzo fucks up the most important job I've ever given him: securing my revenge against the Moretti family after ten years of waiting, plotting, and planning.

I stand from my desk and pour myself a glass of whiskey, knocking it back in one gulp. Gia's shop is my only option. It may be in the center of Palermo and where her friend lives, but I don't care who sees me there. The gossips in this town are relentless and even I don't have the power to control hearsay, but she has left me with no option.

If she won't respond to me, then I have to track her down in person.

I grab my suit jacket off the back of my chair and shrug it onto my shoulders.

Alejandro is in the kitchen, making me dinner. "Are you going out, sir?" he asks, brow furrowed.

I meticulously follow a routine, which I rarely ever break. "Yes."

He looks at the food he's preparing. "Shall I leave the food in the oven for you to heat up?"

The last thing on my mind right now is food. "Whatever." I wave my hand. "I'm not hungry currently. You can leave it in the fridge and I'll get it out later if I want it."

"Of course, sir."

I head for the front door and open it, breathing in a deep breath of cool air. It's cold considering it's early May. May is typically mild, but the weather this year has been fucked up.

Aldo is off today so I have no one to drive me. It's probably best that I walk into town, anyway. I need an outlet for the rage and frustration building inside of me. Gia won't like me showing up at her shop, that's for sure.

I walk down the street toward Palermo center. My little treasure can ignore me as much as she wants, but she can't hide from me. Not in Palermo, or on this island. I own it and rule it.

I take whatever the fuck I want and don't apologize. It's part of the job description and something I've become accustomed to. One thing is for sure: I will have Gia again whether or not she wants me.

12

GIA

It's been three weeks since the fated night. Three weeks since Fabio took control of me, as if he owned me. I hate that I still can't get him out of my mind, despite his sick and twisted ways.

No man has ever made me feel that good. Sex with Fabio was the best I've ever known, and it's hard to forget. The way he took whatever he wanted was intoxicating. All I know is that crossing the line once has to be enough. If we take this further again, then there will be no stopping.

Fabio has called me a few times and sent me about three texts since we had sex, but I've ignored all of them. There's no sense in allowing this to go any further. I already feel so guilty for lying to one best friend and betraying the other.

Most days before Fabio and I had sex, I went down

to the beach in the evenings. Now, I make sure not to go down there in case Fabio is out for a run.

The flower arrangements for a golden wedding anniversary are almost finished. Angelica and Claudia are putting the finishing touches to the centerpiece as I make the flowers for the arches that are to be setup on the beach. "We've not got long to get these to the beach, girls. How are you getting on?" I ask.

They both glance back at me. "Fifteen minutes, tops," Angelica says, and Claudia nods.

"Perfect." I place the last rose into one of the arch dressings and tie it off with natural woven fabric. "What would I do without you two?"

They laugh. "Drown in a sea of flowers," Claudia says.

We all laugh as I grab a few boxes from the back of the shop to put the flowers in to carry down to the beach. Claudia and Angelica continue the finishing touches on the centerpieces, while I box up the rest of the flowers for the event.

I can't believe in over a year since opening I now employ Angelica and Claudia full time. And the way things are going, I might need to find more help. Although, that's not exactly easy when you live on an island. Flower arranging requires attention to detail and a love for all things floral.

Once I've packed the boxes and gotten them on the trolley we use for local transport, I go to check the centerpiece. "It looks amazing, girls."

They both smile at me. "Thanks. I did most of the work," Claudia says.

Angelica punches her in the shoulder. "You are such a liar."

I shake my head. "Is it ready to box up?"

They nod. "Yes, let's get it in a box and then we will head down to the beach," Claudia says, heading into the back to find a large enough box. She comes back with one and we carefully place it in the box before setting it on top of the trolley.

The bell to the front of the shop rings and I look up. My heart feels like it stops beating when I see Fabio standing in the doorway. His dark eyes are fixed on me with an intensity that sends shivers down my spine. "It looks like we've got a customer. Are you okay to get these down to the beach for me? Otherwise we're going to be pushed for time," I ask.

Claudia and Angelica notice who has stepped into the shop and exchange nervous glances. "Sure. We will see you down there?" Angelica asks.

I nod. "Yes, I won't be too long I hope." I walk toward the counter where Fabio is waiting.

"Good afternoon, sir. How can I help you?" I ask, remaining professional, although my heart is beating so fast it feels like I'm having a heart attack. I never expected Fabio to step foot in here.

He clears his throat. "I need flower arrangements for an event I'm hosting."

Claudia and Angelica push the trolley out of the

shop, leaving me alone with the dangerous mobster. At least they won't suspect anything as it just appears as if Fabio needs to order flowers.

The moment the shop door shuts, I shake my head. "What are you doing here?"

Fabio smirks at me. "You left me no choice, bella." He runs a hand through his beautiful gray hair. "You ignored my texts and calls." He shrugs. "What else was I supposed to do?"

"Get over being rejected like any other sane human being?" I suggest.

His expression darkens. "Avoidance isn't rejection. I know you want me." He shakes his head, leaning over the counter. "If you thought you could get into my bed once and then walk away, you were dangerously mistaken, Gia."

I swallow hard at the harsh tone of his voice, wishing it didn't make my hair stand on end. "We can't continue this. It's wrong."

Fabio places his hand over mine, making me tense. "If it's wrong then why did it feel so right?" he asks, posing a question I can't answer.

We stare into each other's eyes, and that heated tension emerges between us. I lick my bottom lip as all the dirty, dark memories of that night come flooding back to me. "Fabio." I murmur his name, glancing down at his hand over mine. "What do you want from me?" I ask.

Fabio lets go of my hand and walks around to the

same side of the counter as me.

"No one except staff can come back here," I protest feebly, despite knowing that this man doesn't care about the rules.

Fabio chuckles softly, a sound that makes butterflies dance in my stomach. "I've missed you, Gia," he murmurs, closing the gap between us.

I shake my head and slip past him into the back of the shop, knowing that it's too public in the front. Anyone could walk in or glance through the shop window and see us getting close.

Fabio chases after me. "I don't mind the hunt, tesorina," he says, eyes frantic as he corners me.

I lick my bottom lip. "Why can't you see that this is a bad idea?"

He smirks at me. "How can it be a bad idea when it feels so good when I'm inside of you?"

I swallow hard, wishing that statement wasn't true. "Because I'm your daughter's friend." I shake my head. "Because we shouldn't do it."

He closes the gap between us, forcing me to move closer to the wall. "I want you, Gia. Do I strike you as a man who cares about the consequences?"

"Not exactly." My back hits the wall. I've got nowhere to go.

Fabio places a hand on either side of me against the wall, boxing me in. "I can't get you out of my mind, tesorina." He grabs hold of my throat in a dominant yet tender grip. "I want you in my bed every night. Do you understand?"

I bite my bottom lip, knowing that can never happen. "I can't—"

He tightens his grip on my throat and presses his lips to my jaw, kissing it. "You can and you will."

I sigh heavily, wishing he wasn't so impossible to have a conversation with when he's like this. "I need to get going. The event down on the beach won't organize itself."

Fabio doesn't let go. "Your employees will handle it, I'm sure." His eyes narrow. "Text them and tell them you're caught up doing my order and won't make it," he orders, grabbing my cell phone out of hand.

"No, I need to see the client."

The look he gives me could kill. "I said text them and tell them to handle it. Now."

I glance at the phone and nod, typing out the text to Angelica.

Fabio moves his hand to my throat, teasing it down into my blouse.

I shudder as he cups my breasts, making me wish I'd worn a bra today.

"You aren't wearing a bra, Gia. Why?" A look of jealous rage enters his eyes.

I stare at him in disbelief. "I find it more comfortable not to wear one. Is that a crime?"

He moves his hands to my hips and pulls me against his hard, muscular body. "No, but if you ever so much as look at another man, I'll kill him," he growls, making the hair on the back of my neck stand on end.

"What are you saying?" I ask, wondering how on earth I landed myself in such a ridiculous situation with a man as dangerous as Fabio Alteri.

"I'm saying that you are mine, Gia. Always." Fabio kisses my lips hard, possessing them. "Now, be a good girl and wrap your arms around my neck." He grabs hold of me and hoists me against the wall.

"Fabio, what the hell are you doing?" I ask, feeling unbelievably exposed as he loses control in a place that's so personal to me. "Siena or anyone could walk in." Sure, it's past closing time, but Siena could come back at any minute. She had to take clients to the other side of the island, but she never mentioned what time she'd be back.

"Fuck Siena. You ignored my texts and calls. You left me with no option." His eyes are frantic as he forces a hand under my skirt and tears my panties in two. "I need you now." He frees his cock from his pants and thrusts into me without another word. My head falls back against the wall as he makes me feel whole the moment he enters me.

My nipples are hard peaks against the fabric of my blouse as he rips open the buttons without a care in the world. He captures my right nipple between his lips, sucking on it and making it painfully hard. "Fuck, Fabio," I murmur.

He growls. "It's sir to you, baby."

A flood of white hot pleasure ignites inside of me. "Yes, sir," I say, looking into his eyes. He captures my left nipple with his lips and lavishes attention on that one.

He fucks me hard against the wall, his muscles straining as he lifts me up and down his cock.

Fabio is like a man possessed as he takes me in the back of my shop without a care. "I've been going fucking insane ever since I last saw you," he says, biting my bottom lip. "Never ignore me again."

He carries me over to a crate in the corner and sets me down on my back, keeping his cock buried inside of me.

"This is crazy," I say.

Fabio shakes his head. "No, you are crazy for ignoring me." He grabs my hips and fucks me on the crate. "Never do that to me again, do you understand?"

I look into his eyes and feel an odd sense of desperation to be cared for by this man. "Yes, sir," I answer.

"Good girl. I want you to come to my bed every night from now on." He shakes his head. "I don't care if you have to sneak out in the early hours. Just make it happen," he says, pumping his cock in and out of me.

The bell at the front dings and my heart leaps into my mouth. Fabio stills inside of me, watching my expression. Siena normally uses the back entrance, but she might have come through the front if she forgot her keys. "Hello, is anyone here?" a man calls.

Fabio places a hand over my mouth and holds my gaze, continuing to fuck me slowly. He's certifiably insane.

I meet his gaze questioningly, trying to ask what the fuck he's doing.

He stares right back at me, fucking me as some guy shouts out front.

I relax the moment I hear the bell ding again, and the door slams shut. "You are crazy."

Fabio smirks. "Yeah, crazy for you, baby," he groans, increasing the tempo of his thrusts. "Crazy for this tight little pussy wrapped around my cock."

His words melt me as I feel the pleasure increase, despite where we are. Fabio has a way of making me forget the consequences when his hands are on me.

He bites my neck. "Have you touched yourself in bed thinking about me?" he murmurs into my ear.

I swallow hard, thinking of the amount of times I've got myself off thinking about Fabio since that night. "Yes, sir, every day."

He groans. "Good girl."

I hate the way my stomach clenches every time he calls me that. It's as though I crave his approval.

Fabio kisses me again, forcing his tongue into my mouth and claiming it the way he claims everything else from me—rough and hard, with no apology.

"I want you to come on my cock, baby," he groans.

I look into his eyes, feeling the pleasure mount.

He plays with my nipples as he continues to pump into me harder. "Come for me."

I feel my climax hit me and bite my lip to stop myself from screaming. My vision blurs as I stare up at the beast who took me without mercy. He demands everything from me as if it's his right, and for some sick reason I love it.

Fabio roars against my skin as he comes undone, pumping me full of his seed. When he finally stops thrusting, he looks me in the eye. "I want you in my bed tomorrow night. Do you understand?"

I nod. "Yes, sir, I understand."

He kisses me. "Good girl," he whispers.

The bell at the front goes off again and my heart leaps into my mouth. We both freeze, waiting to hear who it is.

"Gia, are you here?" Siena's voice rings through the shop.

It feels like all the blood in my body drains out as I freeze against Fabio. We're about to be caught red-handed.

13

FABIO

Gia pushes me off of her, eyes frantic at the sound of her friend's voice.

I must admit that I got a little reckless. It's what Gia does to me.

She nods toward the fire exit at the back. "Out of there, fast," she mouths.

I steal another quick kiss from her. "Don't forget. Tomorrow night," I whisper into her ear, forcing my cock back into my pants before heading out of the back of the flower shop.

I check to see if the alleyway is clear then make my way toward Main Street. It was impulsive to walk into Gia's shop like that and even more impulsive to fuck her in the back.

Before I met her, I always made calculated decisions. It's as if I've lost all of my common sense, blinded by a primal desire for Gia.

It's a dangerous situation because a man who's not in control can't comprehend the surrounding risks. Control is one of the most important things a leader has to possess, and right now I hardly have any.

Gia is dangerous, not only because she's forbidden, but because I can't think clearly around her.

Aida's other best friend almost caught us. If I'm going to keep pursuing this, then I need to be more careful.

I enter Main Street only to be met by a rough-looking man standing in my way and blocking me from leaving the alleyway. "Who the fuck are you?" The guy flashes a crest on the medallion around his neck. The Moretti family crest. I growl, "You are on my turf so I won't hesitate to kill you."

He laughs at that. "I'd like to see you try, old man."

Something snaps inside of me. I step toward him and punch him square in the jaw.

He grunts at the impact, moving his fist to punch me back. I capture it in my palm and squeeze hard enough to crack his knuckles. "No one attacks me in my hometown and lives to tell the tale," I say, searching his eyes frantically. "Who are you?"

He punches me in the side, knocking the air from me.

I step away before he can hit me again and pull out the switchblade in my pocket. "I won't ask again. Who are you?"

"Dario Moretti, son of Rafa Moretti."

My brow furrows. I wasn't aware that Rafa had another son other than Benito. "Perfect. I will kill you and ship your fucking head back to Naples."

Dario shakes his head. "I highly doubt it." His eyes shift behind me and I know that he's got backup.

I move fast, knocking the gun from the hands of the man behind me. I grab him and force my blade against his throat. "You thought your bodyguard could save you?"

Dario pales slightly as I drag the knife across the bodyguard's neck, killing him quickly. "What the fuck?" Dario asks.

I shake my head and move toward the now cowering son of my enemy. "Was it you who killed my capo?" I ask.

His eyes flash with fear. "What if it was?"

I shrug. "It doesn't really make a difference. You are dead either way."

Dario pulls a gun suddenly, aiming it at me.

I hold my hands up in mock surrender. If he thinks pulling a gun on me is enough to get me to back off, then he's gravely underestimated my desire for revenge.

Rafa was foolish to send his son into my territory to attack me. It's a mistake he will regret for the rest of his life.

I fling the switchblade in my hand at him and duck, knowing he may pull the trigger as a reaction.

The blade slides through the side of his neck, making blood spurt out over the wall he's standing next to. The gun goes off as he drops it, and the bullet ricochets off the floor.

Dario hits the floor, clutching his neck. "You bastard," he growls.

I smirk at him, feeling unbelievably thankful that Rafa Moretti finally made a grave mistake. All these years, I've been waiting to hurt him as badly as he hurt me. "You will die a slow and painful death," I say, kicking his head hard enough to knock him out.

I pull my cell phone out of my jacket and dial Lorenzo. He picks up on the second ring. "Boss, what is it?" he asks.

"Morretti's son just tried to kill me in the streets of Palermo. I need you down here to collect him and take him back to my home."

"Fuck," he curses. A few moments of silence ensue. "Of course. I'll be there in five minutes."

"Good. Hurry. He's losing a lot of blood. I can't have him escape torture that easily. This remains between us only." I cancel the call and pull the decorative handkerchief out of my jacket pocket, pressing it against the guy's wound.

The knife cut a minor artery, but he's lost a lot of blood. I never expected my chance at revenge to come to me, but now it has. I won't allow this bastard to escape the pain I need to inflict.

Revenge is at my fingertips, but even once I've killed this man and shipped him to my enemy, it won't be enough. He took two people I loved away, and I will do the same to him.

I can't understand why I don't feel more satisfied as I stare at the man on the floor. Revenge is all I've longed for all these years, and yet it feels like nothing will ever be enough.

I fear that Lorenzo may be right. The deep, dark hole inside of me will never heal and revenge will only make it deeper.

I WALK around the man now strung up in my basement. The answer to my prayers. It astounds me that Rafa Moretti sent his son here onto my turf.

He groans. "My father will kill you for this."

I laugh and punch him in the gut. "Your father will die if he tries." I play with the switchblade, knowing that I'm going to get great pleasure from torturing this man.

It's a sick fact, but what these people did to my wife and then my best friend is inexcusable. They even had the audacity to attempt to kill me in the center of Palermo.

No doubt it was a retaliation after learning that I intended to wipe out their entire family in that restaurant.

The frustrating thing is that Rafa is more cautious

than even I am. He doesn't take risks, and they'd only just relaxed, feeling like they were invincible.

If Lorenzo had fucked it all up permanently, I wouldn't have been able to forgive him.

Lucky for him, it seems Rafa was stupid enough to bring the fight to me.

"The fact is that I will post you piece by piece to your coward of a father." I stab the knife into his arm, making him squeal like a girl. "There is no escape for you, Moretti."

He glares at me with a hatred that matches my own. "You're a sick fuck, old man."

I hate being called an old man. It frustrates me more than I can explain. "An old man that bested you in a fight." I tilt my head to the side. "How old are you, anyway?"

He narrows his eyes. "Thirty-two."

I run a hand across the back of my neck, nodding. "Makes sense why I didn't know of you. You aren't a son from his current marriage, are you?"

He spits at me as an answer.

"It's disappointing. I wonder if he will care when I kill you."

Dario growls angrily, "Of course he will care. He doesn't even know I came here to kill you once and for all."

I walk around him in a circle. "It's me who should be desperate to kill you and your cowardly family." I stab the knife into his side, making him howl. "First your father raped and brutally murdered my wife, all because he wasn't happy that I kept hold of a territory my family have ruled for centuries." I pull the knife out and stab it into his other side. "Then, ten years later, once you've established your own territory, you come back and brutally murder my capo." I pull my knife out and place it under his chin, forcing him to look at me. "Why is it that you are so desperate to kill me , when all I've ever done is kept hold of what is mine?"

Dario knows there is no justifiable answer to that question. They're the ones that have wronged me. They're the ones that need to pay. "And yet, I'm the sick fuck?" I laugh. "The sick fuck is the man that cut my best friend's head off."

"You are pathetic, clinging onto a territory you can't provide stability to." Dario shakes his head. "You have no one to take over."

Salvatore was the man who I had in line to take over, the one who would marry my daughter so that it remains in the Alteri blood line. "I had someone until your family murdered him." I move my wrist quick and slice Dario's ear off, making him squeal in excruciating pain. "This will do as my first gift to your father," I say, picking it up and placing it in a clear plastic bag. "You can believe whatever you want. The Alteris have run Sicily for centuries and that will never change."

I grab a bandage and wrap it around his head, making sure he doesn't bleed out. "I will be back for more each day, slowing carving pieces off of you." I walk to the sink in my basement, and turn on the faucet, placing my blood-stained hands under the water. The clear water stains with blood as I wash them . "Unless you want to tell me how I get your father."

Dario's eyes widen, and he shakes his head, wincing as he does. "I'll never betray my father, you figlio di puttana." He calls me a son of a bitch in Italian, but I don't react.

Instead, I walk calmly away from him, leaving him strung up in my basement.

He may act tough now, but as I carve more pieces off of him, his resolve will slowly waiver. This man will give me the key to my revenge, no matter how far I have to take it.

The ultimate prize would be Rafa Moretti, the man who raped and cut up my wife. The man that I've hated with a passion for ten years. For now, Dario Moretti is the perfect leverage I need to reel in the big fish.

Rafa will die at my hand, or I'll die trying to kill him.

"Boss, everyone is here," Lorenzo says.

I nod and stand from the desk in our central Palermo office building. "It's going to get bloody, Lorenzo." I narrow my eyes. "Make sure you lock the door."

Lorenzo swallows. "Of course, sir." He steps aside to allow me to go first.

I haven't explained to him what I have found. The only other people who know about the theft are the two men that did it and Alex, my spy. At least, that's what I hope. This sit-down should weed out any other rats in my organization.

There are two types of people I hate the most: cowards and thieves. Normally, they are the same.

I walk through the corridors of my office block toward the largest meeting room. Lorenzo's footsteps follow close behind. Lorenzo already gathered my men in the large room to wait for me to arrive. I instantly notice the two men that have betrayed me, sitting near the front. Alfonzo and Buto Esposito are twins. They've been a part of the mafia since they turned eighteen years old.

I can't deny that when Alex brought the evidence to me, it surprised me. The Esposito brothers always struck me as loyal and honest men, but it's clear my judgement was way off with them.

My men stand as I enter the room and take my place at the head of the table. "I've called this sit-down because there are ladri in our ranks."

I keep my gaze moving over the crowd of men, but notice the way Alfonzo pales. "It's with a heavy heart that I have to do this, but the Alteri Mafia can't exist without loyalty. When that loyalty is broken by several members, they need to be weeded out publicly to ensure everyone knows what happens when greed supersedes your loyalty to our organization."

Lorenzo is standing by the door, arms crossed. If anyone tries to run, he'll take them down.

"Before I call out the thieves amongst us, is there anyone who wants to come clean?" I tilt my head to the side, still ensuring my gaze falls on each of my men in equal measure. "Your punishment will be less painful."

A deafening silence floods the room as my men glance around, including the Esposito brothers. They're stupid cowards for not coming clean.

"I should have known the cowards wouldn't come forward." I slam my hand on the table, making everyone jump. "Alfonzo and Buto, stand up."

Alfonzo stands and quickly tries to run. But one of my men, Vanni, stops him. "Where the fuck do you think you are going?"

I nod at Vanni. "Thank you." I stand and walk toward Buto, who hasn't tried to escape. Instead, he stares at me with a dark hatred that I'm not sure I deserve. "So, you thought you could steal from me and get away with it?"

Buto doesn't bat an eyelid, staring at me with unwavering confidence. It's a shame he got greedy, as he is a fearless soldier—a soldier I can't really afford to lose.

"Do you have anything to say, Buto?"

Buto clenches his jaw and glances over at his brother Alfonzo. "It was all me. Alfonzo had nothing to do with it."

I shake my head. "The evidence says otherwise." I

pull a large serrated dagger from my jacket pocket and press it against Buto's throat. "Any last words?"

"Let me be the one to take my brother's life."

My brow furrows. "You wish to take his life to spare him from the pain I'll dole out?"

Buto nods in response, jaw clenched.

I step back and regard the man in front of me, scrubbing a hand across my beard. The ultimate torture would be to let him kill his brother and then let him live, thrown in the dungeon of Palermo prison, never to see the light of day again. His guilt would consume him.

"Fine, kill him," I say, setting the knife in Buto's hand. I want to see if he truly has the guts to stab his twin. They say a bond between twins is stronger than that of normal siblings. It would take some serious guts to take the life of a loved one, particularly one that is identical to you.

Buto takes the knife and walks toward Alfonzo. Alfonzo is shaking and pale—fearful until the end. "Brother, what are you doing?"

Buto grabs his hand and squeezes it. "It's better for you this way. You won't suffer."

Alfonzo swallows hard, shutting his eyes. "Fine, get it over with."

Buto hesitates for a moment before thrusting the knife deep into his heart.

Alfonzo's eyes shoot open wide as he gasps for breath, staring at his brother.

"It's okay, brother, it will be over fast," Buto says, gently laying him down on the ground.

"The same can't be said for you, Buto."

Buto glares at me. "I can handle whatever you throw at me." He stands with his arms outstretched. "I'm ready."

I shake my head. "Oh, Buto, you should have known that killing you both would be too easy." I walk toward him. "Now that you've murdered your own brother, I want you to suffer on this earth for a while, grappling with what you've done."

Buto's face pales for the first time since I revealed that I know the truth.

"You will remain in isolation at first, awaiting torture." I tilt my head slightly. "Did you really think I'd let you both go that easily?" I slam my hand down on the table, making most of the men jump in surprise. "You stole over fifteen million dollars from me."

There's some chatter amongst the men, which irritates me. "Silence."

Everyone falls silent, and I glance over at Lorenzo, who is still guarding the door. "Lorenzo, take him to the basement and lock him up."

Lorenzo steps forward to grab Buto, who tries to bring the knife to his own throat. Thankfully, Vanni is too quick. He knocks the knife out of his hand and grabs his wrists, forcing him into Lorenzo's hands.

"Motherfucker," he growls, eyes frantic now. "I may have stolen from you, but I've always been loyal. The least you can do is torture me and kill me." He stares at me with pleading eyes. "This is not fair."

I shake my head. "You should have thought twice about crossing me, Buto." I turn my back to him and walk out of the door. "If anyone else crosses me, I won't be so lenient."

As I walk out of the meeting room, I hear his tortured cries. I'm numb to them.

The many years of running the family business have turned me to ice inside. It was a ruthless tactic, allowing Buto to kill his brother but then leaving him alive.

If I want this organization to run smoothly, I have to be ruthless in my decisions. My men have to both respect and fear me. Without fear, my control would quickly crumble.

14

GIA

The screams set the hair on the back of my neck on end. Clearly, Fabio forgot his order to me yesterday or he thought I would not turn up.

I've waited in his living room for forty minutes after being let in by Alejandro.

He was leaving and gave me a questioning look, but didn't ask me why I was coming to Fabio's home so late again.

I have contemplated leaving repeatedly, wondering if he'll ever come back upstairs.

The screams are coming from the basement, making me thankful that I didn't use Aida's old way into the house.

I don't think I want to see what is going on down there.

The slam of a door makes me jump, and I hear footsteps coming this way. My heart is racing frantically, and I wonder who he has down there and what they've done.

Fabio stops dead still when he sees me, eyes wide.

There are blood splatters on his face and his white shirt. My heart stops beating when I see a bloody piece of flesh in a plastic bag he's holding. "I think I should go," I say, standing and strolling toward the door.

"No," he growls, making me stop on the spot. "How did you get in?"

I shrug. "Alejandro was leaving when I arrived and he said it was fine for me to go in."

He nods. "Wait in my study. I need to clean up."

I swallow hard, my attention lingering on the bloody bag. "What is in there?" I ask.

Fabio's eyes are wild as he shakes his head. "That's not a question you want me to answer. I said, wait in my study."

The blood drains from my face at the violence in his voice. It scares me more than I'd like to admit. "Okay." I walk to the study, wondering whether I made a mistake obeying him.

It's so easy to forget who this man is when we're intimate. The darkness that festers inside of him is beyond anything I can comprehend.

Aida doesn't know the full details of her mother's murder, other than that it was gruesome and her father found her. I know for sure that he loved Aida's mother dearly.

Aida always mentioned that he had changed since

her death. It's understandable. What I can't quite understand is why he broke Aida's heart and sent her away.

I'd always believed that he loved her just as dearly as her mother. I wait in the study for a few minutes before Fabio arrives.

He clears his throat. "How long were you waiting before I came out of the basement?"

I swallow hard. "About three-quarters of an hour."

"Cazzo," he murmurs. "So, you heard everything?"

"Yes, but—"

He holds his hand up to silence me. "Say nothing more. I won't apologize to you for the man I am. You know who I am, and you still came here tonight." He steps toward me, making me take a step back. "Nothing will change between us, do you understand?"

I take another step back, threatened by the dangerous tone of his voice. "You're scaring me, Fabio."

He narrows his eyes. "It would worry me if I didn't scare you, tesorina." He closes the gap between us fast, grabbing hold of my hips. "Don't be shy with me. You want me, otherwise you wouldn't have obeyed me."

I take in a deep breath, knowing that he's right. No matter how dangerous and depraved this man is, I'm addicted to him. "Who were you torturing down there?"

There's something oddly mournful about his expression. "My enemy." He pushes me against the wall, searching my eyes. "I don't show mercy to people who do me wrong, Gia. If you think I'm a monster for that, then so be it."

I swallow hard, shaking my head. "No, I don't think you're a monster. I think you're a man who has lost too much."

Fabio's eyes dip to my lips and then back to my eyes. "Loss changed me, Gia. My darkness will consume you too. It knows no bounds."

I can't understand why the prospect doesn't scare me. Fabio is a ruthless and broken man, but I long to fix him. "Perhaps my light can help consume some of your darkness."

He kisses me passionately, surprising my me. "Let's consume each other," he murmurs against my lips.

It's a tempting notion, one that I can't say no to. "Okay, sir."

He smiles. "Good girl."

I squeal as he lifts me and carries me out of the study, heading toward his bedroom. "I can walk, you know?"

He chuckles. "I know, but I want to carry you, tesorina."

I hate how my stomach flutters. This man is dangerous and ruthless. The moment I heard those tortured screams coming from his basement, I should have fled. But I know he poses no danger to me.

I GLANCE AT MY WATCH, realizing that it's three o'clock in the morning. Fabio expects me in his bed by one o'clock every night. This weekend is going to be so busy with a huge wedding and quite a few other events to prepare for.

He sent me a text about an hour ago, but I haven't replied. He thinks I'm at his beck and call, which is frustrating. I'm used to being independent, and I won't have that taken away from me by a man—no matter how good he is in bed.

Siena got back from a party about an hour ago and offered to help, but she's bad enough at flower arranging sober, let alone drunk.

My phone buzzes again, and I assume it's Fabio as I grab it to check. I feel my heart skip a beat when I see Aida's name on the screen.

Are you awake? I can never work out the time zones.

I swallow hard, wondering why she'd be contacting me out of the blue. We haven't spoken for a long while.

Yes, working late. It's three in the morning. What's up?

I set my phone down on the counter and wait for a reply, stringing the last bow around a bouquet for the wedding tomorrow.

The phone rings, and it's Aida's name on the front. Guilt coils through my gut at the thought of talking to her. It will be the first time since I started sleeping with her father.

I take the call. "Hey, stranger," I say.

"Hey. I'm so sorry I never got around to calling you

after your birthday." There's a short, awkward silence. "I'm a terrible friend."

"It's okay," I say, as she's not the only one who's a terrible friend. I'm the one who has betrayed her in unspeakable ways. "What are you up to?"

I can hear an engine in the background. "I'm heading to New York for the weekend."

"Oh? With your husband?" I ask, still wondering why she's suddenly called me out of the blue.

"No, he's staying in Boston." She sighs. "My father is attending a party he is throwing tomorrow and I don't intend to be around."

The blood drains from my face at the mention of her father. Fabio didn't tell me he was going to Boston, but perhaps he intended to tell me tonight. "That makes sense. I hope you have a good time."

"Yeah, I wish you could be here. I wanted to let you know I'll be in Sicily in six weeks. Milo and I are coming for a vacation, finally."

I should feel ecstatic at the prospect of seeing my best friend, but the news fills me with dread because of what I've done. The guilt over my actions will be far worse when facing her in person. Six weeks is more than enough time to cut it off and try to forget about her father. "That's great," I say, trying to infuse as much enthusiasm into my voice as I can.

"Wow, you don't sound as excited as I expected," Aida says. "Is it because I've been such a terrible friend lately?"

I shake my head, even though she can't see me. "No, I'm just exhausted. I'm doing the flower arrangements for three events this weekend, and one of them is huge." I sigh heavily. "I'll let Siena know tomorrow. We're both dying to catch up with you." It may be a lie now, but five weeks ago on my birthday it would have been the truth.

"Okay, that sounds great. I'll let you know more details nearer to the time."

"Sounds good. Have a great weekend in New York." I laugh. "Try not to spend too much money."

Aida laughs. "You know me. I can't help it. Talk soon." Aida cancels the call and I breathe a sigh of relief. Hearing her voice amplifies the guilt I feel.

A man frantically knocks on the window, startling me. "Please, I need your help," he calls.

My brow furrows as I kind of recognize him, but can't work out why. I move toward the window. "What is the problem?"

He points down the street. "I need a phone. My girlfriend has tripped and badly injured her leg." He shakes his head. "She might have broken it."

I sigh and unlock the door to the shop. "Okay, you can use my cell phone." I pass it to him, but he shocks me by grabbing hold of my wrist hard. "What the—"

He stabs a needle into my arm. "You shouldn't open the door to strangers, Gia."

I step away from him and turn to run, instantly

feeling whatever drug he pumped into me affecting my senses.

"Steady on," he says, grabbing my arm and dragging me out of the shop.

I glance up at him, squinting as it's hard to see in the pitch black. "Do I know you?"

He doesn't look at me, but I'm sure I recognize him. "My boss knows you."

My stomach churns at the mention of his boss. This guy sounds and looks so familiar, but I can't put my finger on who he is. I continue to struggle against him, knowing that if I don't fight, I could end up dead. "Let go of me," I say, swinging my leg at him and catch him where it hurts.

He grunts and lets go of my arm, giving me the chance to escape. I rush down the street toward a bar, which is still lit up, hoping I can find someone to help me. The drug he pumped me with is infiltrating my blood stream and I almost fall. On my next step, I trip on the cobblestones and fall flat on my face, groaning as I graze my knees.

The slam of a car door draws my attention. I see Fabio marching toward me. His silver hair is unmistakable in the barely lit streets. He looks irritated as he leans down and slides an arm around my waist.

"Fabio?" I say his name questioningly, but he doesn't respond.

Instead, he hoists me over his shoulder and glares at

the man who injected me. "Can't you do anything right?" he growls.

His rough, angry voice is the last thing I hear. The musky scent of him is the last thing I smell, and his dominant grasp on my thigh is the last thing I feel. Slowly, I'm dragged into darkness by whatever drug the man I've been sleeping with has had that guy pump into me.

15

FABIO

*G*ia's late.

It's been ten days since we fucked in the back of her shop. Every night since she has come to my bed by midnight, but it's now three o'clock and she isn't here.

I'm concerned, but most of all, I'm pissed off that she chose tonight not to turn up. In less than an hour I need to board a plane for Boston, and I intended to take her with me.

"Boss, we need to leave, or we will be late," Aldo says.

I meet his gaze. "Fine, but we need to make a stop on the way."

Aldo's brow raises, but he doesn't question me. "Of course."

Gia should have been here. But since she hasn't

arrived or answered my texts or calls, I have no option but to take her by force.

It's not exactly something I wanted to resort to. Drugging a woman and forcing her onto a plane isn't exactly the best way to keep her affections. However, Gia knows the kind of man I am. She knows who she got involved with.

I stand and follow my bodyguard out of my home.

He opens the back door of the town car and I slip inside.

"What stop do you wish to make?" Aldo asks, glancing at me in the rearview mirror.

"Natural Beauty Florist in the center of Palermo." I slide my hand into my jacket and pull out a vile of sedative. "You will go into the shop and get the owner to come out, even if she's in bed. Once out you will give her this sedative and bring her to this car."

Aldo gives me a questioning gaze. "Isn't that Gia Dicampo's shop? Aida's best friend?"

I clench my jaw, realizing that there's no hiding the truth from Aldo. He spent most of Aida's life guarding her. "Yes. I don't like being questioned, Aldo." I run a hand across the back of my neck as I set the vile down in the center console. "Just do your job."

"Yes, sir."

I know how twisted it is that I'm fucking my daughter's best friend. My moral code was obliterated a long time ago. Gia is like cocaine, and I can't keep away from her, no matter how much I know I should.

Spending a weekend away without her isn't an option. She's mine and I intend to take her to Boston. I don't have time to convince her to come, so forcing her is the only option.

Aldo drives down the high street of Palermo and stops a few meters from Gia's shop. "I'll see if I can get someone to answer. What if no one does?"

"Break in and drug her in her bed if you have to, Aldo."

His eyes widen. "Sir." He gets out of the car and walks toward the shop, which is dimly lit.

I watch as he knocks on the windowpane, saying something as if talking to someone.

My heart skips a beat when I see Gia approach the window. She's working late; maybe that's why she didn't turn up.

My unsuspecting little treasure opens the door to him and steps out of the shop, passing him something.

Aldo grabs her wrist and stabs the needle into her vein, drugging her. Stupidly, he allows her to step away from him and she tries to run back into the shop.

Aldo is too fast. He grabs her and drags her out of the shop. A jealous rage infects my blood when I see him put his hands on her.

Gia isn't giving in easily as she fights against my huge bodyguard and breaks free, rushing toward the car.

Her steps are clumsy and she trips on the cobblestones, falling almost flat on her face. I growl softly and get out of the car, hating how inept my men can be.

She's a petite girl, and he's two-hundred pounds of pure muscle.

Gia looks up at me, and recognition dawns in her eyes. I try not to make eye contact, wishing I didn't have to intervene.

I glare at Aldo. "Can't you do anything right?" I grab Gia around the waist and hoist her over my shoulder, carrying her back to the car.

She's out cold by the time we get to it, thankfully.

"I'm sorry, sir, she put up more of a fight that I expected," Aldo says as I gently set her down in the back of the town car.

I meet his gaze. "Just get us to the airport in one piece. Can you do that?"

"Yes, sir." He gets into the driver's side of the car and I slide in next to Gia, placing her head on my lap.

I stare at my sleeping beauty, knowing that she's going to hate me for drugging and kidnapping her. It's not exactly the way most men would whisk their women away on a weekend trip.

Gia is always the busiest on the weekends with her flower arrangements, and I knew she wouldn't agree. But she has two employees who can surely hold down the fort while she is away.

All I hope is that the passion she holds for me doesn't warp into hatred. I don't like being told no and this was the easiest way to avoid it.

Gia groans as the plane lifts into the sky. I expected the sedative to knock her out a little longer, but all that mattered was that she was unconscious until we took off.

I sit on the sofa in the plane with her head in my lap, gently running my fingers through her beautiful blonde hair. She will be angry that I snatched her the way I did, but we didn't have time to argue.

Gia moves suddenly, jerking upright.

"Easy, tesorina," I say, setting a hand gently on her thigh.

Her eyes look glazed over, and she looks around the room in confusion. "Where am I?"

I clench my jaw, knowing she won't like the answer. "On my private jet to Boston."

The answer snaps her back to reality, and she stands suddenly. "Why the fuck am I on your jet to Boston, Fabio?" Her legs wobble since the sedative is still in her bloodstream, and will be for a while.

I stand and wrap my arms around her in support. "Sit down, tesorina. The drug is still in your system."

She pushes me away forcefully before taking a seat in a chair nearby. "Drug?" She shakes her head. "I remember now. You had Aida's ex-bodyguard drug me." Her voice holds a tone of disbelief. "What the hell were you thinking?"

"I knew it was the only way to get you on this

plane." I run a hand over the back of my neck. "You didn't turn up tonight or reply to my texts."

"So you drug and kidnap me?" She shakes her head. "Why the fuck are we going to Boston?"

I sit down next to her, but she moves away. "I have to go to Boston for the weekend for a party Milo Mazzeo is hosting. I want you with me."

Gia stares at me as if I'm insane. "Have you lost the plot?"

I shrug. "I want you with me while I'm out of town."

She shakes her head. "You are taking me with you to Boston, the town where your daughter, my best friend, lives, to attend a party thrown by said friend's husband?"

I stare at her, realizing when I hear it out loud it sounds ridiculous. Especially since we are supposed to keep this affair between us a secret.

"Yes. It's only for a weekend and Milo has confirmed Aida won't be attending the party." I sigh heavily. "In fact, she's so desperate to ensure she won't see me that she's gone on a shopping trip with a friend to New York City for the weekend." I know the reason she's gone out of town is because of me. Aida hates me.

Gia stands from the chair I forced her into. "I have three weddings this weekend and I haven't finished the flower arrangements." She sets her hands on her hips. "I'm not a doll you can do with as you want. I have a life, Fabio."

I wave my hand dismissively. "You have two employees. I'm sure they can manage while you are away."

She glares at me furiously. "No. Bring the jet back down and let me off right now." Her hands are on her hips and she looks positively adorable, trying to make a stand.

I stand up from my chair and walk toward her. A small amount of her confidence diminishes, but she meets my gaze. I wrap a hand around her slender throat and walk her against the wall of my jet. "I thought you understood, tesorina. I always get what I want, and right now I want you with me."

She swallows hard under my hand and shakes her head. "You're an asshole."

I chuckle at that. "I've been called much worse." I move my lips to her jaw and kiss it softly. "You knew exactly what you were getting into when you got in my bed, Gia."

Gia glares at me as I tighten my grip around her throat. "Let me go now."

"Are you looking for a punishment?"

"I'm looking for you to let me the off this fucking plane so I can go back to my life."

I like her tenacity. However, it's clear that Gia has underestimated me. If I want her to come with me, then she will come with me whether or not she wants to. "Punishment it is," I say, wrapping my arms around her and lifting her.

"Put me down," she cries as I haul her over my shoulder.

I ignore her cries as she punches my back hard, trying to get me to stop. It's futile since she's not getting off this plane or out of her punishment. The fact is, she doesn't realize her reluctance is a turn-on for me. My favorite kink with a partner is consensual non-consent. However, this isn't exactly consensual.

"What the fuck do you think you are doing?" she demands as I lower her down onto the bed in the bedroom of my jet.

Before she can move, I clamp a handcuff attached to the bed around her wrist.

Her eyes widen as she tries to free herself. "Are you serious?"

I push the hem of her dress up to her hips and tear her panties in two. "Deadly."

Gia pales, staring up at me as if she can hardly believe that I'm forcing her to accompany me to Boston. I don't wait for her to say anything else, sliding my fingers inside of her.

Gia writhes against me. "Let me go." She shakes her head. "You're a fucking monster." The look in her eyes is one of disbelief, but there's a desire in them too —desire to be dominated.

"I'm surprised you only now realize that." I pump my fingers in and out of her wet pussy, getting her ready for my cock. "You knew exactly who I was when you crossed the line." I slide my fingers out of her, holding her gaze. Slowly, I slip them into my mouth and suck them clean. "Sweet as sin, tesorina."

Her eyes dilate, but she shakes her head. "You are literally insane if you think I'm going to be happy about you dragging me half way across the world because you want to fuck me."

I chuckle at that. "I don't care if you're happy about it or not. You know what I told you, Gia. I get what I want." There is truth to the statement. It's a statement that has governed my relationships with everyone other than my daughter for ten years. But as I say it, it doesn't feel right. Gia isn't a whore who I can do with as I want. She's an independent woman who I'm forcing to submit to me.

My ruthless side won't give up the fight to possess this woman in every way. Gia fighting me only makes me more determined.

I rub her clit, and she cries out, arching her back. "Shit," she says. As she comes undone, her juice squirts all over the clean bedsheets. I love the way she always squirts when she comes. It's fucking hot.

No matter how much she tries to fight, she has no control over her body.

"That wet pussy is ready for my cock, tesorina," I say, unzipping my pants and dropping them to the floor.

Gia doesn't say a word, just watches me intently as I free myself from the confines of my boxer briefs.

"You're a bastard for kidnapping me, Fabio," she says, her attention fixed on my cock.

I laugh. "Few people can get away with calling me names, Gia." I move toward the bed and kneel between her thighs, grabbing her throat. "I can't wait to take that pretty little cunt."

Her eyes widen at the use of that word. "In your dreams."

I raise a brow and shake my head, positioning my cock at her entrance. "In yours, baby," I say, moving forward and filling her with every inch.

She moans, no longer fighting it once my cock is deep inside of her. "Yes, Fabio," she cries.

I tighten my grip on her throat, choking her a little. "It's sir to you, tesorina."

Gia's lip trembles as she licks it, nodding. "Yes, sir."

I move in and out of her, still choking her gently. Her moans are a symphony that set my soul ablaze.

As I gaze into her eyes, taking her roughly, I know that what is forming between us is dangerous. Everyone I care about always comes to harm.

"Fabio." She moans my name as I move my hands from her throat to her hips, driving in harder and deeper.

I rip open the front of her dress and capture her nipple between my teeth, irritated that she ignored my anger over her not wearing a bra before. "I warned you about working and not wearing a bra."

She arches her back, moaning as I lavish attention

on her. "And I told you it's more comfortable without one."

I suck her other nipple, making her moan. "Well, I don't enjoy thinking about all the perverts walking into your shop and looking at your breasts," I growl.

Her eyes widen, and she arches an eyebrow. "Well, you'll have to get over it."

I grind my teeth together and unfasten the cuff around her wrist.

Gia whimpers as I pull my cock from her tight, wet pussy. "What are you—"

I don't give her time to finish her question, grabbing her and roughly forcing her onto all fours. My hand drives down against her ass cheek, hard and without warning.

Gia squeals, trying to escape from me. "That fucking hurts."

I keep my hold on her hips and spank her other cheek just as hard. "Good. I want you to learn your lesson." I spank her other cheek again, and this time she moans. "I own you, possess you, and if I don't like you not wearing a bra while serving male customers, then you will wear a fucking bra." I spank her other cheek again, feeling my dominant, possessive side taking control. I can't help it. Gia turns me into this primal caveman. I slide my cock through her tight, wet entrance again, letting her feel every inch as I sink to the hilt. "Now take my cock like my good little slut," I growl.

Gia moans again, arching her back as I fuck her. Every stroke is harder than the last since all my control has escaped me.

I can't understand what she does to me, but it is unlike anything I've experienced before. This primal need to make her mine and own her drives me.

"Tell me you are mine, Gia," I say, stilling in her tight little cunt.

Gia shakes her head. "No."

I spank her ass again, hard enough to bruise. "I won't ask again," I growl, knowing she's just angry because I stole her away from her work.

When she says nothing, I pull out of her tight, wet heat. Then I clamp the restraint on her wrist again and grab a vibrator out of the nightstand.

I turn it on the highest level and push it against her clit, making her jolt. "Until you tell me what you know is the truth, I'm going to bring you to the edge of climax only to deny you every goddamn time."

Gia glances over her shoulder with wide eyes. "That's fucking torture."

I nod. "My other disciplinary methods aren't working on you."

"Fuck," she says, and I notice the way her thighs shake.

I remove the device and spank her ass again. "Tell me you are mine," I order.

Gia doesn't react, keeping her face forward.

"Fine." I turn the device back on and press it against her pussy, close to her clit.

"Damn it," Gia cries, arching her back as I move the device around her sensitive area. She'll feel the sensation everywhere except where she really wants it. When I let it touch her clit, her body tenses. I turn it off, leaving her panting and frustrated.

"Let me hear you say it, and I'll let you come."

Gia glares at me over her shoulder with an emotion that borders on hatred. "Fine, I'm yours. Now let me fucking come," she says.

I chuckle. "Say it like you mean it."

Gia grunts in frustration, continuing to hold my gaze. "I'm yours, sir, to do with as you want," she says, her voice sultry and delicious.

"Good girl." I slide my cock deep inside of her. "Now, I want you to come on my cock."

Gia moans, arching her back as I feel her muscles instantly clamp around my cock. Her body starts to spasm as I fuck her hard, spanking her already stinging red ass.

"Fuck, I'm going to come," she cries, her body convulsing.

I groan as she tumbles over the edge, squirting her sweet cum all over the bedsheets and my cock. "That's it, baby, come for me," I growl, feeling myself on the edge of climax. "I'm going to fill you to the brim with my seed."

"Yes, sir, please give me your cum," she pants,

arching her back so my cock goes as deep inside of her as possible. I growl as I come undone, biting down on her shoulder. I don't stop thrusting until every single drop is deep inside of her.

Gia is mine, and in time she will come to accept that fact.

16

GIA

Rage coils through me like a disease. It's an emotion I'm not used to feeling.

Fabio dragged me away from my home in the middle of the night as if he owns me. The moment we got here, he locked me in the hotel room and left.

Lies always catch up with you, and right now it feels like I'm drowning in them.

Thankfully, Angelica and Claudia have come to my rescue and have finished the last arrangements. They sent me photos of the finished articles and have confirmed they'll deliver them on time. I don't know what I'd do without them.

Siena keeps ringing me, although I've texted her to tell her I'm in Rome with the guy I met. She was a little disbelieving when I told her I'm in Rome, ditching my responsibilities at the shop. Not to mention, I left it unlocked. I know it's out of character for me, but it's because I had no choice.

Fabio is insane if he thinks this is acceptable behavior. I hate that I still want him physically, even if he is a controlling asshole.

I turn toward the door of the hotel and glare at it, wondering how he locked me in here. I try the door again and grunt in frustration when it won't budge.

"Bastard," I mutter.

Fabio left about two hours ago, telling me he had an important meeting. No doubt with Aida's husband.

A man that is cruel to her, and yet she's fallen for him in ways I can't comprehend.

I walk into the bathroom and turn the faucet of the bath on, letting the water run warm before putting the stopper in. If I'm stuck in here, I may as well enjoy the jacuzzi bath.

There's nothing else to do.

Once the tub is full with balmy, warm water, I slip inside and sigh. The controls for the jets are pretty simple and I set them on a low, shutting my eyes as the water massages my muscles.

I hate that the first thing I see when I shut my eyes is Fabio, moving over me the way he did in the back of his jet. He took what he wanted unapologetically, fucking me aggressively.

He doesn't know how to be gentle, and it has surprised me how much I crave the rough treatment. I slide my finger between my thighs, rubbing my clit as I think about him.

It's insane how insatiable I am lately. It doesn't matter how many times he fucks me, I'm always ready for more. The hunger inside of me only seems to grow the longer this torrid affair carries on. I slide my finger inside myself, thinking about his huge, hard cock pumping in and out of me.

I moan, arching my back as the memories come flooding back. Fabio is a beautiful, silver-haired sex god, even if he is an asshole.

"That's it, baby, finger that pussy for me," Fabio murmurs, startling me.

I sit upright, feeling the heat travel to my cheeks as I notice him leaning against the door frame. "I didn't hear you come in."

He smirks and walks forward. "No, because you were too busy being my naughty little slut and fingering your pussy," he growls, grabbing a fistful of my hair and forcing me to look up at him. He leans down and kisses me forcefully, making me moan. "Now finish up because we've got a party to attend."

I raise a brow at him. "What kind of party?"

"Milo is celebrating being appointed the newest member of the Boston city council. I've picked you up a dress."

"Isn't it risky for me to be seen with you by Aida's husband?" I ask.

Fabio shrugs. "Why does it matter?"

I swallow hard. "Aida mentioned they are coming to Sicily in six weeks."

Fabio's eyes widen. "I haven't been told this." He lets go of my hair finally and paces away. "Milo won't out us to Aida. You will use a different name for him."

"What name?"

"Lucia will do," he says, walking away from me and back into the main hotel room.

The guy is insane for bringing me here. It was a bad idea. I get out of the bath and dry off, feeling a little unsatisfied about having not finished what I started.

When I walk back into the hotel room, Fabio is naked. It's impossible not to admire his physique. For an older man, he's built like an adonis.

He turns to face me. "Quit staring and come and get dressed." He signals to a stunning dusty pink ball gown hanging on the back of the door into the closet.

I walk toward it and run my hands through the expensive fabric. "This must have cost a fortune."

Fabio sneaks up behind me and sets a hand on my hip. "Not half as much as you are worth, tesorina," he murmurs into my ear.

I step away. "Don't think that buying me a dress will make me forget that you drugged and kidnapped me." I glare at the silver-haired fox. "You really are a piece of work, Fabio."

He smirks at me. "You weren't complaining when I fucked you in my jet."

His cockiness only adds to my frustration. I grab the

dress off the hanger and carry it into the bathroom, slamming the door behind me.

He needs to realize that kidnapping someone is not okay. I won't just forgive him for stealing me away from my responsibilities.

I drop my towel and step into the dress, realizing that I can't do up the zipper on the back myself. I grit my teeth, trying to force the zipper up, despite it being almost impossible.

"Fuck," I say.

Fabio chuckles from the other side of the door. "Do you need some help, Gia?"

I glare at the shut door. "No, thanks." I open the door and walk past him, heading toward the hotel room door.

"Where the fuck are you going?" Fabio growls, making the hair on the back of my neck stand on end.

"To find someone to help me with my dress," I say, continuing walking.

His fast footsteps make my heartrate speed up.

Before I can make it out of the hotel room, he has me boxed against the door. "There's no fucking way you are getting another person to touch you, male or female," he growls possessively, grabbing hold of the zipper. "Only I touch you, Gia. Do you understand?"

I shake my head. "No, I don't."

He bites my shoulder enough to hurt. "Then it would seem you need to be punished."

I shudder at the thought.

"It's a shame we don't have time before the party." He kisses the back of my neck, sending confusing sensations through my body. On the one hand, every time he's forceful and dominant, my body reacts. On the other, I know that after what he did, I should resist all of his advances. "Once we return here tonight, though, you are going to wish you didn't challenge me, tesorina." He zips my dress up before grabbing my hips and forcing me to face him. "I made it clear the kind of man I am from the moment we met. You need to accept that I have a claim over you, Gia."

I swallow hard, looking into his dark mahogany brown eyes. I say nothing, as there's no way I'm giving him the satisfaction of agreeing.

He's right about one thing, though. I always knew the kind of man I was getting into bed with, but did it anyway, which means I'm as much to blame in this. A fantasy that was so different from reality drew me to him.

"Now, come and sit on the bed," he murmurs, grabbing my hand and dragging me away from the hotel room door.

I glare at him as he forces me down onto the bed.

He gets dressed, putting on a tailored navy blue tuxedo that makes him look painfully handsome. It would be easier to hate him if he wasn't so beautiful. It would be easier to hate him if my body didn't crave his touch.

Once Fabio is finished getting dressed, he approaches me and offers me his hand.

I glare at it and don't take it, standing by myself.

The move only inflames his rage as he growls and grabs hold of my hips. "This bratty behavior is getting tiresome, Gia. I want you to act the part for me tonight. Can you do that?"

"Why should I do anything for you? You have stolen me away from my home and responsibilities." I shake my head. "I have the fucking right to be angry at you, Fabio." I yank myself out of his grasp and walk toward the hotel door, only to be stopped again before I make it.

When he yanks me around this time, there's a different expression in his eyes that resembles regret. "I'm sorry, Gia." He runs a hand across the back of his neck. "All my life I've taken what I want, when I want. It's hard to change that, but I understand that what I did was wrong." He tilts his head slightly. "I promise I won't kidnap you again in the future."

I hate the way my stomach flips at his promise and apology. Fabio is broken, but is it possible that I can mend him? That's a silly notion. "Thank you," I say simply.

He offers me his arm, and I hesitate a moment before taking it. We walk in tense silence out of the hotel room and down the corridor. The man who drugged me, who I realize now is Aida's old bodyguard,

Aldo, follows us. It makes me a little uneasy as we walk down into the main entrance of the hotel.

"Is the party at the hotel?" I ask.

Fabio nods. "Yes. A lot of very important people from the city will be here." He gives me a pointed look. "So, be on your best behavior, tesorina."

I glance over my shoulder at Aldo, who is staring at us quizzically. He spent so much time following Aida, Siena, and me around shopping malls, beaches, and bars. It makes this feel a little too real that I'm now on the arm of my best friend's father.

"What's wrong, Gia?" Fabio mutters, drawing my attention to him.

"We shouldn't be here together," I say.

He glances at Aldo and nods at him, telling him to move away. "Aldo is making you uncomfortable?" he asks.

I draw a deep breath. "This entire situation is making me uncomfortable. We shouldn't be together in public, even if we are in a different country."

Fabio shrugs his shoulders. "You need to relax, tesorina."

"This is the town where Aida lives. What if she returns from New York?" I ask. Panic sets in as I know she's only a three-and-a-half hour drive from here.

Fabio moves his hand to the small of my back, making me tense. "We best find you a drink."

I sigh heavily, wishing that wasn't Fabio's answer. He doesn't seem as worried as I am about the consequences of what we are doing. The bar is busy as he pushes his way to the counter, forcing me with him. "Chardonnay?"

"I'll just get some water, I'm feeling nauseous." I set a hand on my stomach and my brow furrows. "What's the date today?"

I'm not sure why I ask as I know it's the fifteenth of May. Two weeks late for my period. I swallow hard, realizing that although I was taking the pill, a few months ago I had to stop as they were giving me terrible cramps.

Since I wasn't having sex, it didn't really matter. Once Fabio and I started sleeping together, I never gave it any thought.

What a fucking idiot.

"It's the fifteenth." Fabio wraps an arm more tightly around me. "Are you okay? You look a little pale."

I swallow hard, knowing that I'm not okay. If I'm pregnant with Fabio's baby, then this just became ten times more complicated.

17

FABIO

I can sense that something is bothering Gia. Even though she's angry at me, she has been acting off, following me around with her head bowed.

"Let me introduce you to Milo." I turn to face her.

She shakes her head. "Isn't that a bad idea since I'll probably meet him in Sicily?"

"Milo is a busy man and unlikely to remember you." I signal around the room, knowing that the likelihood is that he won't recognize her. "He meets many people." I glance over at my son-in-law, who is talking with some politicians. "After all, it would be out of sorts for me not to introduce my date."

"Fine." She crosses her arms over her chest defensively.

I set my hand on the small of her back and lead her toward Milo, clearing my throat once I'm behind him. "Milo, I wanted to introduce you to my date, Lucia."

Milo smiles, but when he does, it's not warm. He takes Gia's hand and kisses the back of it. "Lovely to meet you, Lucia."

Gia shuffles uncomfortably, reclaiming her hand. "Nice to meet you," she says timidly.

I hate seeing any man touch her, even though I know the man in front of me is in love with my daughter. It's all I could have hoped for, that they'd fall for each other in the end. Milo Mazzeo may be a cruel man, but thankfully he has developed a soft spot for my daughter.

"Are you enjoying being a city council member?" I ask, wondering if it's all he hoped it would be.

He nods. "It has given me a significant edge on the Irish, that's for sure."

It's hard to comprehend the friction and turmoil that occurs in one city. There are four crime groups battling each other in Boston. The Irish, the Italians, the Russians and the Mexicans. It's hard enough having to deal with enemies outside of my territory, let alone in it. "I don't envy your position, Milo."

He shakes his head. "No, it's a difficult one for sure." He nods toward the back of the events room. "I thought we could have a discussion about my plans tonight." He glances at Gia. "If you wouldn't mind giving us a moment, Lucia."

I feel uneasy about leaving her here, but I catch Aldo's eye and nod for him to keep a watch on her. "Of course."

Gia gives me a concerned look as I walk away from her, but I don't acknowledge her. My one rule when I'm in public is to never make it obvious that I care for anyone. It makes them a target.

I follow Milo toward a set of double doors at the back of the events hall of the hotel. A man opens the door to us, revealing a conference room. Milo sits on one side and I sit opposite him.

"What business do we need to discuss that we didn't talk about earlier?" I ask.

Milo sighs heavily. "The Irish are causing me more trouble than I expected. Is there any chance you can spare some support?"

I tilt my head to the side. "Support in what form?"

He looks a little uncertain about answering. "We don't have anywhere near the manpower you have. Is there any chance you can spare a dozen of your men?"

I have more men since I control an entire island. However, I'm not sure how many of them will appreciate being shipped to America. "How long will you need them for?" I ask.

I have younger men in my ranks who have no wives or children who may accept spending time away in America. Although, it's not standard for my organization to ship men to another country.

"Three months, maximum. Probably less," Milo says.

I run a hand through my hair, considering his suggestion. "What do you offer in return?"

He leans back in his chair, clasping his fingers together in front of him. "I heard you are still having trouble with the Moretti family."

I clench my jaw at the mention of my feud with the Moretti family. A feud that has cost me too much. "I've been having trouble with them for a long time."

Milo nods. "I think I know a way to end that trouble once and for all." There's a darkness in the man I sold my daughter to. A darkness that is more twisted than my own. I've known it ever since we met for the first time in Sicily.

"What do you have in mind?" I ask.

Milo's smirk widens. "The Moretti family knows that I am partnered with you, but they don't know me personally." He runs a hand through his dark brown hair. "My suggestion is simple."

I raise a brow, waiting for him to continue. "Once things die down here in the next couple of months, I intend to visit Sicily. On my trip, I will go to Naples to meet with the Moretti family under a false identity."

I sit up straighter, wondering where exactly my son-in-law is going with this.

"Once in Naples, me and my men will cut the head off the snake." He shrugs. "Then, we should be even."

Milo's offer is attractive, especially since Lorenzo fucked up my latest chance at revenge. I don't forget that Dario is strung up in my basement, but bringing the fight to Sicilian soil isn't ideal. If Milo can take them out in Naples, that would be best.

"What do you say?" he asks.

I nod in reply. "It sounds like we've got ourselves a deal." I tilt my head slightly. "However, I have got his son in Sicily."

Milo runs a hand through his hair. "Do they know?"

I shake my head, since I've been sending the parcels with pieces of Dario anonymously through a trusted source. "They know someone has him, but I don't believe they know who." I shrug. "Although they may suspect it's me."

Milo nods. "It is best to stick with my plan. I think keeping your enemy as far away from your territory as possible is ideal."

"I agree." I am thankful that my son-in-law is smart. He will take good care of my daughter.

Milo smiles and stands, and I follow suit. "Then we have a deal." He holds out a hand for me to shake, and I take it.

A question has been on my mind ever since I sat down with him. "How is Aida?"

The mention of my daughter instantly softens his gaze and he smiles the warmest smile I've ever seen from him. "She is well." His brow furrows. "I'm not sure she wants me to tell you, but I feel you should know."

"Know what?" I ask.

"Aida is three months pregnant." The pride in his eyes fills me with hope. Milo may have an infamous reputation, but it's clear he's got a soft spot for my daughter.

"That's great news. I'm happy for you." I run a hand across my beard. "I assume her leaving town this weekend is because I'm here?"

Milo nods. "Yes. She is angry at you for what you did."

"That's to be expected."

Milo looks like he wants to ask me something, but suddenly a bang outside the door draws our attention. "What the fuck was that?" Milo asks, rushing toward the door.

I follow him, all my thoughts returning to Gia. A round of gunshots goes off, making my heart freeze in my chest.

Milo sprints through the door, drawing his gun. I do the same, all my focus on finding Gia. I assumed this party would be safe, particularly since it's a political event held by the city council.

There are two men with rifles, firing on the screaming and panicked crowd.

I notice Aldo crouching down and firing rounds at the men with machine guns, but Gia is nowhere to be seen. A heaviness sets in as I wonder if I'm about to lose her. If she dies here, it's all my fault. Gia didn't want to come to Boston, but my selfish desire to have her close at all times ruled me.

I draw my gun and drop behind a toppled over

table, next to Milo. "The Irish have the audacity to attack you at a council meeting?" I ask.

Milo's eyes meet mine. "They're becoming more desperate."

Aldo takes out one attacker, shooting him right between the eyes.

I scan the room again, checking the bloody bodies lying on the floor. There's no sign of her elegant pink ball gown on any of them, thankfully.

Where the fuck is she?

I can't lose her too, even if she won't embrace the fact that she belongs to me. Gia has ignited something inside of me I thought had died long ago.

"Where is your woman?" Milo asks.

I shrug. "I don't know. I can't see her."

Milo pops his head up and shoots at the remaining gunman, who continues to fire at any movement in the room. He clips his shoulder, but it's not enough to stop him.

The gunman only aims his gun at us as he shoots the table in front of us frantically. "Cazzo," I growl, rushing toward Aldo to find cover.

I shoot as I run, hoping I can make it over there before he takes me out. The bullets ricochet around me and one of them clips my calf. I ignore the excruciating pain, knowing that I'm dead if I stop now.

Aldo notices me and covers me as I make my way over to him. "Fuck, sir. You're shot." He pulls a clean handkerchief from his pocket. "Hold this over the wound."

I grab it and press it to the wound, hardly able to care about it right now. "The bullet just clipped me. It's a harmless flesh-wound. Where is she?" I ask.

Aldo's brow hitches upward. "The bathroom. She went to the bathroom a minute before they attacked. Hopefully she is safe."

I feel my stomach twist. "I have to get to her, now."

Aldo swallows hard. "Then we need to take this bastard out."

I nod, briefly glancing around the pillar to get a look at the shooter. "I'll take him out, but I need you to cover me."

Aldo's eyes widen. "Sir, I think it's best—"

I hold a hand up, silencing him. "Don't question me right now, Aldo."

He swallows hard and nods, cocking his gun. "Be careful, sir."

I don't respond to his pointless words of caution. Instead, I take a long, steady breath and ready myself.

This bastard needs to die. He's the only person standing between me and the woman I care so dearly about.

I come out of hiding and aim my gun at him, feeling time slow as he turns to face me.

Aldo covers me, shooting at him from an angle as I aim my gun right at his head. Years of practice mean I never miss.

I shoot, still moving across the room, and hit him right between the eyes. He goes down cold as a wayward bullet misses me by two inches.

Adrenaline is firing through my veins as I stare at the lifeless body on the ground. Milo is no longer in his hiding position, and I can't see him.

I don't wait for Aldo, instead heading straight toward the bathroom. It feels like my nightmare started all over again. If Gia isn't okay, I don't know how I'm going to make it through this time.

18

GIA

I stay frozen, hugging my arms around my knees as I remain sat on the closed toilet seat.

The gunshots pierce the air, making my heartrate spike.

Fabio dragged me to Boston, and into the most dangerous situation I've ever encountered.

Why does he think he can force me to go anywhere?

I know the answer: it's who he is. He forced Aida to marry a monster, and now I'm being forced to go wherever he wants me to go.

The gunshots continue to echo down the corridor, making my heart race. Shouts come from the other side of the closed bathroom door.

I am thankful I went to the bathroom when I did. If I'd been in that room, I might be dead right now.

The sound of the bathroom door swinging open

makes my stomach churn. "Check for anyone in the cubicles. I want Fabio and Milo alive," a deep, Irish voice says.

My heart pounds frantically as I realize these men are the enemy. These are the men that have been shooting the place up.

I swallow hard, hugging my knees tighter to my chest.

"Can't see no one, but this cubicle is locked." I hold my breath as the door rocks back and forth.

Footsteps approach and stop outside of the door, followed by knocking. "Anyone in there?" the other man asks.

I bite my lip, knowing that uttering a word may get me killed. Two hands appear over the door and suddenly a man pulls himself up and peers over at me.

"Alright, lass?" he asks, shaking his head. "No need to hide. We're not looking for you."

I swallow hard, staring at the rough, tattooed man peering down at me.

"Open the door and come out for me, now," he orders.

I slowly get off the toilet seat, knowing that defying these men is probably more dangerous. I unlock the door and open it, trembling as I do. "What do you want?" I ask, my voice small.

The man's eyes narrow. "Where are you from?"

My heart skips a beat as I realize my accent is a

giveaway. "I'm originally from Spain." I shrug. "I moved here a year ago."

He shakes his head. "Where in Spain?"

"Barcelona," I say in the best Spanish accent I can muster.

He nods. "Lovely. Okay, well, do you know either of these men?" he asks, holding up a photo of Milo and Fabio.

"Yes, that one is Milo Mazzeo, the new council member." I turn my attention to the other photo, furrowing my brow. "The other man. I'm not sure who he is. I think I saw him talking to Mr. Mazzeo earlier."

The smirk that curls onto the man's lips is manic. "Perfect. Where did you see them last?"

"I saw them in the main events room. What is this about?" I ask.

He shakes his head. "Don't worry your pretty little head about that. You stay right here and lock yourself back in the toilet until later." He nods at the cubicle and I do as he says, locking myself inside.

I hold my breath, waiting to hear the men leave. Their footsteps echo away and the door slams behind them, leaving me shaking. Tears flood down my cheeks as the situation overwhelms me. I gasp for air, desperately trying to get it into my lungs.

Those men were dangerous and enemies of Milo. It proves how little Fabio really cares for me, bringing me somewhere so dangerous.

I hate the way my chest aches as I realize that all

this has ever been to him is sex. He doesn't care if I get hurt, and why would he? I'm nothing to him other than a girl to fuck and use.

I jump at the sound of more gunshots outside of the bathroom, wondering whether Fabio is okay. It irritates me that I care, but I do. What started out as a silly, taboo crush has quickly warped into something more meaningful for me, even if Fabio is an arrogant asshole.

I remain with my back firmly pressed against the door, listening to the steady rhythm of my breathing. The sound of the bathroom door opening startles me away, and I stare at it, wondering if those men have returned.

"Gia?" Fabio's voice is panic stricken.

A flood of relief hits me at the sound of his voice, even if I am angry at him for dragging me into this mess. I can't speak, as I'm in shock over my encounter with the couple of Irish thugs that stormed in here. Instead, I unlock the door and step out.

Fabio spins to face me, eyes wild and frantic. "Grazie Dio," he murmurs, marching toward me. I feel my heart flutter in my chest as he wraps his arms around me, pulling me close. He says nothing, holding me tightly. I feel my muscles relax as I melt against his hard body. Tears flood down my cheeks as I let him hold me.

Fabio pulls away, gazing down at me with a concern that makes my stomach churn. "Are you okay, tesorina?" he asks, cupping my face in his large hands and wiping away my tears.

I swallow hard. "I was so scared. Those two men—"

Fabio tenses, eyes wide. "Did they hurt you?"

I shake my head. "They just came in here and asked if I knew you or Milo." My brow furrows. "They had photographs of both of you."

Fabio's nostrils flare, and rage ignites in his dark brown eyes. "Those fucking bastards."

I notice the blood on his hand. "Are you hurt?" I reach for his hand, but he grabs my wrists.

"It's barely a scratch on my calf, tesorina." He signals at the hole in his pants. "Nothing to worry about."

Milo comes into the bathroom. "You found your date, then?" His eyes dance with amusement. For a man who has just been attacked at a council party thrown for him, he doesn't look anxious. He appears as cool and collected as before. "Now you see the shit I'm dealing with day in and day out."

Fabio nods in response. "Yes, consider my men on the way to help you bring those Irish sons of bitches down once and for all."

Milo's smirk widens. "I can't wait."

I swallow hard, looking between the man I've inexplicably come to care for and the husband of my best friend.

How did I end up here?

My hand settles on my stomach, knowing that I've made so many stupid mistakes since I turned twenty-one. I never should have marched down that beach and broken into a mobster's home, particularly not when said mobster is my best friend's father.

Fabio grabs my hand. "Come on, let's get back to the room."

Milo steps to one side. "I hope to see you before you fly back to iron out the details of our deal. Perhaps we can all have brunch tomorrow before your flight?"

I swallow hard at the thought of spending any longer lying to my best friend's husband about who I am. It makes me sick to my stomach.

"Of course. Shall we meet at the restaurant at eleven?" Fabio asks.

"Sounds good." Milo smiles at me as I walk past him. It's a smile that doesn't hold any friendliness.

Aida seems to have learned to love the man she hated at the start. My first impression of him is that he is intimidating. I can't imagine what she's gone through being thrust into his arms without warning.

Fabio's hand slips down to the base of my back as he guides me out of the events room, which has been cordoned off by police.

"Excuse me," an officer says to us, stopping us from leaving.

"Yes?" Fabio says.

"I don't think we've had your statement." The police officer clicks his pen, flipping to another page on his notepad. "Can I take both of your full names, please?"

I swallow hard, glancing around to see if Milo is around.

Fabio answers for me instead. "Fabio Alteri and Lucia Dicampo." He runs a hand through his silver hair. "We're here on vacation from Sicily, invited by our friend, Milo Mazzeo."

The officer scribbles what Fabio says onto a piece of paper. "Did either of you have any direct contact with the shooters?"

Fabio tightens his grip on me. "No, we were both in the boardroom at the back when the shooting started."

I swallow hard, feeling uneasy that not only has Fabio given him a fake name for me, he's lying to the cops. His lie is convincing too. It makes me wonder how easy it would be for him to lie to me.

The officer nods. "Okay, thank you." He steps to one side. "If we need more information from you, we'll be in touch."

"Of course. Anything you need, officer." Fabio leads me past him and toward the main entrance hall of the hotel.

There's a tense silence between us as he leads me into an open elevator. The doors shut, closing us in together.

Still, he doesn't say a word. I normally enjoy silence, but I need to hear him speak. Fabio needs to apologize to me for thrusting me into the middle of this.

Does he even care that I was in such a dangerous position less than twenty minutes ago?

The elevator dings, signaling my arrival on our hotel room floor. Fabio squeezes my hip as he leads me out of it and along the corridor to our room, opening the door to our room when we arrive.

Once the door shuts, he still doesn't speak, instead walking over to the dresser and pouring himself a whiskey.

"Aren't you going to say something?" I ask, frustrated by his silence.

He pauses mid drink and sets the glass down on the dresser. "What is there to say?"

I shake my head. "Sorry for dragging you to this hellhole of a city would be a good place to start."

He paces toward me. "There's one thing you will have to learn, Gia. I am not one who apologizes lightly." He grabs hold of my hips and pulls me toward him. "I don't regret bringing you here."

I look at him in disbelief. "Perhaps that would have been different if that Irish thug had pulled the trigger of the gun they held to my head."

Fabio's eyes flash. "They were merely trying to intimidate you. You were never in genuine danger because they didn't know you were with me."

I shake my head. "The moment they heard my accent I was in danger. I'm just lucky they believed I was Spanish rather than Italian."

Fabio lets go of me and walks back to the dresser,

knocking back the whiskey. "I wouldn't have allowed anyone to harm you."

Although I haven't yet done a pregnancy test, I'm pretty confident of the results. As I stare at the broken don of the Sicilian mafia, I wonder what his reaction would be to such news.

All I know is that I need to end this before it's too late. Fabio need never find out about our child. We can part once we return to Palermo and never see each other again.

I can't understand why a dull ache ignites in my chest at the thought. The thought of never feeling his touch or kissing his lips again hurts, even if he is an asshole most of the time.

"Come here, bella," Fabio says, his voice softer.

I meet his dark, almost black stare and find myself lured to him for the last time.

Fabio wraps his arms around me, and I wrap mine around his hard, muscled waist. The way he holds me is both forceful and soft.

"What are we doing?" I ask, breaking the silence between us.

Fabio pulls back enough to look me in the eye. "What do you mean, baby?"

"This is wrong. Aida is your daughter and my best friend." I shake my head. "We never should have crossed the line."

He smiles, but it's a sad smile. "You're right. We would hurt Aida if she ever learned the truth, but we won't let that happen." He brushes a hair from out of my eye. "You say it's wrong, but whenever we're together it feels right. Why fight it?"

I feel a piercing pain in my chest as I search his dark eyes, knowing that is exactly what I have to do once we land back on Sicilian soil tomorrow evening. We have to go our separate ways.

Instead of answering his question, I press my lips to his, savoring the way they feel.

Fabio's tongue delves into my mouth with an unmatchable passion. Our kiss turns frantic and wild as he pushes me toward the bed.

He pushes my dress down until there is nothing between us but pure desire, then lowers me to the soft mattress. I'm angry at the man who is touching me softly, but it's impossible to think about it when his lips touch mine.

Fabio holds my hands on either side of my head as he kisses my neck and shoulders, making me shiver. The same dominance is there, but he's being gentler than before.

I can't understand why it makes my chest ache more. Perhaps it's because I know this has to end.

"Fabio," I murmur as he bites my collarbone, sending shock waves through my entire body.

He stops and looks me in the eye. "What is it, tesorina?"

I can't understand why I love him calling me his

little treasure. It makes me feel special. He makes me feel special.

"Fuck me, please," I breathe.

He smiles. "You don't have to ask me twice."

I watch as he frees himself from his pants and moves fast, thrusting himself deep inside of me with no teasing. The deep ache I'd felt is quenched by his thick cock.

There's a desperation as he fucks me hard, moving his hand to my throat as he gently chokes me. I can't understand why I love the sensation so much.

It's forceful but tender. A way of him enforcing his utter dominance over my body.

"Yes, sir," I moan, loving the way it feels as he pumps his hips, slow and deep.

Tonight there's something different in the way he's fucking me. It's full of unspoken emotion—emotion I know we're both feeling. Fabio isn't just a fuck to me. He's been much more than that since the first night I fell into his trap. He has my heart and he could break it as quickly as he claimed it.

It's not too late. That's why I know that this has to end, no matter how much I don't want it to. Even if I'm carrying his child, this can't continue. It's a painful but real fact that I've been ignoring for too long.

19

FABIO

*G*ia stands in front of the mirror, staring at herself with a concerned expression. It's an expression that makes me wish I could read her mind.

"What are you thinking about, tesorina?"

She visibly jumps at the sound of my voice, glancing over at me in surprise. "Don't sneak up on me like that."

I walk toward her and box her in against the sink, placing my hands on either side of her hips. "Are you telling me what to do, Gia?"

Her slender neck bobs as she swallows hard and her cheeks flush a deep red as she watches me in the mirror behind her. "No, I'm telling you that you shocked me."

I press my lips to the back of her neck, kissing her gently. I feel her shiver against me, instinctively arching her back as I move my hands to her hips. "We've not got long until brunch," I murmur, feeling my desire for her spike out of control.

"I know." She looks uncertain about saying anything else. "I'm really uncomfortable about sitting down to eat with Aida's husband." She bites her lip. "Can't you tell Milo I'm not feeling well and go by yourself?"

I tilt my head, regarding the woman in front of me. "What if I don't want to go without you?"

Gia's brow furrows. "It's not a good idea. I'm going to meet him with Aida in six weeks." She shakes her head. "He might forget me from a brief meeting, but having a meal with someone is different."

She has a point. I'm not entirely sure where Milo's loyalties would lie between me or his wife. If he were to tell Aida about our relationship, it would hurt her even more than I already have. I've not been a good father to her for most of her life. I would say that fucking her best friend is probably the worst thing I've done, but I couldn't help it.

Gia has gotten under my skin in ways no woman has ever been able to, not even my late wife. "Face me, baby," I murmur softly.

Gia glares at me in the mirror, but she does as I say. She turns around and looks up at me with those beautiful chestnut brown eyes. "Fine, you may stay here," I murmur before pulling her against me and kissing her passionately. "But I want you to be ready to head back to Sicily once I return."

Gia tenses against me. "I'm more than ready." Her eyes flash with irritation. "I never wanted to come here."

I narrow my eyes. "Don't lie, Gia. I know that deep down that you love it when I take charge."

She pushes me away from her with a surprising amount of force. "No, I don't love it. I may enjoy your dominance in bed, but you crossed a line. You snatched me away from my work commitments, which may not seem important to you but they are to me."

I should have known she'd hold this against me. "Your staff have easily handled your commitments." I step toward her. "If you ask me, you need to learn how to delegate more, Gia."

My business advice only seems to get me an enraged response as she storms away from me. "Unbelievable." She may not want to hear my advice, but as the head of the Alteri Mafia, I run several enterprises. Enterprises that I've had to delegate control of for them to run efficiently. I follow her back into the hotel suite.

"What is so unbelievable about simple business advice?" I ask, narrowing my eyes.

She sets her hands on her hips. "You are being a patronizing asshole, that's what's unbelievable." She glances at her watch. "You best get going or you will be late."

I clench my jaw, wishing I had time to bend her over my knee and paint her ass red. Time isn't on my side. Instead, I close the gap between us and grab her throat forcefully. "Don't mess with me, Gia. I'll have to punish you for your disobedience on the plane."

She glares at me, but her resolve weakens as I press my lips to the edge of her jaw and nibble. "I bet you're really looking forward to it, aren't you, baby?"

Gia shakes her head. "No." Her cheeks redden, signaling that she's lying.

I press my lips to hers and kiss her quickly. "I bet your pussy is already dripping wet," I murmur before turning and walking away. "You better not touch yourself, or I will know."

I don't turn around to look at her and walk out of the hotel room, heading down the corridor. Gia is driving me crazy with her disobedient, bratty attitude.

Milo is already sitting at a table for three. His brow furrows when he sees I'm alone. "What happened to your date, Fabio?"

I shake my head. "Indisposed."

Milo chuckles at that. "I didn't even see her touch a drop of alcohol. You must have had a very eventful night." He winks.

He leans back in his chair as I take my seat opposite him.

"Before we delve into business, I need to address something about your date." He runs a hand through his hair. "It's odd that Lucia looks very much like Aida's best friend, Gia."

It feels like he knocks the air out of my lungs.

How could I be this stupid?

I didn't think that Aida would have grown close enough to Milo to tell him about her friends, and I didn't think Milo would have the time to pay attention.

"Are you going to tell my daughter?" I ask.

Milo shakes his head. "No, it's not my place." He runs a hand over his dark brown beard. "If this is just a silly faze, brush it under the carpet and ensure my wife never learns of it." Milo cracks his neck. "If this is long term, you and Gia need to tell her when we come to Sicily." He shrugs. "It's down to you ultimately, but if I learn it continued and you don't tell her, I will have to come clean." Milo unbuttons his jacket. "Aida is the only person I give a shit about on this earth and I won't watch while you break her heart for the second time by lying to her."

That's fair enough. This has happened because I'm too selfish to put my daughter in front of my own needs. "Understood. I'll work it out before you arrive in Sicily."

Milo clears his throat. "Good. Now, business."

I can't tell Gia what Milo said, as she'd never forgive me for dragging her here. I clearly underestimated how well my daughter and Milo's relationship is going.

A waiter comes to take our order and I order a fried breakfast. Milo orders the same.

"Can you give me a timescale for getting your men out here?" he asks, pouring himself some coffee. "Do you want some?"

I shake my head, not feeling like I can stomach

coffee. Nothing beats Italian coffee. "I can get them to you next week if needed."

Milo smiles, but as always, it's cruel and unfeeling. I can see why he got his reputation. "Perfect. We will obviously have a few meetings while I'm in Sicily to hash out the plans in relation to the Moretti family." He tilts his head to the side. "Hopefully you can reconcile with Aida before I go to Naples. Although that may depend on your decision concerning her friend."

I swallow hard, hating the way Milo makes me feel so guilty without even questioning my decisions. "It's clear you disapprove. As my business partner, why don't you speak frankly?"

Milo's brow raises. "I only hate seeing someone close to my wife betray her." He shakes his head. "Not you, but her friend who she still adores." He waves his hand dismissively. "Let's not dwell on it; you know my stance."

The waiter brings our food, and we eat in silence. There's an awkward tension, but I think only I feel it. It's because I know that I have a huge decision to make.

Gia has become important to me. The idea of letting her go seems impossible. However, my relationship with her will only cause my daughter pain, something I should have given greater thought to before I jumped in bed with Gia.

It's too late now to wind back the clock, but I can do the right thing still.

The question is, do I want to?

20

GIA

I jolt awake as the plane hits the runway.

Fabio sits opposite me and smiles when he sees I'm awake. "We're home."

I sit up straight and glance out of the window, instantly recognizing Palermo airport. "Thank God for that."

Fabio chuckles. "Didn't enjoy Boston?"

I shake my head. "No, nor almost being killed by Irish thugs."

His eyes flash with guilt at the mention of my close encounter with Milo's enemies. "My taking you to Boston was dangerous." Fabio runs a hand through his gorgeous silver hair. "I won't take risks with your life again, Gia. I promise."

I swallow hard, knowing that he won't take risks with my life again because this can't continue. Aida will be in Sicily in six weeks. This forbidden relationship has to end before it's too late. "I know you won't, because this ends today."

Fabio's brow furrows. "What are you talking about, Gia?"

I stand, crossing my arms over my chest. "Whatever the fuck this is between us, it ends today."

Fabio stands and closes the gap between us, looming over me to intimidate me. I won't allow him to. "I thought I told you I'm in charge." He grabs hold of my throat lightly, making my knees shake.

I place my hand over his and pry his fingers from my throat. "No. If I don't want this, then you can't force it on me." I walk away from him, shaking my head. "The only way this is going to continue is if you kidnap me and tie me up against my will." I turn and glare at Fabio, wondering if he is capable of doing such a thing.

Fabio looks hurt. "Don't tempt me, tesorina."

"If you did, I'd hate you forever," I say.

The dangerous don just stares at me as if contemplating kidnapping me and whether I'm serious. "Hate is a very strong word."

I nod in reply. "It is, but taking away someone's free will is the quickest route to hatred."

Fabio tilts his head, as if trying to work out how serious I am. "Do you really think you could ever hate me?"

As I stare at the silver fox I've grown inexplicably fond of, I know that I could never truly hate him. No matter what he has put me through, my feelings for him are the opposite. Another very good reason to get out of this while I still can. However, if he were to kidnap me and hold me against my will, I'm sure my feelings would quickly change. "I don't know, Fabio. All I know is this must end."

Fabio looks hurt as he stares at me with a longing that makes my stomach clench. "I understand." His lack of protest surprises me, but it's clear that he has no intention of holding me against my will. "Will you allow me one last kiss, tesorina?" he asks, making my heart ache. He moves toward me slowly, waiting for my answer.

I don't want to kiss him again, as all it will do is make me wish I didn't have to break this off. Fabio may have crossed the line by kidnapping me and whisking me off to Boston when I had responsibilities, but it doesn't change the way I feel about him. "Si," I murmur.

He grabs hold of my hips hard and pulls me against him, lifting my chin up to look into my eyes. "Sei bellissima," he breathes before pressing his lips to mine.

At first, the kiss is soft as he gently probes my lips with his tongue. Once I open them for him, the passion and longing in the kiss heightens. I claw my nails into his back as he gropes my ass possessively, making me wet between my thighs.

My chest aches at the thought of never kissing this man again. The thought of never feeling his hands on my body or the exquisite sensations when he moves inside of me. It hurts breaking this off, but I know it's the right thing to do.

The right thing to do would have been to never walk down that beach on the night of my twenty-first birthday. When I took that walk to give Fabio a piece of my mind, I was drunk and truly intended to do that.

It was a stupid thing to do, but I never expected to feel the way I did when he looked into my eyes. Or for him to feel the same way and make a move.

After that kiss, I could have had more willpower and stayed away. Instead, I took things further. I was the one to make the next move. It was my fault, and that's why I need to be the one to do the right thing.

Fabio breaks away from me, his eyes dazed with lust. "Gia, are you sure about this?" he murmurs.

I nod and take a step back, pressing my hand to my lips. "Yes. We can't keep doing this to Aida."

Fabio swallows hard, eyes lingering on my body. Finally, he takes a step back and nods. "You are right, tesorina. Even though I wish you weren't."

His admission that breaking things off is the right thing to do only makes it hurt more. "Goodbye."

"Ciao, bella," he says, eyes full of remorse.

I wonder if he regrets the time we spent together, but don't question him. Instead, I turn and walk out of that plane and onto the runway without looking back.

There are taxis parked in the rank out front and I take one, rushing away from the man I've fallen for.

As I watch the airport fade into the distance out of my window, I know that life will never be the same.

I press a hand to my stomach, knowing that I have to stop wondering and find out the truth.

Am I carrying a mobster's baby?

SIENA JUMPS to her feet as I enter the apartment. "What the fuck were you thinking?" she asks, not giving me a chance to step through the door.

I sigh heavily and slump onto the sofa. The last thing I feel like doing right now is explaining myself. I didn't have a choice. "I wasn't thinking," I say.

Siena shakes her head. "What the hell happened? You realize you left the shop unlocked?"

I swallow hard, knowing that it's difficult to explain. "Did I?" I ask, shaking my head. "He turned up without warning and insisted I go to Rome with him for the weekend," I say, hating how much I've been lying to everyone I care about. "I thought I'd locked the shop."

Siena shakes her head. "You didn't even take your fucking purse." I look up at my friend, whose eyes are full of anger. "I thought you'd been kidnapped or something."

Pretty accurate. "I'm sorry. I got caught up in the moment."

Siena's brow furrows. "Who the fuck is this guy, Gia?"

I wish that I'd never walked down that beach on my birthday. "No one. It's over now."

Siena gapes at me. "Wait. So you skip town on one of your busiest weekends for this guy, only for it to be over just like that?"

I shrug, feeling the weight of what I've done weighing heavily on my shoulders. The deep sadness I feel at ending it with Fabio is soul crushing. "Sorry, Siena. I've had a long day and I don't really want to talk about it." I rub my face in my hands and stand. "I need to freshen up." I walk toward the bathroom, knowing that I have to find out once and for all if I'm pregnant.

Am I carrying Aida's half sibling inside of me?

I pull the pregnancy test out of my bag. It may be my first time doing one, but I know deep down that I don't want to see the results, hence my pathetic attempt at procrastinating. I bought the test while Fabio was at brunch with Milo, but I couldn't bring myself to do it at the hotel.

I take the test out of the packet, follow the instructions, and put the cap back on, placing it down on the sink counter. My heart is pounding hard as I wait for the result to show, praying that the second line doesn't appear.

My stomach sinks, but I'm not surprised when the second line appears—positive. The thought of being pregnant at all right now is daunting, but particularly when that child is Fabio Alteri's. The leader of the Sicilian mafia. My best friend's father.

Fuck.

No one can ever learn the truth about my child's father. There's no way I'd ever have an abortion, so it looks like I'm about to become a single working mom. I guess the apple doesn't fall far from the tree after all.

My mom ran the shop and had me, so I'll to do the same.

It will be hard seeing Fabio around town, knowing we can never be together as a family. I know that was always a stupid fantasy.

Even before I fell pregnant, I'd fantasized about a world where we could be together openly. A world where he wasn't my best friend's father.

I'm about to repeat my mom's mistakes all over again.

21

FABIO

I slam my knuckles into his face, shattering his nose with a sickening crunch.

"Do you regret betraying me yet, Dino?" I ask, slowly circling the man tied to the chair as the rage grows.

Dino is the man that fucked up my chance at a revenge. Lorenzo found out how the Moretti family learned of our plan, and it all came down to this asshole.

He spits out blood and then glares at me. "I did what anyone would do: accepted the money from whoever paid the best." He shrugs. "The Moretti family paid best."

I grab hold of the back of his neck and squeeze hard, forcing him to look at me above him. "A mistake you will regret for the short remainder of your pathetic life," I growl.

I'm not normally one to get this angry over a lowlife like Dino. Yet, ever since Gia called our affair off, I've been a loose cannon. Rage has become my new normal. It's been two weeks since she broke it off, and it feels like with every day that passes the rage grows.

Dino's fight escapes his eyes. The first sign of fear, an emotion he mostly certainly should feel. "I can make it right, Fabio." I let go of his neck, knowing I have no interest in giving him a chance to make anything right.

He knew exactly what he was getting himself in to when he betrayed me and sided with the Moretti family. Milo will take my enemies out once and for all. I trust him to stick to his word, as he has a dozen of my men helping him sway the war in his favor.

The Irish are experiencing too much loss at the hands of the Italians. It's only a matter of time until they're forced to surrender. Milo will be here in four weeks with my daughter. He says it's going to be tough to convince her to meet with me, but I need to explain to her why I did what I did.

I slam my fist into his jaw repeatedly, hardly registering the damage I'm doing. As I punish the man that robbed me of my revenge, it feels like I'm no longer in my body. For a while now I've felt detached from the present, as if watching myself from above.

Gia breaking our relationship off has me unhinged. It's like losing everything all over again, even if she is still alive. Twice I've had Aldo drive me by her shop purposely, and I watch her as she works on her flower arrangements.

"Boss." Lorenzo's voice pulls me back into my body.

I stare down at the man I'd been torturing, swallowing hard at the bloody mess. His blood coats my knuckles and splatters my clothes. Dino is hanging on by a thread. I turn to face Lorenzo. "Finish it," I say, walking away from the man who I'd almost beaten to death without even realizing it.

As I walk out of the basement, I realize how far I've fallen. This isn't me.

I'm not a man fueled by rage and violence.

Ever since the Moretti family killed Salvatore, I've been spiraling, and Gia breaking things off was the last straw.

I wipe the blood from my knuckles onto my bloodied white shirt, heading toward my bedroom.

Dino shouldn't have betrayed the Alteri Mafia. If he hadn't been such a greedy piece of shit, the Moretti family would be dead.

Gia may have told me to stay away from her, but two weeks have passed and my longing to be near her hasn't subsided.

I won't let her tell me what to do. I own Sicily, and if she wants to remain in Palermo, she will reconsider her decision.

Aida won't like it, but I won't give up my only shot

at a semblance of a happy life because of who the woman is that I've fallen for.

Gia feels the same way I feel about her, that I'm certain of.

The door to my room is unlocked, and I enter, stripping off my jacket and shirt. I shove them into the laundry basket in my room. I've got blood everywhere, even on my pants, so I take those off next and stuff them in too. My housekeeper is used to bloody clothes.

I walk into my bathroom and turn the faucet on the shower on, letting it warm up.

Gia has unraveled me. Her defiance isn't something I'm used to dealing with, but it's alluring and sexy. In fact, I think it's one of the reasons I'm so hooked on her.

We connect on so many levels, not only sexually but emotionally. It's a connection I've struggled to find with anyone, even my late wife.

I grab my cell phone and type out a text to Gia, knowing she probably won't respond.

I need to see you tonight. Please reply. I miss you.

Those words are words I've never said to a living soul before. As the leader of a powerful crime organization, it's hard to consider emotions of any kind.

However, only the truth will get her back, and telling her I miss her is the truth. Plain and simple. There's no need to embellish it.

After a few moments staring at the screen, I send

the text. The water in the shower has already warmed and I step under the spray.

The water turns crimson as the blood washes from my face, hands, and neck.

Brutality is a part of my world—a part I seem to have become desensitized to. The blood washing down the drain doesn't affect me. It's simply another day at the office.

I know how fucked up that is. It's sick to think that my world has become so twisted. Gia made the right decision to get away from me, but she made a wrong one when she broke in here. Now that I've had her, I can't let her go.

I may have given her space these past two weeks, but that's all she is going to get. I can't stay away from her any longer.

The water finally runs clear as I turn my attention to my cock, which is as hard as a rock. For a man who is about to be fifty years old in a month, I've jerked off more than I have since I was a teenager in the past two weeks.

I fist myself thinking about my sweet little treasure. She thinks she can walk away from me. Gia needs to learn that there's only one ruler in Sicily and that's me.

I'll take what I want, when I want. The ugly reality of being tangled up in this kind of work is that it's easy to get used to everyone saying yes to you. Gia saying no only makes me want her more.

I groan as my cock throbs against my hand. The

image of Gia's face and perfect, firm breasts imprints into my mind. Two weeks of not having my beauty writhing and crying beneath me has been two long. No matter how many times I jack myself off, I'm never satisfied.

I won't be satisfied until my cock is buried in Gia's tight little pussy again. It's clear that now that I've had her, I'll never be able to get her out of my mind. My feelings for her have been clear since the moment we met. No woman has made me feel this way, not even my late wife.

I have fallen in love with my daughter's best friend. It's wrong on so many levels, but it feels right whenever we are together.

I fist my cock harder, feeling frustration and arousal building. My balls ache for release as I think about how good Gia's tight virgin asshole felt wrapped around me. "Cazzo," I growl as my release hits me. I shoot rope after rope of creamy cum onto the shower floor, wishing it was deep inside of Gia.

The idea of Gia finding another man and settling down with him or having a family drives me insane. Now that she's not with me, it makes that idea more likely. Any man would be lucky to have her…until I found out and throttled him for touching her.

If there is one thing I've learned from all of this, it's that life is never simple. Gia is all I want. I can't keep away from her, so that means I'll have to come clean to Aida.

I thought a second chance wasn't in the cards for me, but Gia makes me want things that make no sense. I want a second chance at having a family and protecting them successfully this time.

A family with Gia would bring far too many complications. Namely, that my daughter is her best friend. But that doesn't stop my mind from fantasizing about a future with her—a future I know I don't deserve.

Gia deserves a man that brings her safety and stability, but my heart won't let her go. She's been mine since the moment she broke into my study on the night of her twenty-first birthday. I have to make her see why this can't end. We are made for each other and that's a simple fact.

22

GIA

I glance up, swallowing hard when I see who I've just walked into.

Fabio stares at me with a look that is almost frantic. "I can't do this anymore, Gia."

My brow furrows as I glance back toward the main street, worried that someone might see us. "Do what?" I ask, returning my attention to him.

"Stay away from you," he mutters.

My stomach twists as I stare into the dark brown depths of Fabio's eyes, knowing that I don't truly have the power to stay away from Fabio, either. The past two weeks have been torture, and when I got his text last night, I almost caved and sent a text back—almost.

"Aida will be here in Sicily in less than a month." It's the only response I can come up with.

Fabio slides his large, rough hands onto my hips,

gripping me tightly. "That's not a reason for me to stay away."

I swallow hard, painfully aware of how easily anyone could see us down this alleyway. Fabio isn't difficult to recognize, being six foot six tall with silver gray hair. He's always impeccably dressed, and he exudes confidence. "It is a reason for both of us to stay away from each other."

He tightens his grip on my hips. "I can't stay away from you, no matter the consequences."

I feel my heart skip a beat. "Fabio—"

He kisses me passionately, making my stomach clench. The last thing we should do is kiss down an alleyway in Palermo.

I push him away. "Not here," I breathe.

He chuckles, smiling down at me. "That's not a no."

I narrow my eyes at him. "It's also not a yes."

Fabio slides his hand lower, cupping my ass cheeks firmly. "You know you can't resist, tesorina."

I grit my teeth, knowing that he's right. No matter how much I try to fight it, I long for his touch. It angers me how little self-control I have when it comes to him. "Not here," I murmur again, but the fight has escaped me.

"What are you scared of, baby?" he asks, his voice as soft as silk.

I bite my lip, remembering the secret growing inside of me. What started out as a hot and forbidden affair has turned into something so much more complicated. "We can't be seen."

Fabio pulls me tighter against him, letting me feel the hard press of his cock against my abdomen. "Why not? We both want this, so let's stop hiding."

I stare in shock at Fabio, wondering if he hit his head. "Because Aida will find out, one way or another." I shake my head. "Is that what you want?"

A flash of guilt enters his dark brown eyes. "Not exactly. I'd rather she hear it directly from me." He sighs heavily, loosening his grip. "I can't stay away from you, Gia." He turns his back on me and runs a hand through his beautiful silver hair.

I know the feeling, although I've been handling it better than Fabio. As I take in his appearance, it's impossible not to notice how tired he looks. The dark rings around his eyes are an instant giveaway, along with the dullness of his normal bright eyes.

"Fabio, how could we ever explain this to Aida?" I can't lose my best friend over a man, even one I feel so strongly about. Aida has been there since I was little. We've been through everything together.

He grabs my hand and brings it to his lips, kissing the back of it. "We'll work it out, together. I can't lose you too, Gia." There's raw emotion lacing his voice.

"What do you mean?"

He shakes his head, and I can tell he doesn't want to open up to me. "It doesn't matter."

I pull my hand from his. "It does. If you want this to continue, you need to be more open with me."

Fabio's jaw clenches. "Very well, but not here." He glances behind me at Main Street. "Meet me at my house at eight o'clock tonight."

I narrow my eyes at him. "I won't be staying the night."

Fabio chuckles. "I wouldn't be too sure about that, bella."

His confidence is attractive, but I am not going over there for sex. If he won't open up to me, then he won't be getting what he wants. I need to know more about the broken don and why he pushed Aida away. He's tortured by his past, and I've always been drawn to broken people. Perhaps it's in my DNA.

My mom wasn't exactly the best judge of character. My dad was a waste of space who left her penniless when I was very young. Any partners after that were all guys who didn't deserve her or treat her well.

"I'll see you later," I say, turning to walk away.

Fabio grabs my hand and pulls me back to face him. "Not before I get a taste, tesorina."

I narrow my eyes. "That's not the deal."

"Fuck the deal," he growls softly before wrapping his fingers around my throat and pushing me against the wall of the alleyway. "I want to taste you now, baby, and I always get what I want."

I swallow hard, looking up into his dark, almost

black eyes. It's crazy how much I've missed this man. His dominance is addictive.

"Yes, sir," I say.

He smirks at me. "Good girl," he purrs.

Fabio teases me, pressing his lips to the edge of my jaw, before snaking down over my neck softly.

I shudder, loving the way it feels to be pinned against the wall by this man. His weight holds me in place, making it impossible for me to escape. "Fabio, not here—"

He silences me, placing his lips over mine and forcing his tongue into my mouth.

I groan as he deepens the kiss. Fabio's hard cock throbs in his pants against my abdomen, making me long to feel him inside of me. After a few minutes of making out in the city center of Palermo, Fabio breaks the kiss. "Cazzo, bella, facciamolo qui."

I shake my head, eyes wide. "No fucking chance, Fabio." He just said let's do it here, which will never happen.

He chuckles again. "Calm down, baby, I'm messing with you." He bites my earlobe, before whispering, "But I'm definitely fucking you later whether or not you want me to."

A shudder pulses down my spine at his words. Before I can protest, he turns away from me and walks briskly down the alleyway, away from the city. I swallow hard, watching after him.

The right thing to do would be to stay home tonight

and ignore his invitation. Although I don't seem to be able to do the right thing at all lately.

My palms are sweaty as I stand in front of Fabio's villa, feeling anxious about tonight.

I can't help but wonder if this is a ploy to reel me back into his trap. The moment I give in to his demands, I relinquish any control I still hold.

I press the bell and tap my feet on the floor, waiting for Fabio to answer.

He appears quickly, dressed in a pair of black pants and a beige shirt that is only buttoned up halfway, giving me a teasing view of his muscled, tattooed chest. "Buonasera signorina," he says, making goosebumps prickle on my exposed arms. His eyes drag slowly down my dress, which I ensured isn't too revealing.

"My beautiful treasure," he murmurs, his eyes lighting with hungry desire. "Come in." He steps to one side, allowing me to walk past him and into the wolf's den.

I get a waft of his masculine scent, which makes me want to jump him already. "Are you going to tell me what you meant earlier, then?"

Fabio laughs. "Straight to the point. I think it's why I like you so much."

I hate the way my stomach flips.

"Come and have a seat." He gestures for me to sit on the sofa.

I sit down and he sits next to me, taking my hand in his. "You want to know what I meant when I said I can't lose you too." There's a far off, sad look in his eyes. "You obviously know what happened to Aida's mother, Lianna?"

I shift, feeling a little uncomfortable at the mention of his late wife. She was a lovely woman. She was the kindest person I ever met. I feel a little guilty that I've been sleeping with Fabio, even if she died ten years ago. "Yes," I say simply.

He nods. "That was my first loss, but recently, I lost my best friend."

My brow furrows. "Who?"

"Salvatore Greco, my capo." Fabio drops my hand and runs it through his silver hair. "My enemy murdered him over a year ago now. Two months before I sent Aida away." His jaw clenches. "I did what I had to do to protect the only person I cared for in this world. God knows I didn't make the right decisions for Lianna or Salvatore."

"You broke her heart, Fabio," I say, knowing how upset Aida was at the things he said to her. "You told her you didn't want her around because she reminded you of her mother."

His eyes flash with what looks like rage. "I did what was necessary. The Moretti family was moving in on Sicily. It was too dangerous for her here." He pauses a moment, as if searching for a way to explain what he did to me. "I know Aida. If she knew I had a shred of good in me, she'd try to fight for it." He sighs heavily. "She wouldn't have gone so easily." Fabio shakes his head. "In fact, I may have caved and allowed her to stay. But the risks were too high." He stands and paces the living room. "Milo gave me the power to get the Morreti family to back off, and he took Aida far away from the feud, keeping her safe from the bloodshed."

I knew there had to be more to it than him deciding to ship her off for personal gain. "You did it to protect her?" I ask.

Fabio glances at me again. "Yes, I sacrificed the last good thing in my life in order to ensure that she didn't meet the same terrible fate as everyone else I've loved." His jaw clenches at the word as he stares at me. "Now, I have someone else to lose and it frightens me, Gia."

I swallow hard, hearing Fabio admit to being afraid. The broken don is scared to lose me. My heart skips a beat as I wonder if he's implying that he loves me.

"What are you saying, Fabio?" I ask.

He sits next to me again, grabbing my hands. "I'm saying that you are my world, tesorina. I can't let you go, no matter what the consequences are."

I look down at our hands, knowing that I feel the same. "What do you propose we do then?"

Fabio smiles at me. "When Aida comes to Sicily, we tell her the truth."

I think about the secret I'm also keeping from him.

His baby that I'm carrying. "Do you think she will hate us?"

Fabio shrugs. "I don't know. She hates me already. All I know is that I can't stay away from you, Gia. The thought of you ever being with another man brings out my murderous tendencies."

I raise a brow. "Murderous?"

He nods. "Yes, I'd kill any man that tries to fucking touch you."

It's a sick and twisted declaration, but one that makes me feel special and protected.

I nod. "Okay, we will come clean when Aida comes to Sicily." I search his dark black eyes. "Does that mean you want to be with me for the long term?"

He laughs. "Of course. Do you think I'd risk your friendship with my daughter over a fling?"

I shake my head and he pulls me close, kissing me. "I want you, Gia. Always. No other man will ever touch you while there's still breath in my lungs." He kisses me again, making me dizzy with happiness.

Fabio may not have said those three words, but he might as well have. We both love each other. The question is, what will he think about the news I've yet to share with him?

Is he prepared to become a dad again?

23

FABIO

Dario Morretti stares at me with a dark hatred. A hatred that I know all too well. "Why don't you stop playing with your food, Alteri?" he growls.

I laugh at that. "And miss an opportunity to cause a Moretti pain?" I shake my head. "I don't think so." I punch him in the gut.

"Stronzo," he growls.

"You can call me an asshole all you like, Dario. It will not change the fact that I'm going to continue torturing you for a very long time." I pull my knife and slice into his bruised flesh, making him squeal like a girl. "Your family took everything from me and it's only a matter of time until I take everything from yours."

"My father will kill you before you have the chance," he spits angrily.

I laugh at him, as this time I guarantee I'm going to

come out on top. "I had considered sending your head to him as a warning, but I think I prefer presenting his head to you. Then I'll cut your head off and send it to your mother along with your father's head." I circle the strung-up Moretti. "After all, you had the courtesy to do the same to my late wife and my capo."

A glint of fear ignites in Dario's eyes. "I had nothing to do with your wife's death. I wasn't even in Italy."

I shake my head. "It doesn't matter. The fact that you're a Moretti means you're involved because of your blood alone." I stab the knife into his hand, which is already missing four fingers, which I've sent to his father, making him screech as blood shoots from it. "Let's be clear here. You came to Palermo to assassinate me, so don't tell me you're fucking innocent." I pull the knife out of his hand and stab it into the other. "By the time I'm through with you, you will wish you were never born a Moretti. I can assure you of that."

The darkness inside of me grows and twists the more blood I draw and bones I break. I no longer have a soul. I sacrificed it a long time ago.

"You're a sick old bastard," Dario spits, wincing as he speaks.

"Maybe. I don't care if I am. Your family took everything from me and I won't rest until I take everything from your family." I slice the knife across his cheek, making him wince. "I've got nothing left to live for."

That statement would have been true a couple of

months ago. Now it's not true. Gia makes life worth living again. However, I don't want my enemy to know that, even though I have him trapped in my basement.

I clench my bloodied fists and slam my hand into his face, knocking him out. Once he's unconscious, I walk away and leave him bleeding. Dario Moretti made a grave mistake when he came here on a vendetta, no doubt trying to prove he's as worthy as the two children from Rafa's current marriage.

Lorenzo is standing in my kitchen when I ascend from the basement. His eyes widen when he sees that I'm covered in blood. "Having fun?" he asks, raising a brow.

I glare at my stand-in capo. No one knows that I have Dario Moretti locked in my basement, other than Lorenzo. The last thing I need is for word to get out; it always has a way of getting back to Rafa. "Yes. What do you want?"

He shuffles some papers in his hands, searching for something. "Mayor wants you to sign off on the hotel you didn't give permission for." He passes it to me.

I shake my head. "I'm not having the Russians moving in on Sicily. Did he say why?"

Lorenzo shrugs. "I feel he has a financial interest in it."

I sigh heavily, knowing the mayor of Palermo is as greedy as they come. "Do I have to bribe the bastard, then?"

Lorenzo nods. "It would seem like it. Would you like me to go on your behalf?"

"Two million euros and no more, though." I run a hand through my hair. "That man has had too much money from me already."

"Sir." He bows his head and walks out of my home, leaving me alone with my darkness. I glance down at my bloodied clothes, knowing that I need to get cleaned up quickly. Gia will be here in half an hour.

I don't want her to see how pitch-black the darkness within me truly is. She hasn't seen the harrowing side of my job and I never want her to.

THE NEXT MORNING Gia sits on the terrace outside my home, looking out at the sea. I feel my chest ache at the sight of her. It's been two weeks since we decided to carry on with our torrid love affair, and now we're two weeks away from Aida and Milo arriving in Sicily.

I've yet to tell her that Milo knew the truth. It won't help anything and will only worry her that he might change his mind and tell Aida.

I know he won't. Milo is not impulsive or reckless. He's smart. He's probably one of the smartest men I know. Salvatore would have cherished my Aida, but at least I know she's found love even if I forced it upon her.

I pour a cup of coffee and head out onto the

terrace. "Buongiorno, tesorina," I say, taking a seat by her side and placing my hand on her thigh.

Gia glances up at me, and I can tell something is bothering her.

"What's wrong?"

She shakes her head. "Nothing."

I tighten my grip on her thigh. "Don't lie to me, Gia. I can tell when something is bothering you."

Gia sighs heavily. "I'm worried about telling Aida. She will be here in two weeks."

I nod. "I know, but we have to come clean." It has been bothering me, but it's the only thing we can do.

I want to be with Gia for the rest of my life. If I were to lose Gia too, I don't know if this life would be worth living.

"The thought of losing my best friend scares me." She glances down at her hands. "I've known Aida my whole life pretty much."

It's impossible not to feel guilty for crossing the line with her. "I know." My brow furrows. "You still have time to call this off," I say, feeling my chest ache at the thought.

Gia meets my gaze with wide eyes. "Is that what you want?"

I shake my head. "No fucking chance. All I'm saying is that you have a choice."

"I know, and I choose you. I just feel guilty about it."

My heart swells hearing her say she chooses me. "Is that all you're worried about?" I ask.

There's a flash of panic on Gia's face for a moment. "Of course. What else would I be worried about?"

I look at her through narrowed eyes, wondering why she won't open up to me. There's something else on her mind, but she won't tell me. In time, she will learn that there are no secrets between us. If she is to be mine, then she needs to learn how to trust me as her master and protector.

"I've got a day off today," I say, taking her hand in mine. "What do you say about spending it together?"

Gia glances at her watch. "I've been putting too much on Angelica and Claudia lately. It's only a matter of time until I drive them away."

"Surely they can manage one day. You work seven days a week, tesorina. Maybe it's time you employ more people to help at the shop."

Gia glances at me thoughtfully. "Perhaps. I'll check in with Angelica and find out if they can manage."

I smile. "What would you like to do?"

Gia shakes her head. "What can we do? We can't go out in public until we tell Aida."

"We can go out on my yacht." I nod toward my smaller day yacht moored down the pontoon on the beach. "Do you like boats?"

Gia folds her arms over her chest. "I've never been on a boat."

"Let me take your boating virginity then, tesorina." I stand and hold a hand out to her. "What do you say?"

Gia places her hand tentatively in mine, allowing me to lead her down the beach and to my boat. "What if I get seasick?"

I laugh. "No one gets seasick in the Mediterranean in the summer. We're not going out far."

Her shoulders visibly relax at my assurance and I help her into the boat. She takes a seat on the plush, built-in sofa and I stand at the helm, firing up the engine.

I pull the boat away from the beach and head toward my favorite spot in all of Sicily. The Torre Salsa Nature Reserve has the most beautiful unspoiled beaches, which are often almost private.

Gia is so worried about us being spotted, making this the perfect place to go, since it's on the other side of the island.

"There are drinks inside if you want one," I call to her.

Gia smiles and stands from her seat. "Sure, what do you want?" she asks, strolling into the yacht. Normally I'd get one of my men to drive, but I didn't want anyone around today.

Other than Aldo, my men don't know about Gia and that's how I'd like to keep it. "A beer, tesorina," I call in response.

It may be ten o'clock in the morning, but my dependence on alcohol over the years has grown. For me, a beer is nothing more than a soda.

When I lost Lianna, whiskey was my best friend, until Salvatore snapped me out of it. He saved my life, but I've felt myself reverting to my old ways ever since his death.

Gia returns with a beer and a soda. "Can you teach me how to drive?" she asks, looking at the steering wheel.

I smile at her. "Sure. Stand in front of me and grab the wheel."

She takes the wheel and I close her in against it, placing my hands over hers. "It's pretty simple, tesorina. Easier than steering a car," I murmur into her ear, feeling my cock get hard against her ass.

Gia moans softly. "Fabio, I was being serious."

I chuckle at that. "So am I, but as soon as you come close, my cock gets hard."

Gia arches her back, driving me insane.

"Non hai idea di quanto sei sexy," I whisper into her ear, which means she does not know how sexy she is.

Gia spins around and kisses me, breaking my attention from the water.

I pull away. "Sorry, baby, I've got to concentrate until we get to our destination."

Gia pouts slightly before dropping to her knees. "Okay, sir, but I can suck you off while you concentrate on the water."

I groan as she unzips my pants and frees my throbbing, hard cock.

Gia pumps my shaft in her hand two times before wrapping her gorgeous, thick lips around me.

"You are my dirty little whore," I growl as she takes my cock into the back of her throat, eagerly pleasuring me.

She looks up at me with her beautiful chestnut brown eyes, sucking on my cock like her life depends on it.

I could die happy right now.

All I want to do is fuck her, but I have to direct the boat.

It makes me regret not getting one of my guys to drive, but I feel Gia is a little too modest to fuck in front of someone else.

"Fuck, your mouth feels like heaven, tesorina."

She pulls her mouth off my cock and gazes up at me. "You taste so good, sir."

I groan, knowing that I can't wait for the forty-minute boat trip to the other side of the island. I cut the engine and grab hold of her chin. "You're such a dirty girl, Gia." I let go of her chin and grab the anchor, throwing it overboard. "I need to fuck you right now."

She bites her bottom lip in a way that drives me insane with lust. "Yes, sir."

"Now lie down on the lounger for me," I order, watching her as she does as I say. It's clear she's in a submissive mood right now, following my every order.

"What now, sir?" she asks, glancing up at me.

"Bikini bottoms off."

Her eyes flash with lust as she pulls them down her hips, flinging them to the floor. She opens her thighs wide, letting me see her tight little pussy, dripping already.

"I want you to play with yourself," I order.

Gia's brow furrows in confusion, but she does as I say.

I watch as she slips her fingers between her thighs and rubs her clit. It's a vision I never want to forget.

I fist my cock in my hands, watching her as she dips her fingers into her pussy. Her moans are like music to my ears. "Are you ready for this, baby?"

Gia's eyes open and fix on my cock. "Fuck, yes. I'm so ready," she says, eyes dilated.

"I'll be the judge of that," I say, walking toward her and kneeling between her thighs. "You are soaked." I kiss her inner thigh, making her shudder.

"I'm wet for you, sir," she purrs, knowing exactly what I want to hear.

"You're always wet for me, aren't you, baby?"

She licks her lips. "Always."

I bury my face between her thighs, devouring her sweet nectar as it drips from her wet pussy. Her back arches and she cries out, lacing her fingers in my hair.

It's rare that I fuck her unrestrained, but right now I don't have the patience to tie her up. I need to take her here and now.

"Fuck, sir, that feels amazing," she moans, arching her back more.

I tease the tip of my teeth over her clit, making her cry, "Oh, fuck." I stop and reach for her breasts, tearing her bikini top off of her. "You are so beautiful, tesorina."

"Ti prego, Fabio," she begs.

I stop playing with her nipple and look her in the eye. "What do you want?"

"Your cock."

I chuckle. "Once you tell me what you are."

Gia groans. "Sono la tua puttanella."

"Good girl. That's right, you are my little whore, always hungry for my cock." I stand and fist myself before grabbing her hips and forcing her onto her knees. "I'm going to give you it."

Without another word, I thrust every inch of my throbbing dick deep inside of her.

Gia cries out my name, making my balls ache.

I move in and out of her hard and fast, spanking her firm, round ass cheeks as I do. "That's it, baby, take my cock," I growl.

Gia arches her back, forcing me as deep as possible. "Yes, sir," she cries.

I grab hold of her throat and pull her upwards so that she's almost looking at me. "My dirty little whore is so fucking wet," I murmur into her ear. "I think you've been fantasizing about me fucking you all morning, haven't you?"

Her eyes roll back in her head. "Yes, sir."

I let go of her throat and pull my cock out. "Stand up," I order.

Gia stands, gazing at me with hazy, lust-filled eyes.

I sit down on the seat and gesture for her to come forward. "Sit on my cock."

Her eyes light up as she moves forward, straddling my lap. My eager little whore slides right over my cock without a moment of hesitation.

Gia moves up and down, but I grab her hips.

"You may be on top, but that doesn't mean you're in control."

Her eyes dilate as she stills on my cock, waiting for me to take control of her exquisite body. "Choke me, sir," she murmurs, her voice small but certain.

I blink twice, wondering what happened to the inexperienced woman I'd met on her twenty-first birthday. "Do you like that, Gia?" I ask, gently sliding my hands up her chest. "Do you like it when I choke you and fuck you at the same time?"

She bites her bottom lip. "Yes, sir."

I groan as I wrap my fingers around her throat and squeeze just hard enough to hurt and partially block her airway. "Fuck, Gia. You are perfect." I thrust my hips upwards, fucking her as I choke her throat.

Gia moans, eyes rolling back in her head as I take her without mercy. Our bodies meet in a clashing of flesh on flesh as I drive us both toward the cliff edge.

I loosen my grip on her throat and grab her hips instead, making it easier to fuck her harder.

"Fuck, I'm going to come," she cries.

"Good. Come for me, baby," I growl, knowing I'm close.

Her juices flood around my cock as she releases, making me groan. Gia shudders on top of me as she comes undone, her body tensing.

I roar as my cock explodes deep inside of her, mixing my seed with her cum. It's raw and dirty and fucking beautiful.

"You are so fucking hot when you come for me, Gia."

She moans softly as I move her off me and place her on the sofa. I kiss her lips, drowning in the intimacy of the moment. We kiss lazily under the sun, neither of us caring how exposed we are.

24

GIA

My phone dings and I check it.
So excited to see you tomorrow!

I hate that I'm not excited. Aida is arriving in Sicily tomorrow, which means shortly after Fabio and I are going to have to tell her the truth.

I fear losing my best friend, but I know I can't live without Fabio. He's the father of the baby growing inside of me—a baby I've yet to tell him about.

It's all so messed up.

Siena passes me a cup of hot cocoa before sitting down next to me. "You looked stressed," she says.

I shrug. "No, I just didn't sleep well last night."

Her brow raises. "No, because you were out with some mystery guy. What's being going on with you lately?"

I sit up straighter in my seat. "What do you mean?"

She shakes her head. "You're gone more nights than

you are here. Unresponsive to texts and calls. I don't know. Who is this guy? Is it the same one you said it was over with?"

I raise a brow. "Wow, a lot of questions."

Siena shrugs. "It feels like since your birthday we hardly talk. You've pulled away from me."

I take her hand and squeeze it. "Sorry, I wasn't trying to be distant. I've had a lot on my mind lately."

Siena smiles, but it's a little forced. "You've had a man on the brain, which is so unlike you. Why won't you tell me who he is?"

I shake my head. "It's complicated."

Siena pulls her hand away. "I get it. You don't value me as a friend. Ever since Aida's been gone, we've grown apart. It's as if..."

"As if what?"

"As if we were only ever friends because of Aida."

I stare at her with wide eyes. "That's not true at all. Aida was just the most laid back out of all of us."

"Yeah, and we clash. We never should have been friends, but Aida was like our glue. Now that she's gone we're falling apart."

I shake my head. "No. It's my fault that I've been distant. I'll try to fix that."

Siena gives me a disbelieving stare. "You will try to fix it but can't tell me who this guy is that you are dating?"

I swallow hard. "It's not the same guy from Rome." I shake my head. "I will tell you in time, but please just have patience." I know I can't tell Siena before I tell Aida. Aida needs to be the first to hear it, and straight from me and Fabio.

I'm not sure what Siena is going to think of me when I come clean. Perhaps I won't only lose one friend, but two. "Why don't I pick up our favorite from Tierry's? Then we can have a girl's night in watching movies."

Siena looks at me for a few beats before finally cracking a smile. "Seriously? You haven't stayed home for ages, so yes."

I know Fabio won't be pleased, but I will see him tomorrow at his ball. "Yes. I'll get it now."

"And ice cream," Siena says as I walk away.

I look back and smile. "Of course."

As I walk out of the building and down the street, I type a message to Fabio.

I'm having a girl's night with Siena. She is suspicious. Will see you tomorrow.

I send it and then text back to Aida.

Can't believe you will be back tomorrow.

It's not exactly making me sound excited, but I can't keep lying to her. The fact is, I'm scared to face her. I'm a coward.

Tierry's pizzeria is busy, but I catch Tierry's attention. "Ciao, Gia. The usual?" he asks.

I smile. "You bet."

He nods and heads to the kitchen to give them our

order. It's summer and the tourists are crowding the streets, but Tierry always gives locals priority.

My phone chimes and I check it.

I'm not too happy about that, tesorina. Who said you could have a girl's night?

I roll my eyes and text back.

I can do what I want, Fabio. You don't control me.

The bubbles ignite as he types back to me.

I do own you, but have a good time. You'll get a punishment for this tomorrow night.

I can't help the excitement that tingles across my skin at the thought. I've grown to crave Fabio's punishments and his rough ways.

My phone dings again, and this time it's Aida.

I know. Can't wait!

I sigh heavily, stowing my phone back in my purse.

Tierry appears a few moments later with our pizzas. "Can I get you anything else?" he asks.

I nod. "Yeah, have you got a pint of salted caramel ice cream left?"

He smiles. "For you, of course." He grabs the tub and returns, ringing up my order. "Twenty euros, bella."

I pull out a twenty-euro bill and hand it to him. "Thank you, Tierry."

"Buon appetito," he says as I turn away. I begin fighting through the crowd and back onto the street. The summer is the worst time of the year because it's too crowded, even if it does wonders for my business and all the businesses in Palermo.

A man stands in my way, glaring at me. "Excuse me."

He narrows his eyes at me. "Are you Fabio's whore?"

My brow furrows as I stare up at him. "Who the fuck is Fabio?" I ask, playing dumb.

"Fabio Alteri."

I laugh at that. "No chance. He's old enough to be my father." I try to dodge around him, but he steps in my way.

"How do you explain this?" He thrusts an envelope into my hand and then walks away.

I stare at it, wondering who that guy was. How did he know about me and Fabio?

I take a peek inside the envelope, and my heart stills. There's a photo of me and Fabio getting intimate on his yacht. Accompanying it is a note, but I don't read it here. It's too public. Instead, I slip the envelope into my purse and continue walking back toward the apartment.

My heart is racing as I open the door and Siena jumps up, looking excited about the pizza. I hate that this has suddenly cropped up, as it means I need to see Fabio tonight. This may be a threat from his enemy.

"That was quicker than I expected," Siena says.

I smile, but it feels forced. "Yeah, Tierry always

prioritizes the locals though. Here, take the pizza and ice cream. I just need to freshen up."

I head into the bathroom and grab the envelope out of my purse. There are six photos of us fucking on his yacht and a threatening message.

We're coming for you.

I pull my cell phone out and take a photo of the message and one of the photos, sending it to Fabio.

Some guy just ambushed me in the street and gave me an envelope with photos of us inside and this message. Shall I come over with it after Siena goes to bed?

I tap my foot nervously on the floor, waiting for him to reply. The bubbles appear.

Are you okay? Did he try to hurt you?

I'm fine. He just gave it to me and walked away.

The bubbles appear again.

Come over as soon as you can. Bring the envelope.

There's no way I can bail on pizza, movies, and ice cream with Siena. I will have to wait until later.

I'll come when I can. See you later.

I unzip the inner pocket of my purse and slide the photo and note in there, securing it.

"Hurry, Gia, the pizza is getting cold," Siena shouts.

"Coming," I call back, staring at myself in the mirror. It's crazy the way my life has taken such a turn since I met Fabio. Pregnant at twenty-one years old with a mobster's baby. A mobster who happens to be my best friend's father. To top it all off, we're now being threatened.

I sigh heavily and return to the living room, where Siena is already tucking in to her spicy pizza that she always orders. I love pizza simple, just tomato and cheese.

"I couldn't wait for you. You took too long," Siena says.

I laugh and sit down next to her, grabbing my box and tucking in. She already has pretty woman playing on the television—her favorite movie.

I try to relax, but I'm too on edge. The exchange with one of Fabio's enemies only brings home how dangerous he is, even here in Sicily. I saw firsthand the crazy shit Fabio is involved in while in Boston.

It makes me wonder what kind of danger I'm in merely being connected to him.

Fabio is waiting on his terrace as I come along the beach. When he sees me, he rushes through the gate and onto the beach.

"Are you sure you are okay?" he asks, cupping my face in his hands.

I reach for his hands and pry them away. "Yes, the guy just came up to me and asked if I was your whore."

Fabio's jaw clenches. "Fucking bastard. No one calls you that."

I raise a brow. "Except for you?"

He growls softly. "Except for me." He grabs my hand and leads me back into his villa. "Where is this envelope?"

I dig it out of my purse and pass it to him.

He sits on the sofa and I sit next to him, watching his face fall as he flips through the six photos. If Aida were ever to see them, I'd never forgive myself.

"You said there was a note."

I nod and pull the note out of the pocket inside my bag. "Here."

His jaw clenches the moment he sees it, and he scrunches it up. "Motherfuckers."

"What is it?" I ask, setting a hand on his arm.

"I'd recognize that handwriting anywhere." He stands and paces the floor. "The same handwriting was on the bloodstained note I had dropped at my door the day they murdered Salvatore. Rafa Morreti is here in Sicily."

My brow furrows. "How do you know?"

He holds up the note. "Because that's his writing."

"He could have written it and given it to that guy in Naples. It doesn't mean he's here for certain."

Fabio glares at me angrily. "That's the stupid kind of bullshit attitude that will get you killed."

I'm taken aback by his sudden outburst. "Don't take this out on me. It's not my fault they are threatening us."

"Other than the fact that you couldn't wait to get

my cock in your mouth before we got to our destination."

I glare at Fabio since he's being an asshole. We both wanted it. If he is going to blame me for this, then he can fuck off.

I stand. "I'm leaving." I walk past Fabio, only for him to grab the back of my neck suddenly and pull me back to face him.

"You're not going anywhere, Gia." His lips are only inches from mine. "It wasn't your fault, but you will spend the night with me here." His breath falls on my face. "It's not safe anywhere else."

The way he grips my neck is possessive and rough, and it makes me melt.

"Fabio," I breathe his name.

"Gia," he murmurs back.

Someone clears their throat behind us, forcing Fabio to let go of my neck. I jump away from him.

"Sir, I'm sorry to interrupt, but we found something suspicious at the port," the man says.

Fabio walks toward him. "Lorenzo, what did you find?"

He passes him some kind of coin and a knife. "A Napoli piastra and a knife on the floor in the warehouse."

"Moretti is sending me a warning." Fabio chucks the knife onto a nearby table. "He's here."

Lorenzo's brow furrows. "How can you be sure?"

He walks toward me and grabs the crumbled note

from the coffee table. "This is proof he's here. Rafa wrote this note."

Lorenzo takes the note, and his face pales. "Do you think they are going to strike tomorrow?"

Fabio shrugs. "Have all the men on high alert. We need to plan for every eventuality."

Lorenzo nods. "Sir."

"Make sure that you double security for tomorrow. I want every man we've got on this."

"Of course," Lorenzo says, bowing his head slightly.

"That will be all." Fabio waves his hand toward the door.

I watch as Lorenzo walks out.

"Who is that guy?" I ask.

Fabio seems to only just realize that I'm still here. His eyes widen slightly. "My capo." He runs a hand through his hair. "Or interim capo." He shakes his head. "I haven't decided whether he's worthy of the job, yet."

I can sense the tension in Fabio's shoulders as I walk toward him. My stomach twists as I wrap my arms around his waist, hugging him tightly.

Fabio wraps his arms around me in return. "I can't risk losing you, amore mio."

My heart skips a beat at hearing him calling me my love. It's the first time he's used that expression. "You won't lose me," I say, glancing up at him.

He looks at me with such a tortured stare. "You

can't be sure of that, tesorina." He sighs heavily. "I've lost so much already. Maybe it would be safer if you stay away from the ball tomorrow night."

I push away from him. "No chance. Siena would never forgive me if I bailed."

Fabio's jaw clenches. "Would you rather disappoint your friend or end up dead?"

I swallow hard, finding my mind going to the baby growing inside of me. It's reckless to put myself in danger because of the baby, but surely they win if we cower away. Perhaps that's what they want. "If I don't attend out of fear, then your enemy wins. Is that what you want?"

Fabio grabs my hips and pulls me against him again. "All I want is for you to be safe. I can't lose you, Gia." He kisses me softly and tenderly, making my chest ache.

I still don't know how to tell him the truth. I'm pregnant with his child and I'm scared that might change the way he feels. The last thing I want is to be abandoned, just like my mother was—just like I was.

25

FABIO

"Sir, security for the ball has been doubled." Lorenzo crosses his arms over his chest. "Do you really believe the Moretti family would be stupid enough to attack you at such a high-profile event?"

I shrug. "I don't know what to believe anymore, Lorenzo." I run a hand through my hair, feeling uneasy. Rafa has been leaving warnings, trying to scare me. "Is Milo here yet?"

Lorenzo shakes his head, glancing at his watch. "He was supposed to be here an hour ago, but I know there have been hold-ups at the airport."

The six weeks since I last saw my son-in-law have flown past. It's now time for him to deliver his end of the bargain. His last message suggested that the war he's been fighting has ended, as he sat down with the leader of the McCarthy clan to agree on a truce.

It's odd to think that they can go from killing each

other one minute to agreeing to a truce the next. An enemy made in Italy is an enemy for life. There are no truces to be made.

My maid, Concetta, appears in the doorway. "Sir, there is a man here to see you. He said his name is Milo."

I nod. "Thank you, Concetta."

She bows her head and continues on her way down the corridor toward the bedrooms to clean.

"I don't need you here for my meeting. Make sure all arrangements are in place for tonight. Prepare for any eventuality."

Lorenzo nods. "Sir." He walks out and passes Milo, who is standing with his capo, Piero, to one side.

"Lorenzo, perhaps you can keep Milo's capo company and learn something useful from him."

Lorenzo turns back around. "Sir?"

"Piero, this is Lorenzo, my interim capo. He can show you around while Milo and I talk."

Piero exchanges a glance with Milo, who nods in response.

"It's good to see you, Fabio," Milo says, approaching me and shaking my hand. "How have you been since we last met?"

I shake his hand firmly. "As well as can be. I hear the war is over with the Irish?"

Milo nods. "Thanks to you, we overpowered them. They were losing too many men and Malachy didn't have a choice but to sit down and agree to the terms of a truce."

I signal to the sofa, and Milo sits. I take the chair opposite him. "Do you still intend to meet with the Moretti family in Naples?"

Milo leans back in the chair. "Yes, but it's been difficult convincing them to agree to a meeting. They are cautious."

I run a hand across the back of my neck, as I know firsthand how cautious they can be. It's taken me ten years to even get close to having my revenge on them.

"I'm confident we are close to agreeing on a date and a place to meet, though." He glances at Piero, who is standing outside on my terrace. "My capo is in talks with them."

A short, awkward silence falls between us. "How about your personal situation? I have not made Aida aware of what I learned in Boston six weeks ago."

I knew it would come up at some point, but I didn't think he'd be so quick to ask. "Gia and I are still together. We intend to come clean to Aida while she is here in Sicily."

Milo looks disappointed. "She will be hurt by it terribly. I am only glad that I will be there to pick up the pieces." He looks me in the eye. "I guess it must be serious to consider coming clean."

I nod. "Yes. I haven't felt this way since my late wife died."

Milo nods. "Fine, but I'm not sure how you are

going to convince Aida to meet with you." He shakes his head. "She's pretty adamant that there is no way she will see you while we are here."

"I will find a way. Let me worry about that." I clench my jaw. "Aida deserves my apology for the way I acted the last time I saw her."

Milo doesn't acknowledge that. "This is our address. You didn't get it from me, but if you think it will be easier to just show up, you have my cell number to check to see if we're in." He passes me a piece of paper with an address scribbled on it.

"Thank you, Milo."

Milo shakes his head. "It's nothing. For my child's sake, I hope she can forgive you."

I hope she can forgive me, too. Although it feels impossible, considering what I'm going to have to tell her. "It's wishful thinking," I say.

Milo's brow furrows. "Aida has the biggest heart of anyone I know. It may take time, but I believe she will forgive you and her friend." His brow furrows. "However, there is no need to implicate me in this."

I hold my hands up. "Of course not. I haven't even told Gia that you know. It will remain our secret."

Milo nods, satisfied. "Now down to numbers." He reaches into his inside pocket and pulls out a piece of paper. "I owe you three million dollars for your guys, isn't that right?"

"Yes, you have the bank details."

Milo writes something down on the paper. "How much will you pay me for killing your enemy, though?"

I narrow my eyes at him. "There was never mention of payment for that. I simply have to pay the wages of my twelve men and expenses. I don't think it's unreasonable to ask for that."

Milo tilts his head. "True, but what about the risk to my life if I go to Naples and they know who I am?"

I feel a little irritated that Milo is only now trying to back out of our deal. As my son-in-law I owed him help, but he offered this. "You taking out the Moretti family wasn't my idea. Why the cold feet now?"

Milo sits back in the chair and places one leg over the other. "It's risky. I'm due to be a father." He shrugs. "Perhaps the risks aren't worth the reward."

Rage coils through me, but I try to keep a handle on it. "The reward which you've already had." I shake my head. "Make it six million and we can call it even. I won't send you to Naples." Milo clearly isn't man enough to follow through on his word.

He sits up straighter. "Woah, I didn't say I wouldn't do it. I just want to be compensated if I wipe out your enemy." He runs a hand through his dark hair. "I would have paid a fucking arm and a leg to end the feud with Malachy months ago, and your feud with the Moretti family has been going on far longer."

I grit my teeth together and glare at my son-in-law. I'll give it to him, he's got balls trying to shake me down for a job he hasn't done yet. "We'll discuss it once you get a meeting with them. Until then, you pay me my three million dollars."

Milo chuckles. "You are as stubborn as I am."

I clench my fists by my side. "Milo, you maybe my son-in-law, but it would be wise not to disrespect me in my home."

Milo bows his head. "Of course. I was merely jesting. We will agree to a figure when I get the meeting with Rafa Moretti." He folds the paper away and stows it in his pocket. "Do you have any further business to discuss?"

"Yes, I want to move the coke by plane. It takes too long to come by sea."

Milo's brow furrows. "It's far more expensive by plane."

I nod. "Yes, but we can't keep up with demand. If we don't speed up supply, then we're losing out to the competition." I run a hand across the back of my neck. "The simple question is, can you arrange it?"

Milo regards me for a few beats before nodding. "I believe so, but it will take me some time to arrange everything." He pulls his cell phone out of his pocket and starts typing. "I'll ask my men in Boston to start making arrangements, but it may take a month."

"That's fine. If we want to capitalize on the European market, then we need to get the product in faster than the competition."

Milo smiles. "I have always admired your ambition, Fabio." He stows his phone back in his pocket and stands. "I'm sure we will have a few more meetings before I leave for Boston in two weeks. I'll keep you posted on developments with the Moretti family and moving the coke by plane."

I hold out a hand to him. "Thank you."

He takes my hand and shakes it before turning and walking away.

I can't deny that working with Milo Mazzeo has always worried me. The first sign that our partnership may not always run smoothly is him trying to shake me down for something I want.

In Boston, he never mentioned me paying him to kill Rafa. Either way, time will tell whether we can continue to work together without problems.

The larger problem is if the Moretti family is going to strike me here on my soil. I didn't voice my concerns to Milo, since it doesn't involve him. The last thing I want is for him to think I fear the Morreti family and their threats.

The Alteri family has held control over Sicily for centuries. One Napoli bastard won't change that. Not as long as I still have breath in my lungs and my heart is still beating.

26

GIA

My heart is pounding frantically in my chest as I walk along the beach toward Aida's rented villa.

Siena is quiet. It's probably the one time I want her to talk to keep my mind off of facing my best friend after everything I've done. I think she's pissed at me that even though I spent the evening with her last night, I still snuck away after she went to bed.

I'm torn in two directions. A part of me is ecstatic that my best friend is here. In fact, I'd say I'm excited to see her after all this time. The other part dreads it because despite my attempt to call things off with her father, it didn't last long. Also, her husband, Milo, is here. Hopefully, he won't recognize me.

It's as if Fabio is a magnetic field and I'm a magnet, unable to resist the pull of his charm. I notice the villa at the end of the beach and two figures down by the sea. Milo and Aida. They are still too far away to make out their faces.

Siena appears to be in her own world at the moment. I wonder if she's still angry about how I've been acting lately. "Are you okay?" I ask.

Siena meets my gaze. "Yes, I'm fine. Why do you ask?"

I shrug. "You're a little quiet."

She laughs at that. "I'm too loud or too quiet for you. I can't win."

I laugh too. "True. Sorry. I'm so anxious to see Aida."

Siena nods. "Me too."

When I glance back at the two people in the distance, I can make out Aida's face. I realize that I need to act natural, and in this situation I would run to her. "There she is. Come on," I say, breaking into a jog in her direction. "Aida, oh my God!" I shout.

Aida stands and walks toward me, meeting me with a tight hug. All the while, this niggling guilt tugs at my insides, making me sick to my stomach.

"It's been too long since I last saw you," she says, her voice cracking with emotion. When she pulls away, I see the tears streaming down her face.

"We have both missed you," Siena says as Aida pulls her into a hug.

"Boston is a shit hole compared to here," Aida says, making both of us laugh.

I pause when I see Milo standing behind Aida,

staring right at me. There's a glint of recognition in his eyes, but he quickly moves his attention to Siena. "Aren't you going to introduce me?"

Aida rolls her eyes.

I think she expects us to laugh, but neither of us does. "Gia and Siena, this is my husband, Milo." Aida turns to Milo. "Milo, this is Gia and Siena, my two best friends."

"It's lovely to meet you," I say in unison with Siena.

Milo nods. "Good to meet you too." Milo glances at Aida. "I'll let you three catch up." He possessively grips Aida's waist and whispers something into her ear, making me instantly suspicious of what he's saying. He then kisses her neck and walks back toward the sea, to my relief. If he recognizes me, then he hasn't said anything to Aida, yet.

"At least your arranged marriage landed you with a hot husband," Siena says.

Aida laughs.

I grab Aida's hand and look her in the eye. "Aren't you intending to see your father while you are here?"

Aida shakes her head. "No chance in hell. After what he did to me, I'm not sure I'll ever want to see him again."

I feel disappointed at her answer, but I guess it's not surprising because of the way Fabio acted to get her to leave. "I think he regrets what he did to you, Aida." The moment those words leave my lips, I'm kicking myself.

How the hell would I know?

I'm so nervous that I'm digging myself a hole already.

Aida's brow furrows. "Don't tell me you ignored me and went to speak to him?"

I shrug, feeling the panic inside of me increasing. "I'm sorry. I couldn't sit by while he ripped my best friend away from me like that." The guilt feels like it's going to eat me alive.

"Did he say he wished he hadn't done it?" Aida asks.

He has said that, but I know revealing too much will only increase her suspicion. "He admitted what he did and how he went about it was wrong."

Aida shakes her head. "If that's the case, I'd expect him to track me down and apologize. There's no way I'm running to him."

Siena pipes in. "Yeah, what he did was not okay."

I nod, keeping my stupid mouth shut.

"I don't want to spoil my time here thinking about him." Aida glances toward the sea, where Milo is swimming. "Will both of you join us for dinner tonight?"

My stomach churns as I glance at Siena.

"We're supposed to attend your father's annual ball tonight. Isn't Milo invited?" Siena asks.

There's no chance in hell I can miss Fabio's ball. He's expecting me to be there, even though we won't be able to be open about our relationship.

Aida looks hurt at the mention of the ball. "Yes, but Milo isn't attending out of respect for me."

An awkward silence falls between us.

"Never mind. We can have dinner tomorrow night," Aida says, the reluctance in her voice clear.

The relief I feel is monumental. It's Fabio's fiftieth birthday tomorrow, and I want to be with him tonight.

"I can't believe we have to wait an entire day until we can catch up," Siena says.

Aida glances at her watch. "You better get ready, or you'll be late for the ball. If you feel up to it, you can spend the day with us tomorrow. We've hired a yacht."

I notice Siena nod out of the corner of my eye. "That sounds amazing, doesn't it, Gia?"

I shrug, knowing that the chances of me making it are slim. "I'm not sure I'll be able to make it tomorrow. I'll try." My phone rings and I take it, walking away.

"Ciao, bella," Fabio says on the other end, making my stomach flutter.

"Fabio, now isn't a good time. I'm with Aida."

There are a few moments of silence. "How is she?"

I keep walking, forgetting that I haven't even said goodbye. Fabio has me twisted up and the guilt I feel around Aida is crushing. "She is angry at you still." I sigh heavily. "She's going to hate me when she finds out."

"She might not be happy at first, but I think she will be more forgiving than you think in time."

I hope he's right, but the fact is, we have both been

selfish. We had many chances to end this once and for all, but constantly came back to each other. "I hope so," I mutter, feeling a tugging at my chest. "Tonight we can't even speak, can we?" I ask.

Fabio sighs. "No, not until the ball has ended." He clears his throat. "Then I will have you in my bed."

I feel myself getting hot already at the prospect.

"Gia, wait up," Siena calls after me, making my heart skip a beat.

"I best go. I'll see you later."

"I can't wait, tesorina," he murmurs, before hanging up.

Siena catches me up as I stow my phone in my pocket. "Sorry, I had to take the call. Work."

Siena's brow furrows. "That was super rude, Gia." She shakes her head. "You didn't even say goodbye. What has gotten into you lately?"

A gorgeous forty-nine-year-old mobster.

"I really don't know, Siena." I shake my head. "I'm the worst friend ever, aren't I?"

Siena laughs. "Possibly. Although, Aida didn't exactly win any prizes when she couldn't even pick up our call on your birthday."

I shake my head, knowing that doesn't come close to what I've done. I am the worst friend ever, not only to Aida, but to Siena too. "That was nothing."

Siena shakes her head. "It's not nothing. It's hard to accept that Aida has this whole new life that we're not in, isn't it?"

I meet Siena's questioning gaze and nod. "I guess so." I won't be in it at all when I tell her that for three and a half months, I've been fucking her father.

Not to mention, I'm pregnant with her half-sibling.

He hasn't once mentioned birth control, which I found a little strange. Perhaps he thinks I'm sensible enough to have thought of it myself when we first started fucking.

All I know is that I don't want to mess what we have up, but not telling him is probably exactly the way to do it.

Every time I think about telling him, I chicken out. It's been a week since I had my first ultrasound. I stowed the photo from it under my pillow.

Sicily and its residents are so traditionalist. When I told the doctor doing my ultrasound that the father wasn't involved, she gave me the dirtiest look ever.

To ensure I didn't risk being recognized, I went to a private clinic on the other side of the island. The last thing I need is for Fabio to find out about my pregnancy through idle gossip.

"Gia?" Siena says my name, breaking me out of the daze I'd fallen into.

"Sorry, what?"

Siena shakes her head. "I said, do you want to go shopping for a dress this afternoon?"

I smile at her. "It's been a long time since I hit the shops."

"Is that a yes?" Siena asks.

I nod. "Yeah, why the hell not?" I'm not sure what I'm going to wear tonight, but nothing I own fits me quite right. I've got a feeling it's because of the very slight bump that's forming.

Before long, there will be no hiding the truth from Fabio. I need to come clean to him tonight, after the ball. All I can do is hope that he still wants me once he knows the truth.

27

FABIO

*G*ia is breathtaking.

Even with her mask on, I can pick her out a mile away. Everyone else at the party fades into the background, while she shines brighter than the sun.

I've lost my heart to her. It's a fact I've been painfully aware of for a while now. When the Moretti family murdered Lianna, I vowed I'd never love again the way I loved her. Her loss was too painful. Yet, I love Gia more than I've ever loved anyone.

Her eyes meet mine from across the vast ballroom and a small, knowing smile twists onto her lips. A smile that makes her shine brighter.

I feel a tug in my chest, wishing I could walk over there and whisk her onto the dancefloor. Despite the masks, it's obvious who I am. My size and my distinct silver hair are a giveaway. Siena, my daughter's other best friend, is on her arm as they move deeper into the room.

I lose sight of her in the crowd. It irritates me that she's wearing such a gorgeous, tempting dress, but I can't spend the night by her side. She's fair game to any man in this place.

If I so much as see a man talking to her, I know I won't be able to stay away. He will feel the force of my wrath. My possessive nature is uncontrollable when it comes to Gia. I'd go so far as to say I'd kill any man who touches her.

"Fabio, buon compleanno per domani," Luisa says. "Are you feeling old yet?"

I smile at the city counselor, knowing that I have to be on my best behavior when amongst the bureaucrats of Palermo. "I felt old a decade ago, Luisa." I kiss her cheeks. "How are you?"

She laughs, but it's a fake and irritating laugh. "Oh, you are funny, Fabio. You don't look a day over forty." Her eyes narrow. "What is your secret?"

"Whiskey," I say.

Luisa laughs as if it's a joke, which it wasn't. "Are you going to be attending next month's council meeting?" She sets her hand on my arm again in a flirty manner, irritating me. "We haven't seen you at the last few."

I pull my arm away and put some distance between us. "I've been very busy. I can't say for certain if I will attend next month." I clear my throat. "They can direct any urgent matters to Lorenzo, my capo. If you would excuse me." I walk away from her, finding her company insufferable.

I may not spend the night by Gia's side, but I sure as hell can stay close to her. I walk toward the bar and spot her instantly. Her beautiful blond hair falls in waves down her exposed back in the stunning dusty blue ballgown she is wearing.

I notice men staring at her, and it angers me. All I can do is watch as she chats with Siena. Hopefully, none of these idiots consider going near her. Despite where I am, I feel like a loose cannon ready to go off at any minute.

I walk up to the bar and stand next to her without looking at her. Gia shuffles uncomfortably, and I can feel her attention on me. It is impossible to stay away from her when she looks so beautiful.

"I'll have a whiskey on the rocks," I say after I catch the attention of the bartender.

They ignore the fact that there were people waiting before me and get my drink.

Siena clears her throat. "So where is this man you've been seeing? Is he going to be here tonight?"

Gia shakes her head. "No, not tonight," she says quietly, glancing in my direction.

Siena suddenly notices me. "Fabio Alteri?"

I feel a little taken aback and nod. "Yes."

She shakes her head disapprovingly. "You ought to track down your daughter and apologize to her for what you did." She sets her hands on her hips. "Are you even sorry?"

I stare at Gia's friend. "I don't like being addressed like that, Siena."

Siena looks shaken that I know who she is. "Shit, this mask doesn't help hide my identity then, does it?"

It's hard not to laugh at that. "You underestimated me if you thought I don't know who everyone in here is."

Gia is staring at me, a little dumbfounded.

"My daughter's two best friends."

The bartender returns with my drink. "Can I get you anything else?" she asks.

I turn to Siena and Gia. "Can I buy you two a drink?"

Siena shakes her head. "No thanks. I'm not accepting a drink from a man who broke my best friend's heart. Right, Gia?"

Gia looks torn, but mutters her answer. "Right." It's amusing, as she has taken far more than a drink from me.

"Make sure these two have drinks on me all night," I say to the bartender before grabbing my whiskey. "Looks like you don't have a choice now." I exchange a lingering glance with Gia, before walking away reluctantly.

"What a cocky asshole," I hear Siena say as I leave. She's lucky that she's Gia and Aida's friend, otherwise she may not have gotten away with me hearing such a remark.

Milo isn't here tonight, but his capo is. In respect for his wife, he declined the invitation. I expected as much, but I would have preferred he were here.

I approach Piero. "Having fun?" I ask.

"It's not too bad. I rarely get to go to a work party without the boss." He shrugs. "It's weird to be honest, but Aida wouldn't come so Milo wouldn't."

I am thankful that my son-in-law is so devoted to my daughter. It's the least that she deserves after everything I've put her through. Although I loved my daughter, I wasn't exactly present for her childhood. My vendetta for revenge has ruled my life.

"What was your first impression of Lorenzo?" I ask, still uncertain about him as Salvatore's replacement. No one can ever live up to the man I lost.

"He seems like a good man from our brief encounter. Why?"

I sip my whiskey. "He's not been my capo long. I'm not sure he's up to it."

Piero clears his throat. "It's tough to put your trust in someone else when your last capo was so long standing, but I think you ought to give him a chance." He reaches into his pocket, making me tense on instinct.

He pulls out an envelope. "Do you know who could have written this?"

I take the envelope, instantly recognizing Rafa

Moretti's writing on the front. "Where did you get this?"

"A letter posted through Milo's door this afternoon. He wanted me to show you."

I open the envelope and read the note.

You will die here, along with the rest of your family.

"As soon as he received it, he moved to a new address." Piero slips a card into my pocket. "This is the address. He's worried your enemy is going to strike tonight."

I glance around the room, searching for Gia. She's nowhere to be seen. It makes me infinitely nervous that the Moretti family may strike here, and she's in attendance. They know that I'm fucking her, since they have photographic evidence.

Rafa would love to get his hands on another one of my lovers and end her life. The last time I stood in front of him, he had my wife's blood all over him. He's one sick bastard—sicker than me, and that's saying something.

He raped my late wife while she bled out on our bed. I'll never forget the scene when I found her. It fuels my thirst for revenge, but that thirst has diminished ever since I met Gia. It feels like I'm making all the same mistakes again, driving her into danger rather than away from it.

"I assume Milo had heard nothing back from the Moretti family about a meeting?" I ask.

Piero shakes his head. "No. The first week they were

regularly in contact, but for the past five days there's been total silence from their end."

My brow furrows as I try to work out what that means. Perhaps they found out Milo's true identity and intend to end both of us.

He's foolish if he thinks he can take down the Alteri family and Mazzeo family in one strike.

Milo has a dozen of his best men here with him on the island.

Hopefully, Rafa has gotten cocky and has brought the fight onto my turf. If he has, I'll end him once and for all.

The only thing I'm scared about is Gia getting caught in the crossfire. It makes me wish she had listened to me last night and stayed away from the ball.

She could have lied to her friend and told her that she was feeling ill, but instead she's here in probably the most dangerous place for her.

Milo's threat is proof enough. The Moretti family has come here for me.

"Shall I get you another drink?" Piero asks, nodding at the empty tumbler in my hand.

"Sure."

Piero walks toward the bar. I do a more stringent sweep of the room, trying to find Gia among the growing crowd of people.

It's no use. I can't find her.

A sense of unease twists at my gut. I haven't stayed close enough to her.

Suddenly, it feels like the ground trembles as a blast erupts through the room. Debris and smoke flood the entire room and screams erupt shortly after.

The force of the blast knocks me to the ground, and I hit my head. Everything goes dark. All I see in that moment is Gia's face.

28

GIA

The explosion rocks the ground, sending me straight over onto my ass.

My heart skips a beat as I hear gunshots in the distance. I glance around, but I can't see Fabio. Siena is by my side, but she's unconscious. I try to wake her, but she's got a nasty cut to her head.

"Fuck," I mutter, glancing around the rubble-filled room.

Fabio was right. The Moretti family is here and they're only here to harm anyone connected to Fabio. They know about us, which means I'm in more danger than ever before.

I should have listened to him when he told me it was best that I stay away from this ball. The shooting grows louder and I remain on the floor, unsure of what to do.

Screams and shouts fill the air as I try desperately to wake Siena.

"Come on, Siena, wake up." I gently rock her, hoping she's going to be okay.

She grumbles, but doesn't open her eyes. I swallow hard, glancing at the entrance to the events hall of the hotel. It's only a matter of time until they make it in here.

I glance around again, searching desperately for any sign of Fabio.

There are so many bodies lying on the ground, covered in debris.

Siena groans again, coming to her senses. "Gia?" she asks.

I kneel next to her again. "I'm here, Siena. You are going to be okay. Just keep quiet and keep your head down." I swallow hard. "Gunmen are here. It's best you stay still."

Siena struggles to move. "What about you?"

"I'm going to get help. Just stay here."

Siena says nothing else, letting her eyes fall closed.

I stand and head in the direction I last saw Fabio: by the bar. The smoke from the blast still fills the room. Disorientated people scramble around me, trying to find the exit.

The bloodied bodies lying on the ground make me fear the worst.

What if Fabio didn't survive the explosion?

They blew the bar to pieces. Glass is shattered all over the floor and the bartender who served us earlier is lifelessly hanging over it.

I swallow hard, finding it difficult to believe that a feud could have brought so much bloodshed to innocent people.

That's when I notice the distinctive silver hair. My heart sinks into my stomach when I see that he's lying face first on the ground.

"Fabio!" I cry his name, rushing to his side and dropping to my knees. I gently rock him, trying to get him to wake up. "Please, Fabio." Tears fill my eyes when he doesn't stir.

I use all my strength to turn him over onto his back, noticing there are no open wounds. His pulse is there thankfully, so he's just been knocked unconscious by the blast. I sit with his head in my lap, gently brushing his face.

"Please wake up."

Fabio grumbles something, making hope bloom in my chest.

"Fabio?"

His eyes flicker open and he looks dazed for a few moments, before recognition flickers to life in his eyes. "Gia. What happened?" He tries to sit up, groaning.

"An explosion. I don't know how, but there are gunmen here in the hotel."

His eyes widen and he sits up straighter. "Moretti," he growls.

"Careful, you obviously took a blow to the head."

He pushes me away and stands up. "I'm fine, tesorina. You need to find somewhere safe to hide." His eyes are wild and frantic. "They know your face."

I shake my head. "I'm not leaving your side, Fabio. The safest place for me is with you."

Fabio's jaw clenches. "No, it's not. The safest place for you is as far away from me as physically possible." He grabs my hand and practically drags me to my feet. "Run to the bathroom on the second floor and wait for me there. Do you hear me?"

I stare at him with cool defiance. He may boss me around in bed, but that's because I like it. When it comes to everyday life, I draw the line. "No. Siena is hurt, and I'm not running." I yank my hand from his and turn my back on him.

He grabs me by the back of my neck and pulls me toward him. "Don't defy me here, Gia. This is life or death. It's not a fucking game," he growls, the fear in his eyes clear.

"I know it's not a game, but I'm not your puppet you can order around. If you don't want me by your side, I'll help my friend."

The gunshots are getting closer still. "Don't you hear that? They'll kill you, tesorina." He tightens his grip on my neck. "I can't let you walk around here and get shot."

I feel weak and pathetic as he drags me toward a door behind the bar. He flings the door open and nods at a set of stairs. "Those stairs will take you to the corridor on the first floor. You take them and you find the ladies' bathroom. Do not come out until I come and get you. Do you understand?"

"Perfectly," I say behind clenched teeth.

The gunshots are so close now it feels like they're on top of us.

"Now go. I want to see you disappear up those stairs."

I turn and rush up the stairs, only to smash straight into someone's chest. I squeal when I see it's a tall, bald man wielding a machine gun.

"Gia?" Fabio calls my name.

"Aren't I the luckiest man tonight? The girl I was looking for has run straight into my arms." He grabs me by the throat and turns me around, holding the gun to my head. "Walk," he barks.

Fear coils through me as I slowly walk down each step, knowing that my life hangs in the balance. I can only assume the man who has me is one of the Moretti family.

Fabio stands in the doorway with his gun aimed at the man behind me, but if he shoots, he risks killing me.

"Well, well, Alteri. It looks like your lovers are always drawn to me," he sneers, tightening his grip on my throat so hard it feels like I might pass out.

"Let her go, Rafa. This is between you and me."

Rafa Moretti. The man who killed Aida's mother. The man that Fabio has been so desperate to kill all these years.

I swallow hard. Fabio should have listened to me instead of sending me to hide. The fear in his dark brown eyes is poignant as he glares at his enemy.

"I don't think that's how it works, do you?" Rafa releases his grip on my throat, but keeps the gun to my head. "You have something of mine, and I want it back," he growls.

Fabio pales slightly, shaking his head. "I don't know what you're talking about, Moretti."

He cocks the gun pointed to my head, making my heart skip a beat. For the first time in my life, I'm staring death right in the face.

It's a harsh and poignant feeling. A feeling that is very difficult to put into words. All the things I still want to do hit me hard, making me wish I'd lived differently.

"You have my son, Dario. We know because we tracked his last movements to Palermo."

The screams I've heard coming from Fabio's basement finally make sense. He's got Rafa's son down there, and he's been torturing him repeatedly. Fabio gives nothing away. "I haven't seen your son, Rafa."

"Liar," Rafa cries, kicking the back of my knees and forcing me to the ground. "I'll shoot this bitch right here and then fuck her while she bleeds out right in front of your eyes."

All the blood drains from my face at such a sick threat.

"Just like I did to your whore of a wife."

I can't imagine how much it hurt when he found his

wife raped and murdered. Fabio still looks far cooler than I feel. "I'm sure you would, but she is nothing to me." The coldness in his tone cuts me to the core. "Do what you want with her."

His words hurt me. I know those words are not true, but it doesn't make it any less painful to hear. I love Fabio with all my heart. All I want is for the both of us to survive this and have a family together.

"You're a terrible liar, Fabio." Rafa points the gun at my throat. "Where should I start with you?" he asks, glaring down at me as he stands by my side. "I know you love riding cock like a whore. Perhaps we can give this old man a show?"

I spit at him. "Never."

That results in a hard slap right across my face. It's so hard that it makes my ears ring.

"Keep your hands off her," Fabio growls angrily.

Rafa laughs. "Doesn't sound to me like she means nothing to you. I'm going to have a lot of fun with her." He grabs hold of me and drags me to my feet. "Don't move a muscle or I'll blow her pretty little head off." He drags me toward a fire exit at the back of the small galley kitchen.

It feels like all hope is lost as he opens the exit and drags me away from the man I love.

Fabio doesn't stand a chance at saving me. I only wish that we had longer to spend together. Rafa knocks me in the back of the neck and everything goes cold. Darkness descends and I know that there is no hope.

29

FABIO

It feels like my world stops still when I see Rafa descend those stairs with Gia in his arms, a gun pointed at her head. It was like my worst fucking nightmare come true.

That bastard won't take the love of my life from me. Not this time.

Rafa wants something that I've got—his son. That means Gia has more chance of surviving, at least long enough for him to get what he wants.

Rafa disappears with Gia out of a fire exit. I rush after him, knowing that I'd die trying to save her life. No matter what it takes, I won't let history repeat itself.

When I rush out of the door, I see he's already bundling her unconscious body into the back of a vehicle.

I pull my gun and shoot the two front tires out from the car.

"Cazzo," Rafa swears. I shoot at him next, missing him by barely an inch. He ducks down and takes cover, aiming his machine gun at me and firing.

I dive behind a wall nearby, since it's my only cover from his attack.

Gia is in that vehicle. I have to get to her before they take her away from me forever. The car isn't driving on those wheels, so I've bought myself some time if nothing else.

"Alteri, come out of hiding and face me like a fucking man," Rafa bellows. The sound dredges up my deep, fiery hatred for him.

It's been too long since he killed my wife. I should have had my revenge on him years ago, but I'm cautious. Every move I've made since that day has been to put the Alteri empire before any attempts to get my revenge.

"Why don't you put down the machine gun and face me like a man, Rafa," I call.

There are a few moments of silence. He's unlikely to agree to hand to hand combat, as he's a coward. Only cowards rape women who are bleeding to death. He delights in pain and blood—it gets him off.

I may like pain, but not like Rafa, who enjoys watching a woman suffer while he fucks her to death. It makes sense why he's been through his fair share of wives all these years.

"Fine. You put down your gun and come out. Maybe then I'll consider putting down mine."

I laugh at that. "No chance. I know you will shoot me the moment I show my face."

The fire exit opens and Piero and Lorenzo appear at it. Shooting ensues as they quickly rush to join me behind the wall. "Sir, what's going on?" Lorenzo asks, eyes wide.

"Rafa Moretti has my woman. I'm not letting him take her."

Lorenzo's brow furrows. "Woman?"

I shake my head. "Now is not the time to explain." I glance at Piero. "Any ideas of how to go about this? You are used to this kind of tension in Boston."

Piero nods. "The only way is for one of us to provide a distraction while one covers and the other sneaks in and gets the goods."

I clench my jaw at Gia being called goods, but he's right. There is no other way to get her out of there safely.

"Any takes for the distraction?" I ask.

Lorenzo nods. "I still need to prove myself to you, sir. I'll do it."

Piero and I exchange an uncertain glance. "Nah, it makes more sense if I distract and you cover me, Lorenzo," Piero says. He then looks at me. "You get your lady and try not to get shot."

I nod in response, feeling a twinge in my chest. Piero reminds me very much of Salvatore. He's smart, unlike Lorenzo. It makes me wish he were still here.

"I'll strike three seconds after you go out."

Piero takes in a deep breath. "Let's hope I don't get shot this time." He shakes his head. "I've been shot too many times to count." He rushes out into the open, firing his gun toward Rafa and his men.

Lorenzo covers him, firing round after round at any of the shooters.

As I go the other way around the wall, my stomach sinks. Rafa is two hundred meters ahead, dragging Gia behind him.

Motherfucker.

He no doubt lined up another vehicle somewhere else and thought he could sneak away. I sprint like my life depends on it, closing the gap between us. Once I'm within firing range, I narrow my eyes and shoot at both knees, bringing him to the ground. "Cazzo," he growls.

I shoot the hand he's holding the gun with, making him drop it. "Not so fast, Moretti," I say, walking over to him and grabbing Gia, who clutches for me.

Her breathing is labored as I push her behind me, blocking her with my body, even though Rafa no longer has his gun.

"What are you going to do to me, Alteri?" Rafa spits, glaring at me. "How can you get your revenge?"

I stare down at him, knowing that nothing I can do to him makes any of the losses any better. "Knowing that you are no longer breathing is revenge enough." I lift the gun in front of me and shoot his other arm. Rafa squeals. "Just so you know, I have your son, Dario." I smirk at him. "First, I'm going to kill you and bring your head to him, then I'm going to kill him and ship both heads to your wife."

Rafa growls like a beast. "Don't fucking touch my son."

"You shouldn't have touched my wife or best friend." I step closer to him. "I'll then kill the rest of your pathetic, useless family until the scourge you laid on this earth is wiped away completely."

Despite Rafa being shot in both arms, he brings one arm up and swipes a knife across my face. "Fuck," I growl, holding a hand to my face.

I grab hold of his arm before he can attack me again, bending it backward. "Motherfucker," he cries, dropping the knife to the floor.

"Gia, pick up the knife," I order.

Her face is as white as a sheet as she goes to get the knife. I notice her hands are violently shaking.

"Give it to me." I hold my free hand out.

She places it reluctantly in my hand, taking a few steps away from me.

"This is for my wife," I say, slamming the knife deep into his rib cage, just below his heart.

He screams in pain, blood bubbling up his throat and into his mouth.

"This is for Salvatore and Aida," I say, thrusting it in a few centimeters higher, but still missing his heart.

More blood travels up his throat as the knife hits major arteries.

"And this is for the love of my life, Gia." I slam the

knife right through his heart, making his eyes widen. It's only a matter of seconds until he loses consciousness, and I let him drop to the floor.

I drop the knife too, feeling a deep relief spread through me. It's finally over.

Gia stares at me in shock, no doubt struggling to understand the darkness she just witnessed. "Come here," I murmur.

She shakes her head. "I need a moment to process what I just witnessed."

I stalk toward her. "You witnessed a man saving your life because he loves you." I wipe the blood from my hands before grabbing her hips. "It was him or you. I couldn't watch while I ripped you away from me."

Gia nods slowly. "I know. I just..." She trails off, looking uncertain.

"What is it, Gia?"

"This is far from over, isn't it?"

Piero jogs to meet us. "His men are all dead." He looks at me with surprise. "You killed Rafa?"

I nod. "Yes. What did you expect me to do with him?"

He shakes his head. "You did the right thing. I just expected you to want to kidnap and torture him." It's what I thought I would have wanted too, but as I stood in front of him, I knew the only way to end this was to end him.

If I kept him alive, I risked the chance of him escaping—a chance I would not take.

"No, it wasn't worth it. I needed him gone. Have you got an ID on the guys you killed?"

Lorenzo approaches, blood dripping from his arm where he was shot. "Benito and Adria Moretti, as well as two of his men."

I feel satisfaction hearing that we also killed his son and daughter. It's less work for me in the future.

Piero runs a hand through his hair. "I would help with the clean-up, but I really need to report back to Milo."

I nod. "Of course. Let him know what happened. Tell him we will visit tomorrow. He knows why." I turn to Lorenzo. "Get the men to clear up the mess back here before the press find out."

Lorenzo and Piero go in opposite directions, leaving me and Gia. I drag her back into the hotel, putting distance between us and the carnage we just left behind. I wash the blood from my hands in the sink in the back kitchen of the hotel.

"You didn't answer my question," Gia says quietly.

I dry my hands and turn to face her, cupping her cheek in my hands. "No, it's not over yet, but it will be soon."

She shakes her head. "There's something I should have told you a while ago, I just haven't found the right time."

"What is it?"

"I'm pregnant, Fabio. Almost three months pregnant, to be exact. It seems it happened the first night we had sex."

Hearing she's been keeping such important news from me feels like a punch to the gut. "When did you find out?" I demand.

"Just after we got back from Boston. I intended not to tell you and raise the baby alone, since we broke it off that night." She shrugs, glancing down at the floor. "When we got back together, I wasn't sure how to tell you."

"Gia, you should have told me." I lift her chin to gaze into her eyes. "Why didn't you?"

She sighs. "I was scared you wouldn't want anything to do with me or the baby once you found out."

I growl softly, grabbing her hips firmly and pulling her against me. "Then you don't know me very well, tesorina. I'm not your father."

Her eyes well up at the mention of the father who skipped out on her and her mother when she was little.

"I love you, Gia. I want to have a family with you."

Her eyes widen at my proclamation of love. It's the first time I've said it so frankly, despite meaning it on other occasions. "I love you too, Fabio." Tears flood down her cheeks. "I love you more than anything in this world."

I smile, hearing her say that to me. "Then this is good news, baby. We are going to have a family of our own." I kiss her softly at first, before deepening the kiss.

My tongue delves into her mouth, desperately searching it like a man possessed.

I've never felt like this before. Our love is so pure. Even if I don't deserve a love like this, Gia makes me want to strive for the light. She makes me want to be a better man.

The snap of cameras going off behind me brings me back to reality.

"Fuck," Gia says as the paparazzi take photos of us embracing. We both break away from each other, but I know the damage is done.

They will plaster our pictures across the news within an hour, meaning Aida will not hear it first from us. I'm about to break my daughter's heart for the second time, and it's made worse by the fact that it isn't going to come from us first.

Only the media would descend on this carnage like vultures, picking anything they can from the utter destruction.

30

GIA

The word is out around Palermo, meaning we didn't get to Aida first.

Fabio holds my hand as we walk toward the secluded beach villa Milo rented.

"We should have come here before the ball," I say.

Fabio's jaw clenches. "It is what it is. We'll be okay."

I tighten my grip on his hand as we come to the front of the villa. Fabio is the one to knock on the door, letting go of my hand.

My stomach is a mess as we wait for someone to answer.

Milo comes to the door. "Fabio, she's pretty upset."

Fabio nods. "Understandable. I didn't expect an attack at the ball last night." He runs a hand across the back of his neck. "We would have come here before if we had known."

Milo nods and opens the door wider. "Come in and say your piece. I can't guarantee she will want to listen, though."

Fabio sighs. "I know how stubborn my daughter can be. She got it from me."

We walk into the house, keeping our distance so as not to rub it in Aida's face.

Aida is sitting on the terrace, her arms wrapped around her knees.

"Wait here, and I'll tell her you have arrived," Milo says.

My stomach churns as we watch Milo disappear onto the porch with her. Aida visibly tenses, before glancing in our direction. The anger in her eyes cuts me to the core, and she quickly looks away.

"This will not be easy," I mutter.

Fabio gently squeezes my hand. "Nothing worth fighting for is ever easy."

If that was supposed to ease my anxiety, it doesn't.

Milo returns, looking a little irritated. "She will listen to you although she doesn't want to." He's looking right at me. "But, Fabio." He shakes his head. "It's too soon I'm afraid."

Fabio looks hurt. "Fair enough. I'll wait here for you then."

Milo nods and signals for him to take a seat on the sofa.

I stare out of the open doors to the terrace, scared to face Aida, particularly alone. *Stop being a coward and tell your friend the truth,* I think. I walk out onto the terrace and sit down on a chair opposite my friend.

"Before you say anything, I know it's purely my father's fault. He's clearly groomed you or something."

I shake my head. "No, Aida. He hasn't groomed me." I sigh heavily. "I'm so sorry that this has happened, and we didn't come first and tell you."

"Sorry you got caught you mean?" Aida asks angrily.

"No. Fabio and I had planned to come and tell you, but after the attack at the ball we got photographed together."

Aida stares out to sea, keeping her eyes off me. "How and when did it start?"

"On the night of my twenty-first birthday, I got drunk and went to tell your dad off." I shake my head, thinking back to how stupid I was then. Who breaks into a mobster's home? It's a sure-fire way to getting shot. Thankfully Fabio recognized me, otherwise it could have been a different story entirely. "I crawled through your secret tunnel, ready to tell him off, but then there was this chemistry that we both felt."

Aida glares at me angrily. "He's old enough to be your damn father."

I nod in reply. "I know. Nothing happened that night. I ran away after he kissed me, but we couldn't keep away from each other. The rest is history." I swallow hard. "I really didn't want this to happen. It just did." I set a hand on my stomach, knowing that

Fabio and I agreed to tell her about the child. "I'm pregnant, Aida. With Fabio's child."

Aida sits up straighter. "Are you fucking kidding me?"

I shake my head. "No. I never wanted to hurt you, Aida. We fell in love and despite our best efforts to stop, we couldn't."

Aida looks out at sea, avoiding looking at me. "That man is a cruel-hearted, sick son of a bitch. I hope you are happy together, as I want nothing to do with either of you." She pauses. "Or your baby."

Pain claws at my chest. "I understand that's how you feel. Fabio never wanted to hurt you. He explained why he did what he did, and if you speak to him, I think you'll come to realize he's not as bad as you believe."

Aida snaps at that. "He told me he couldn't have me around because I remind him of my mother. A woman he has clearly gotten over since he's fucking you now," she spits.

"He did it to protect you. To ensure you left Palermo and didn't come back." I run a hand through my hair. "The Moretti family was trying to take Sicily."

Aida doesn't look like she's listening. "I don't want any of your stupid excuses for him. It's clear he has you brainwashed." She shakes her head. "Out of all the people who could betray me, I never thought it would be you."

No matter what I say, she's not open to listening at

the moment. It's understandable. All I hope is that she comes around in the end.

"I'm truly sorry that I hurt you, Aida." I stand from the seat, feeling the tears filling my eyes. "I want you to know that no matter what, I'll always love you. Maybe in time you will give us both a chance to make this right with you."

She says nothing in response, gazing out over the blue sea.

"I hope I see you again sometime," I say, before turning around and heading back into the villa.

Milo gives me a forced smile. "I told you it wouldn't be easy."

I shake my head. "I never expected it to be."

Fabio stands and grabs my hand. "I guess you will have to repay my favor another way, since I killed Rafa in the end."

Milo runs a hand across his neat beard. "Hmm, I'm sure you will think of something. Are we still on for our meeting in a week?"

Fabio nods. "Yes, see you then." He drags me toward the door, leaving Aida and Milo alone. As soon as we're out, Fabio sighs. "I'm sorry you had to face her alone."

"It's fine. She's not open to listening at the moment and that's understandable." I glance at my phone, which has loads of missed calls from Siena. "I don't think it's only her who I've pissed off though."

"Siena?" Fabio asks.

"Yes. Perhaps I should see her now."

Fabio shakes his head. "You've had enough explaining yourself for one day. Text her and tell her you've been to see Aida and that you will speak with her tomorrow." He opens the door to the car that brought us over here.

I sit in the back and type out the message to Siena.

I'm sorry that you had to find out via the news. I've just been to see Aida. I'll speak to you tomorrow.

I hesitate before sending the text.

Fabio gets in to the car next to me, squeezing my thigh. "What exactly did Aida say?"

"She's angry and thinks you groomed me, but I assured her you didn't." I rest my head back on the headrest. "It's going to take a lot of groveling, I think, if she's ever going to forgive either of us."

Fabio chuckles softly. "Do I strike you as a man who grovels?"

"No, but you are a man who believes family is important. So, you should do whatever is necessary to get your daughter back."

Fabio lifts my hand and kisses the back of it. "You're not wrong, tesorina."

We sit in silence in the back of the car, all the way back to Fabio's villa. Once there, the driver takes the car away, leaving us alone. "I dismissed my staff for today. I felt we would want our privacy."

I raise a brow. "What for?" I ask.

He smirks at my question. "I'm going to make love to you all day and night, that's what for."

My stomach churns. "I'm not sure that's a good idea after what has just happened."

Fabio laughs. "So, now that everyone knows, it's not a good idea for us to fuck?" He shakes his head. "That makes no sense, baby." He grabs my hand and pulls me through the front door, locking it after him. "I want to make you squeal."

I swallow hard. "What about the man strung up in your basement? Dario Moretti?"

Fabio tilts his head slightly. "What about him?"

"Aren't you going to put him out of his misery?"

"Lorenzo already took him away to handle it. The only people in this house are me and you, tesorina."

I can't help but feel nervous about being intimate with Fabio. When he killed Rafa Moretti, I witnessed how dark his soul is. It's pitch black.

"It freaked me out a bit, seeing you like that," I admit.

Fabio walks to the counter in his kitchen and grabs a tumbler, pouring whiskey into it. He takes a long drink before slamming it down on the side. "The things I've witnessed in my life have made me this way, tesorina. You don't get by for as long as I have in this world without tearing out your soul multiple fucking times." His eyes meet mine. "I'm broken and dark in ways you can't understand." He walks toward me. "If that is something you can't accept, then tell me now. All I know is I love you. The thought of losing you makes my world even darker."

I stare into his dark, haunted eyes, knowing that I want him, even with all the darkness that comes as part of the package. I shake my head. "No, I can accept it. I love you too, Fabio." I swallow hard. "Although the town will tear us to shreds with gossip. Our age gap is taboo enough for them."

Fabio growls softly. "I'd like to see them try. If they so much as print one bad word about you, I'll have their heads on a fucking spike."

I swallow hard, knowing he may be talking literally.

"Don't worry, I won't literally do it, but I have power in this city and I won't hesitate to use it if they smear your name." He wraps his arms around me and kisses me deeply, making my knees shake.

When we part, we're both breathless.

It's intoxicating the way Fabio makes me feel, and I'm sure in that moment that I'll never get enough of him.

31

FABIO

I fumble with the velvet box in my jacket pocket. It's not the first time I've proposed, but it sure as hell is the most anxious I've ever felt.

It's been two weeks since I killed Rafa Moretti. Two weeks since Gia told Aida the truth. In those two weeks, I've learned that I never want to live another day without Gia by my side. I have to marry her—it's the ultimate way to prove she belongs to me.

Aida unfortunately didn't agree to meeting either of us again before she left. I fear I've lost all chances of rebuilding the relationship I once had with my daughter. Milo is ever the optimist on that front, which surprised me. He told us to give it time, and that's all we can do now—give Aida the time and space to process what has happened between us. Neither of us chose for this to happen and I hope in time she will realize we never meant to hurt her.

Gia is late for dinner on my yacht. She texted half an hour ago, saying that she had to work overtime. It doesn't matter how much I implore her to get more help, she's as stubborn as me. I love her for it though. Her drive to succeed in what she is passionate about is sexy as hell.

"Fabio?" Gia calls my name from the beach, making me smile.

"Up here, amore mio," I call.

Gia comes up the stairs and her mouth falls open when she sees the romantic setting. My staff arranged the deck with rose petals, candles, and a table for two with silver service. "I think I'm a little underdressed," she says, pointing at the casual clothes she wore to work. "I assumed when you said a date, you meant takeout pizza or something."

I laugh at that. "Do I strike you as a take-out date kind of guy, Gia?"

She shakes her head. "No, I guess not."

I let my eyes drag down her perfect figure. "If you ask me, you are overdressed."

Her brow raises. "Shall I change?"

I shake my head. "No, come and sit down." I pull out a chair for her and she sits.

"What's for dinner?" she asks, reaching for the lid of the silver platter in front of her.

I place my hand over hers. "Not yet, tesorina." I don't sit back down, knowing that putting off the question will only make me anxious. Instead, I drop to my knees, holding her hand.

"What are you—"

I pull out the box and flip open the lid to reveal an elegant, baroque-style engagement ring—a ring that belonged to my grandmother.

Gia's eyes widen and she stares at it in shock. "Fabio…" she murmurs.

"My little treasure, it has been a crazy few months, but the one thing I'm certain of is that I can't live without you." My chest aches as I rarely open up like this. I've been closed off for ten years. "I love you, and I want to spend the rest of my life with you. Will you marry me?"

A few painstaking moments of silence follow. "Of course I'll marry you," she says, her voice cracking as tears well in her eyes.

I feel a flood of relief at hearing her agree to my proposal. "This ring was my grandmother's. It has been in the family for generations and we believed it to be lost until about three years ago when my men rediscovered it." I pull the ring out of the box and slip it onto Gia's finger. It fits perfectly since I checked the size of her mother's ring that she wears and had it resized. "I can't wait to spend the rest of my life with you, tesorina."

I stand and pull her to her feet, kissing her passionately. The kiss turns heated as she claws at me desperately. I break the kiss. "We've got time for that after dinner," I murmur.

She pouts at me, making my cock harder than it already is. "I'm not hungry for food."

I groan and grab her hips, pulling her against me again. "That's because you're a naughty girl, Gia," I whisper in her ear. "And you know what naughty girls need, don't you?"

Gia licks her bottom lip. "Yes, sir. They need to be punished."

I spank her firm ass hard before kneading it in my hand. "That's right, baby. First, we have Alejandro's famous ravioli." I lift the lid from her plate. "It would be a real shame to waste it."

Gia tilts her head slightly, contemplating whether to protest. Instead, she nods and sits down in front of the platter. "I'd rather eat something else, though." The look in her eyes makes my cock even harder.

"You are pushing for a proper punishment, aren't you, tesorina?"

She bites her bottom lip again. "No, sir." She picks up her fork and stabs it into the ravioli, seductively bringing it to her mouth and wrapping her thick lips around it.

I ignore her teasing for now and tuck in to my food, knowing that I haven't felt this happy in a long time. The last time I felt this happy was the first moment I held Aida in my arms when she was born. I can't believe that I'm going to get to do that again with our baby.

Gia is mine. I knew it the moment she ran from my house that night. Despite our age gap and the fact that Gia is my daughter's friend, this has felt right from the moment I set eyes on her in my study. We both knew it was pushing boundaries, but no matter how much Gia tried to put a stop to it, fate drew us together.

"Did you have a good day at work?" I ask.

Gia tilts her head slightly. "Busy. It's always busy." She sighs heavily. "I think with the baby coming, I'm going to have to hire more staff."

"Hmm, I told you to do that a couple of months ago."

Gia rolls her eyes. "Alright, Mr. Know-It-All. No need to rub it in."

She no longer has to run the shop for financial stability, but I know she would never give it up. It's her world, but she needs to take it easier. "I don't want you to be stressed during your pregnancy. Perhaps I can find some applicants for you?"

Her brow furrows. "I don't think anyone you know is going to be suitable. Flower arranging and mobsters don't exactly go hand in hand."

I raise a brow. "Many of the mobsters who work for me have wives like you."

Gia looks thoughtful. "That's true. Well, I already applied to post the job in the local paper, but I guess you can make some enquiries." She glances at the ring on her finger. "When do you want to get married?"

I shrug. "As soon as possible. I want everyone to know you belong to me."

She laughs at that. "I think everyone already knows since it was in the paper."

"It's not the same as marriage." I finish my ravioli. "Now, it's time for dessert."

Gia's gaze heats and her throat bobs as she swallows, bringing the thought of her swallowing my cock to the forefront of my mind.

"How am I going to punish you tonight, amore mio?"

Her cheeks flush. "However you see fit, sir."

My reluctant little brat has quickly turned into the perfect little submissive whore. "Good girl," I say, contemplating how I want to punish her. "Come here."

She stands and walks toward me. "Where do you want me?"

I tilt my head slightly, wondering if she's ready to indulge my favorite kink. "I want to try something new tonight. If you will indulge me."

Gia looks a little uncertain, but nods. "What is it?"

"Have you ever heard of consensual non-consent?"

Her brow furrows. "No, I don't think so."

"Well, it's pretty much what it says. We agree to play act non-consensual sex." I pause at the confused look on her face. "As if I'm raping you."

Gia's eyes widen. "Oh." She says nothing else as her face reddens.

"Do you want to try it?" I ask when she still doesn't speak.

Gia looks at me hesitantly before nodding. "Why not? I'm not sure how good at it I'll be."

"I beg to differ. Just pretend you're pissed at me and don't want to fuck, but I'm not listening to you."

Gia laughs. "As if that hasn't happened before?"

"True. If you want to stop, you shout out red. Otherwise, I'm doing whatever the fuck I want to you no matter how much you protest. Got it?"

Gia nods. "I think so."

I stand and grab her throat tightly. "I'm going to fuck you so hard they'll hear you screaming in Palermo."

Gia shudders. "No, please, you can't do this to me," she protests rather convincingly.

I move my mouth so it's an inch away from hers, staring into her eyes. "I can do whatever the fuck I want. I own you and I own this fucking Island."

Roughly, I grab her hips and lift her with one arm, using the other to clear the dining table we'd just sat at onto the floor. Gia gasps as crockery smashes as it hits the floor. "What are you going to do?" she asks, her voice frightened.

"Fuck your tight little pussy." I wrap my hand tightly around her throat. "Then, I'm going to fuck your perfect little asshole."

Gia tenses against me. "No, you can't do this. Please, someone help," she cries.

It's clear that I'm a sick man for craving this kind of play, but Gia performs as perfectly as I expected.

I tear her panties from her and lift the hem of her skirt, rubbing her clit roughly. Then I slide a thick finger inside of her wet pussy. "Your pussy is soaking wet, you whore," I growl, thrusting my finger in and out of her. "I can't believe you like this."

I undress her so she is entirely naked, letting go for a moment to grab some rope.

She pushes away from me and gently runs toward the exit. "I won't let you—"

I grab her around the waist and hoist her from the ground. "You're not going anywhere." I wrap the rope tightly around her wrists and tie them behind her back, before tying the rope around her breasts to stimulate pleasure in such a sensitive area. I push her to her knees forcefully. "Suck it."

She glares up at me and keeps her mouth shut.

I force the head of my cock against her lips, smearing precum on them. "I said, suck it," I growl.

When she still doesn't, I turn and reach for the open mouth gag I'd brought in here earlier. "You should have done as you are told, while you had the chance." I've used it with her once, but that wasn't in this kind of situation. I force the device through her lips and fix it in place. "Now I can fuck your throat and you can't do anything to stop me."

Gia's eyes flash with desire, but she tries to hide it. She can't talk with the gag in her mouth.

Slowly, I slide my cock through the gag and groan as my hot, throbbing flesh touches her tongue. I grab a fistful of her hair and thrust my hips, rocking back and forth into her throat.

Gia gags, saliva spilling all over my cock and balls as I take her throat without mercy. She turns me into a primeval savage whenever we fuck. I groan as her eyes dilate at the roughness I'm treating her with. There's no doubt we're both broken—both fucked up, but it works so well when we're together.

I pull my cock from her throat and grab her chin between my finger and thumb. "I'm going to fuck you now, mia puttana." I spit into her open mouth, which makes her squirm. Slowly, I unfasten the open mouth gag from the back of her head and drag her to her feet, using the ropes.

Forcefully, I press my lips to hers and kiss her hard. "Such a good little whore, aren't you?"

"No, please, I don't—"

I cut her pleas off with a spank to her firm ass. "Don't lie." I thrust three fingers deep into her pussy. "You are soaking wet."

She whimpers as I force her around and bend her over the table. My cock is harder than stone as I thrust into her as deep as possible. "Take it like a good girl," I growl.

"No, please, stop," she cries.

I groan and tighten my grip on her hips, fucking her hard and deep. Our bodies clash against each other, filling the air with the slap of skin against skin. "Such a good whore," I groan, grabbing her firm breasts with my hands and playing with her nipples.

She whimpers, a sound which I can only describe as pure pleasure rather than reluctance. I feel her muscles tightening as she gets closer to release. "Fuck, I'm going to come," she cries.

I still inside of her and bite her shoulder hard. "Did I say you could come yet?" I ask.

She groans. "No, but—"

I spank her ass. "Don't come until I tell you to." I move in and out of her again, feeling her muscles flutter around my cock. It's only a matter of time until she sends me over the edge, and I'm not ready until I bury my cock deep in her ass.

I pull out of her and retrieve a bottle of lube.

Gia remains still on the table, unable to move from the restraints.

I return to her and grab her hips possessively.

"Please stop. What are you going to do now?" she asks, glancing over her shoulder at me.

I pour the lube onto her tight, puckered hole. Instead of answering her, I slide a finger into her lubed hole, making her cry out, "No, stop." She tries to wriggle away from me.

I place my free hand over her mouth to stop her protests. "Don't pretend you don't love me fingering your ass." I add another finger, gently prepping her tight little hole for my cock. All the while, I hold a hand over her mouth and she groans behind it. "You are such a dirty little whore taking my fingers in your ass."

Once I've got four fingers easily into her hole, I let go of her mouth and lube my cock. I'm harder than a rock at the prospect of coming in her tight little ass. "Keep your legs apart for me," I order, positioning the head of my cock at her gaping entrance.

She does as I say, and I push forward, allowing her ass to swallow my cock inch by inch. It drives me wild, seeing the way her puckered hole clings to my cock. "Oh fuck," she cries.

As I drive in and out of her tight hole, she forgets about the reluctance and embraces the sensations entirely. "Fuck my ass, sir," she cries, arching her back so my cock sinks even deeper.

I roar as all my self-control escapes my grasp. Every thrust into her is harder than the last as she takes my cock willingly. "Do you like me raping your ass like that, you slut?" I ask

"Fuck, yes," she cries.

Our bodies clash together frantically as I drive us both toward the edge. There's no more teasing as our passion and desire become unbearable.

"Oh, fuck, sir, I'm going to come," she screams.

"Come for me, my dirty little whore," I order, knowing I can't last much longer in her tight-as-sin asshole.

Her body tenses and then convulses as she tips over the edge. It's as if she is trying to milk my cock as her muscles clamp down so hard around my shaft. Her pussy squirts as she comes, driving me even more insane.

"That's it, baby, make me fill your ass with cum," I growl.

She is panting frantically as I climax, pumping rope after rope of thick cum into her tight ass.

"Yes, sir, fill my ass," she cries.

I don't stop until I've drained every drop into her. Once I do, I collapse against her back, trying to regain my breath.

When we finally come down from our mutual pleasure, silence descends between us. I hope I didn't go too far with her. Consensual non-consent can be rather confusing, especially for someone so new to such rough treatment.

I undo her restraints, stroking the red skin where the rope had rubbed her. "Are you alright, tesorina?" I ask, lifting her from the table and gently carrying her to the bed inside the yacht. "I didn't hurt you, did I?"

Gia shakes her head. "No, it's just—"

"What is it, baby?"

"I don't know. That was oddly arousing but it shouldn't have been."

I chuckle softly at that. "I know. So you enjoyed it?"

"Yes, but I feel a little confused about it all." Her brow furrows. "Is that normal?"

I wrap my arms around her and hold her close. "Totally normal." I sigh. "I'm glad you enjoyed it."

She nestles against my chest and her eyes fall shut. I hold her tightly, knowing there is no other time in my life that I've felt this happy. Gia completes me in ways I never believed possible.

EPILOGUE

Gia

Two years later...

"Luca, be careful," I call as my son runs across the sand toward the cresting sea.

He is only eighteen months old, but he is growing too fast. He laughs gleefully as he falls into the sand, getting it all over himself.

Concetta, our nanny and housekeeper, rushes after him. "Come on, little Alteri," she says, picking him up and dusting him off. "Time to get ready for bed."

I smile at Concetta, wondering how I'd cope without her. My feet ache and my belly is already swollen despite only being five months pregnant with our next child.

It's hard to believe that I'm married to my best

friend's father, a man who should have been totally off limits. But it's definitely true when they say you can't choose who you fall in love with.

Aida has learned to accept this new dynamic, but it wasn't easy. It took a lot of groveling from both me and Fabio to get her to understand our situation. In the end, she accepted that we never did this to hurt her and that our love was unexpected. Siena was quick to forgive me, but she pulled away a lot after finding out, until a vacation that turned into a nightmare for her. It was a vacation that had a very unexpected outcome, but that's a story for another time.

I rest back in my lounger and sigh heavily.

"Buonasera, amore mio," Fabio says behind me, his voice as smooth as silk.

I smile and sit up, holding a hand out to him. "You are home early."

He takes my hand and joins me on the huge daybed. "I told Lorenzo to deal with things while I take a couple of hours to spend with my wife." He shrugs. "I think he's ready to take on more responsibility. Finally."

I roll my eyes at him. "He's been ready for a while, and you know it. You're just overprotective about the control of your organization."

He chuckles. "Well, that's something we have in common then, isn't it?"

"My flower shop is different. It's not a multi-million-euro enterprise." I have trouble giving over control over anything at the shop, even though I know Angelica and

Claudia are trustworthy. I've since expanded and employed two trainees, since I haven't had the same time since Luca arrived.

Fabio sets his hand over mine and squeezes. "How are you feeling today?"

I shrug. "Tired and cranky. The usual."

Fabio laughs and shifts to sit behind me, placing his legs around me. "How about I give you a massage?" He gently kneads my shoulders.

"Hmm, that feels good," I murmur, letting my head fall back against his firm, muscular chest. He makes me feel so small.

Fabio's lips tease the edge of my earlobe as he moves his hands to my breasts, gently kneading them. "I'm so fucking hard for you, tesorina."

I feel my thighs getting slick as my desire for my husband grows. It's crazy that two years on from our engagement, we're still as desperate for each other as ever. "Concetta is still here and putting Luca to bed," I warn.

Fabio doesn't stop touching my breasts, clearly not concerned about her being around. "Concetta knows not to bother us."

It always surprises me how little he cares that people may see us getting intimate. It's as if he wants people to see us. "You are too reckless."

He undoes the lace ties on the back of my sundress, pulling it down so I'm wearing nothing to cover my breasts. My nipples are hard and aching as he gently plays with them. "I need to have you right now."

"Fabio, wait until she has gone home," I murmur.

Fabio growls softly and grabs the back of my neck. "You know I don't like being told what to do, baby."

I purse my lips, loving the way his roughness always gets me hot. "How about a compromise?" I suggest.

He groans softly. "Why do you always have to disobey me? Is it because you love being punished?"

A shiver races down my spine at the mention of punishment. I can't understand why I crave his discipline so much, even now. "Possibly," I breathe.

"Goodnight, Mr. and Mrs. Alteri. See you tomorrow," Concetta calls from the patio door, making me tense.

Fabio turns to face her. "See you tomorrow, Concetta," he replies.

I hold my breath, waiting for him to confirm that she's gone. "I told you we should've waited."

Fabio chuckles. "Do you think she hasn't seen us getting intimate in over two years?"

I glance back at him with wide eyes. "I hope not."

Fabio shakes his head. "Sorry to disappoint, but I know for certain that she has."

Heat floods through my body to my face, which feels like it's on fire. "How?"

He shrugs. "I saw her in the window's reflection a few months ago while we were fucking in the living room as she left. I doubt that was the first time."

I gape at him, knowing that there's no way I'm going to look Concetta in the eye now that I know. "You could have kept that information to yourself. How am I supposed to face her now?"

Fabio lifts me onto his lap as if I weigh nothing. "Forget about it," he murmurs into my ear, grazing his teeth along the base of my jaw. "I need to fuck you."

I shift uncomfortably in his lap, unable to forget what he just revealed. "What if someone sees us?"

He bites my bottom lip. "Good. I want everyone on this fucking island to witness that you belong to me," he growls, grabbing my wrists behind my back and kissing me hard. "I'm going to fuck you right out here in the open, tesorina."

I shudder as I feel the hard press of his enormous cock beneath me. "That's a bad idea."

He lets go of my wrists and tears the dress off me before sliding his fingers into the knot of his tie. Fabio undoes his tie and straightens it, binding the fabric around my body to restrain my arms. "It doesn't matter if you think it's a bad idea, baby. I'm in control."

I swallow hard as he lifts me from his lap and bends me over on the daybed, spanking my ass hard with his hand. "This is what you want, isn't it, tesorina?"

"Yes, sir," I moan as he teases his hand gently over my stinging skin.

Fabio spanks my other ass cheek harder, making me yelp. "I bet you are soaking wet." He slides his finger into my panties and through my aching slit. "Fuck, your pussy is ready for my cock, baby."

I groan and arch my back, inviting him inside.

Fabio spanks my ass a few more times until my skin is on fire and no doubt red raw. He grabs my hips so hard I know he'll leave bruises. "It's time for me to taste what is mine."

I shiver in anticipation, waiting for him to taste me. His tongue delves between my thighs, making me gasp. Fabio teases me there for a moment before moving his attention to my clit. One flick of his tongue lights up every nerve inside of me.

I moan deeply as he sucks my clit, before lightly dragging his tongue back to my pussy and delving inside to taste me again.

Fabio groans, making my stomach clench. His tongue delves inside of me, pushing me closer to the edge in an instance. The pressure builds fast as he devours me frantically. His tongue moves higher again, circling my clit and making me cry out. Two thick fingers delve inside of me, making me buck my hips toward his mouth. My husband is turning me into a frenzied mess.

"You taste sweeter than honey, baby," he growls against my clit, licking me more.

I writhe against the restraints, wishing I had an ounce of control. I don't. I'm totally at Fabio's mercy, and it's heaven. He curls his fingers inside of me, making me squeal his name. "Yes, Fabio," I cry.

Fabio doesn't stop as I head toward the edge of the cliff top, drowning in a sea of pleasure as he continues to finger fuck me. "I want you to squirt your cum all over me," Fabio growls, making my eyes roll back in my head.

I clamp my eyes shut, unable to think past the hot white pleasure pulsing through my veins. "Fuck," I cry as he hits the spot that makes me come undone. A flood of hot juice squirts from my pussy all over his fingers and onto the daybed.

Fabio buries his face between my thighs, lapping up every drop hungrily. "You are so fucking perfect, Gia," he breathes before devouring me more. "I need to fuck your perfect pussy right now."

I shudder at the sound of his pants unzipping, wishing I could see him. Suddenly I feel the thick, swollen head of his cock against my sensitive entrance. "Fabio…" I murmur his name, needing to feel him stuffing me with every inch of his cock. Ever since I've become pregnant, he's more insatiable, and so am I.

"I want you to fight," he murmurs into my ear, sending shivers right to my core.

I'm surprised how much I love it when he suggests roleplaying non-consent. It's hotter than anything I've experienced before.

"Let go of me, you bastard," I cry, trying to move away despite the tie making it difficult.

Fabio growls and grabs my hips so hard I know they'll be bruised by the morning. "Where are you going, little girl?" he asks, dragging me back toward him on the daybed. "I'm going to fuck you even if you don't want me to."

My heart skips a beat as he shoves every inch of his cock inside of me with one stroke. "No, please don't do this," I cry, trying to fight away from him.

He wraps a muscular arm around my waist and holds me against him. "You can fight all you like. I'm going to take what is mine." He places his hand over my mouth, stopping me from crying out.

Fabio's hips piston hard and fast as he takes me roughly, exactly how I crave it. "You're so wet you must enjoy being fucked against your will," he groans into my ear, letting go of my mouth and gripping my throat instead. "Such a dirty little whore."

I moan deeply, struggling to keep the act of non-consent going. "No, I don't like it. Please stop," I cry, but it sounds half-hearted now.

He spanks my ass hard and fucks me even rougher. Our bodies meet in a violent clash of skin against skin as Fabio takes me like a beast. His grunts and groans are enough to send me right to the edge as he continues to spank my ass red raw.

"Fuck, no, I can't do this," I cry.

Fabio groans and yanks my hair hard enough to hurt. "That's right. Come on my cock while I rape your pretty little pussy," he growls.

That's all it takes to send me over the edge. I squirt

all over his cock, coming undone with a violent orgasm that rocks my entire body.

Fabio growls as he comes along with me, filling me with his thick cum. "Take my cum like my good little whore," he murmurs into my ear before biting my ear lobe.

The pain only makes my orgasm heighten as he continues to fuck me through it. When we're finally finished, we remain still and silent, panting for breath.

I take a moment to recover from my explosive orgasm and the rough play we just engaged in. It is such a confusing sensation when we indulge in non-consent. The love between us is clear, but we both crave the roughness of it.

Fabio lies on the daybed and pulls me close to him, kissing the top of my head. The sun is dipping below the horizon, sending a deep red haze across the sky. It's breathtaking. "Beautiful," I say, gazing out at the view as Fabio's muscular arms hold me.

"Not half as beautiful as my wife," he says.

I glance up at him to see that he's staring at me rather than at the sunset. "I love you," I say, feeling my chest ache at the words.

He smiles and kisses my lips softly. "I love you too, tesorina."

It never occurred to me that I'd always been missing something in my life until I broke into this villa on my twenty-first birthday. The discipline and structure that Fabio brings to my life is everything I've always needed.

He broke me and then put me back together. His rough ways and tendency for ignoring boundaries should have put me off, but for me, he is perfect.

Our love was unexpected and complicated, but we made it out the other end stronger because of it.

Thank you for reading Ruthless Daddy, the third book in the Boston Mafia Dons Series. I hope that you enjoyed reading Fabio and Gia's story.

The next book in this series follows Malachy's sister, Alicia, and his best friend, Niall. Vicious Daddy is available to buy on Amazon or to readable with Kindle Unlimited.

Vicious Daddy: A Dark Brother's Best Friend Mafia Romance

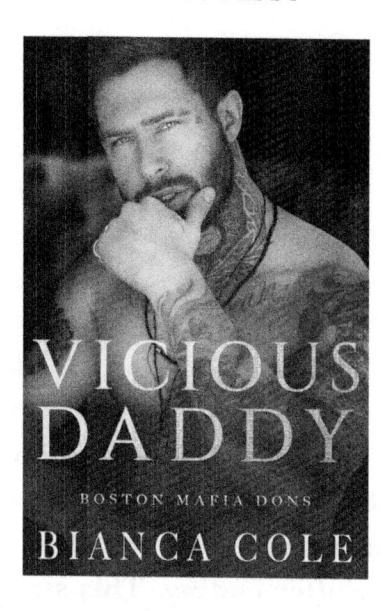

He's off-limits and totally forbidden, so why can't I stay away?

Niall Fitzpatrick is my brother's best friend.

He's also his second in the McCarthy clan.

We've known each other since we were children.

I never looked at him as anything other than my brother's hot friend.

Until one night, we find ourselves alone while Malachy's out.

Desire and passion flares, and we end up crossing a line.

After that night, everything changes between us.

We can't stay away from each other, no matter the consequences.

My brother is insane.

He won't take kindly to us sneaking around behind his back.

Then, I have a shock I never expected.

Despite thinking I was past the accidental pregnancy stage, I was wrong.

Our secret leads to a web of lies we both struggle to keep track of.

Now I'm keeping one from the man I love too.

Will I figure this all out before our lies tear us apart?

Vicious Daddy is the fourth book in the Boston Mafia Doms Series by Bianca Cole. This book is a safe story with no cliffhangers and a happily ever after ending. This story has some dark themes that may upset some people, hot scenes, and bad language. It features an over-the-top possessive, and vicious Irish mobster.

GLOSSARY

ITALIAN EXPRESSIONS

- Tesorina - Little treasure
- Amo il tuo sapore - I love how you taste
- Ti prego - Please
- Come sei bagnata - You're so wet
- Sei la mia puttana - You're my whore
- Succhiami il cazzo - Suck my cock
- Succhiatelo da soli - Suck it yourself
- Mettilo in bocca - Put it in your mouth
- Cazzo, e'incredible - Fuck, it's incredible
- Ti scoperò col mio cazzo e urlerai di piacere - I will fuck you and you will scream with pleasure
- Guardami - Look at me
- Mi fai impazzire - You make me crazy
- Cazzo, come sei stretta - Fuck, you're so tight
- Piegati - Bend over

GLOSSARY

- Grazie Dio - Thank God
- Si - Yes
- Sei bellissima - You're so beautiful
- Ciao, bella - Goodbye, beautiful
- Buonasera signorina - Good evening, miss
- Sono la tua puttanella - I'm your little whore
- Buon compleanno per domani - Happy birthday for tomorrow
- Amore mio - my love

ALSO BY BIANCA COLE

Wynton Series

Filthy Boss: A Forbidden Office Romance

Filthy Professor: A First Time Professor And Student Romance

Filthy Lawyer: A Forbidden Hate to Love Romance

Romano Mafia Brother's Series

Her Mafia Daddy: A Dark Daddy Romance

Her Mafia Boss: A Dark Romance

Her Mafia King: A Dark Romance

Bratva Brotherhood Series

Captured by the Bratva: A Dark Mafia Romance

Claimed by the Bratva: A Dark Mafia Romance

Bound by the Bratva: A Dark Mafia Romance

Taken by the Bratva: A Dark Mafia Romance

Royally Mated Series

Her Faerie King: A Faerie Royalty Paranormal Romance

Her Alpha King: A Royal Wolf Shifter Paranormal Romance

Her Dragon King: A Dragon Shifter Paranormal Romance

Her Vampire King: A Dark Vampire Romance

New York Mafia Doms Series

Her Irish Daddy: A Dark Mafia Romance

Her Russian Daddy: A Dark Mafia Romance

Her Italian Daddy: A Dark Mafia Romance

Her Cartel Daddy: A Dark Mafia Romance

Boston Mafia Dons Series

Cruel Daddy: A Dark Mafia Arranged Marriage Romance

Savage Daddy: A Dark Captive Romance

Vicious Daddy: A Dark Brothers Best Friend Mafia Romance

Wicked Daddy: A Dark Captive Mafia Romance

ABOUT THE AUTHOR

I love to write stories about over the top alpha bad boys who have heart beneath it all, fiery heroines, and happily-ever-after endings with heart and heat. My stories have twists and turns that will keep you flipping the pages and heat to set your kindle on fire.

For as long as I can remember, I've been a sucker for a good romance story. I've always loved to read. Suddenly, I realized why not combine my love of two things, books and romance?

My love of writing has grown over the past four years and I now publish on Amazon exclusively, weaving stories about dirty mafia bad boys and the women they fall head over heels in love with.

If you enjoyed this book please follow me on Amazon, Bookbub or any of the below social media platforms for alerts when more books are released.